T0245792

MALICIA

MALICIA

STEVEN DOS SANTOS

PAGE STREET YA

PAGE STREET YA

First published in 2024 by

Page Street Publishing Co.

27 Congress Street, Suite 1511

Salem, MA 01970

www.pagestreetpublishing.com

Distributed by Macmillan, sales in Canada by The Canadian Manda Group.

28   27   26   25   24   1   2   3   4   5

ISBN-13: 978-1-64567-787-1

ISBN-10: 1-64567-787-7

Library of Congress Control Number: 2022952211

Cover and book design by Laura Benton for Page Street Publishing Co.

Cover illustration © Aleksey Pollack

Printed and bound in China

TO KATHLEEN MORRISON PAGAN,
my oldest and dearest friend, who was with me during my
own visit to the darkness represented by Malicia, and helped
guide me into the light with all of her support, understanding,
and patience. Love you, Kathy!

La Cueva de los Duen

Chupacabra Chill Zone

Valley of las C

Lugaru Lake

Creature Canyon

It's a Small Underworld

Malici

Ratoncito Hall   El Asilo

Doc

Serial Springs

Bor

MALICIA

Graveyard

s

The Inn of Madness

rousel of Chaos

Paranormal Place

ntain

El Bacá Cathedral

Angel Falls

Bayou

Gates

Caribbean Sea

heme Park

RAYMUNDO

"Hundreds of people were slaughtered here at Malicia, the world's largest and now defunct theme park dedicated to all things horror . . . and owned by my family."

I peer across the Caribbean Sea at the island looming just ahead, blocking the clouds and gorging on the scant slivers of light cutting through the gloom. It's shrouded in heavy mist like un fantasma, the ghost of Halloweens past, digging up every painful memory I've ever had.

Turning, I try and keep it together as I face my three companions, huddled together in the cramped, motorized gondola, anxious eyes glued on me. Joaquin, Sofia, and Isabella, the Quisqueya Club, my best friends in the whole world. And right now, the lifelines to my sanity.

I avoid their scrutiny and stare directly into the camera

Isabella has focused on me, concentrating on getting the narration right for what must be the fiftieth take.

"Among the victims were my mother—" a lump forms in my throat—"and my brother, Rudy." I glance at the island, then back at the camera. "The perpetrators were never apprehended, and the reason for the massacre has remained a mystery. Tight security measures enforced by a private American security company, working in tandem with the local government of the Dominican Republic, have also prevented any leaked footage of the interior of the park from ever going viral. But this weekend, all of that is going to change. Today is Thursday, October 28th. By Sunday, October 31st, Halloween night and the anniversary of the massacre, the secrets of Malicia will all be revealed . . ." I pause a few seconds for dramatic effect before yelling, "Cut!"

Isabella looks up from her camera, which is protected by a waterproof case, her bright white smile a gorgeous contrast against her smooth dark skin and curls. "¡Qué chevere! So cool. You nailed it this time, Ray. This Malicia exposé is def getting me into Northwestern's journo program."

I hock up a thick loogie and launch it far into the sea. "Easily nine point five stars."

Sofia turns toward me and sighs. "Really, Ray, I accept the whole rating everything like a movie thing, but couldn't you have gone with a one to five scale instead?"

"IMDB uses the ten-point rating scale. So, I'm staying true to my filmmaking ambitions."

Joaquin clears his throat. His light brown eyes flutter as he looks away. "I just want to say, we all respect and admire you, Ray. We know how hard it is for you to come back here. . . ."

I shrug it off. "Hey, pain fuels creativity, pana. If coming back here's going to break through that writer's block and let me finally get this screenplay done, it's totally worth it. The story of what happened here has to be told the right way, not like some tabloid shit story."

Carajo. I'm a real jablador. I hate to bullshit my friends this way. Filmmaking isn't why I really dragged them here for Halloween weekend. Joaquin squeezes my shoulder. "With my co-producer skills, we're going to do this cinematic justice, tiguere. Screw high school. Next year, we're UCLA bound!"

Joaquin and I have this thing where I call him pana, and he calls me tiguere, kind of like Timon and Pumbaa from *The Lion King*, only Dominican style. I give him a wink, and he elbows me in the chest playfully, before I wrap him in a bear hug, mussing his wavy, dark hair.

Sofia dazzles us all with a smile that brightens the surrounding gloom. "I guess I'm the odd woman out this weekend."

I tilt my head. "What do you mean, doctora?"

"Well, Izzy's working on her big Malicia exposé, you're working on your autobiographical screenplay, and Joaquin's scouting locations, composing shot lists, and whatever other techno thingies you film school boys do regarding said Malicia movie. I'm just the ex-girlfriend along for the ride."

My lips form into a pout. "Awww. Is my jevita Sofia feeling neglected?"

"Don't worry. I can take care of myself. I've brought something big and hard to keep me company." After a suggestive beat, she reaches into her pack resting on the deck and rummages through it, pulling out a large, thick medical volume entitled *The Quintessential Guide to Medicine*, Third Edition, by Richard Bach. "Columbia University's pre-med program waits for no one. There's a reason my name means *wisdom*."

Isabella chuckles. "So what? The name Isabella means *gift of God*." She takes a little bow.

Joaquin clears his throat. "Well, my name does mean *raised by god*, so that trumps you, Izzy, just saying." He shoots me a smile. "And Ray's name means—"

"He who is perpetually starving." I cut him off with a wink.

Joaquin's phone beeps and he stares at the screen intensely. "Still no new hurricane advisory. According to the last one, Edgar was already a Category Four. If it should change course . . ."

Sofia stuffs Bach back into her pack and rushes over, snatching his phone to get a better look before giving it back. "Category Four? That's like winds over a hundred miles per hour, right?"

"Sustained winds of one hundred and twenty-nine and above, to be exact," Joaquin says.

Isabella gives him a side-eye. "You definitely know your hurricane stats."

"I like to have the pulse on anything that might potentially kill me."

My eyes flit to the darkening skies, and I glance at each of them in turn. "We'll be safe in the underground tunnels if the course shifts and we take a direct hit."

Joaquin pops a pill in his mouth and downs it with a long swig of bottled water. "How can there be tunnels on an island?"

"They used dynamite to blast through the volcanic rock underneath Malicia Island. But I'll leave it to the Quisqueya Club to make the decision on whether we move on or go back."

When no one protests, I gun the engines and speed toward Malicia.

The island's silhouette becomes more distinct, revealing the all-too-familiar and odd contours of its climate-controlled dome. It's designed to look like a creepy mausoleum, shrouding the abandoned, crumbling buildings within. The entire park is built around a massive mountain and surrounded by an enormous perimeter fence, patterned after a gigantic, gothic graveyard.

I bank sharply and the craft lurches, dousing us in chilly ocean spray.

Sofia's long black hair comes loose from its bun, plastering against her neck and shoulders; her soaked tank top and shorts hug the curves of her body. Joaquin hasn't fared much better, his dark wavy hair a mess, T-shirt clinging to his slim, swimmer's build like a second skin, exposing that cute little scar on his hip. The two of them cling to each other, shivering and laughing.

I chuckle. "Sorry for the turbulence, gente. There are towels in the center console."

Isabella's been recording every nanosecond of our approach. She turns the camera on me. "Your turn to be exploited, Ray. Beefcake sells. You look like a real papichulo with all those muscles bulging out of that wet T-shirt, rugged jaw, five o'clock shadow, and long jet-black hair whipping in the wind. It's like the seductive hero from one of those steamy romance novels come to life. Viewers will love it!"

I chuckle and hold out my palm to block my face. "Azarosa."

"You're a plague on my life, too." She giggles and goes back to recording our approach.

I blow her a kiss. "Just promise me if something bad happens on Malicia, you won't decide to go all *Blair Witch Project* while you're running for your life. Shaky cam is so not cool anymore."

She gives me the middle finger salute.

I flick a few switches on the console and there's a burst of radio static. "This is *Gondola 666* on our approach. Do you copy, Malicia?"

No response.

"Malicia, can you hear me? Hay alguien ahí?"

My eyes narrow at the continued static. "The work crew was supposed to be waiting for us."

Sofia shrugs. "Could they be on break?"

Isabella chuckles. "Maybe they're all dead."

The gondola's speakers crackle with a deep voice. "*Gondola 666*. We . . . hear you. Te escuchamos."

My muscles relax and I let out a sigh. "Carlos, eres tú? Soy Ray Delvalle. We've started our approach. Is everything okay? Está todo bien?"

More static. Then Carlos finally responds. "Malicia los espera . . ."

Malicia is waiting for us. . . .

There's a click, followed by endless static. I flick the radio off.

Sofia shakes her head. "Is he always that . . . uh . . . cryptic?"

I try and shrug it off. "Carlos is the head foreman in charge of the operation here. The crew has been working twenty-four-seven with my father cracking the whip from the home office. And with this hurricane lurking, he's probably just exhausted and annoyed at having to babysit us this weekend."

They all seem to buy my explanation, but none of them know Carlos personally like I do. He's usually extremely friendly and talkative, un tipo that will bend over backwards to help, especially me, the boss's son.

I flick a different switch on the gondola's dash. Ahead, the massive cemetery gates surrounding the park slowly creak open with a loud, unnerving grind, as our tiny ferry slips through.

Qué vaina! Almost forgot. I take the microphone attached to the gondola's front panel and turn the key in the adjacent activation slot.

"Welcome to Malicia," my best John Hammond in *Jurassic Park* voice booms through the park's crackling speakers. "Prepare to meet your doom."

My eyes flit to my pack and the hidden instruments tucked inside for the ritual I intend to perform. I wonder what they'd say if they knew my other reason for dragging them on this trip was to summon the dead? They'd probably add one more victim to the Malicia Massacre. The gondola slips through the enormous gates, which creak and grind before slamming shut behind us.

JOAQUIN

eart racing. Breathing labored.

Now that we're finally here, my façade starts crumbling as my anxiety levels spike.

It's Thursday. The 28th. All these months of plotting and planning have come down to these last three days. By Halloween night it will all be over, one way or another. But will I have the cojones to go through with it? And will I finally be free?

I clutch my own hands to stop from fidgeting. When I can't swallow, I panic, getting up to rummage through my pack for another bottle of water. I twist the cap off, chugging half of it down. That foggy, disconnected feeling's kicking in big time. What did the therapist call it? Depersonalization. Part of my Generalized Anxiety Disorder, aka Oh my GAD this sucks.

My dumbass therapist would be suffering from GAD, too, if she were fighting for her very life and soul.

I scan the scenery on either side, filled with the remnants of ancient trees, creating a canopy above us that blocks out much of the gray sky. Long strands of Spanish moss dangle from them, brushing across the gondola and tops of our heads with a low hiss, raising gooseflesh.

One particular symbol catches my eye. It's not carved into the wood like the others. It's been etched in red paint—blood? A circle with horns on each side and a letter B at its center. Its mark.

I press my hand against that spot on my hip.

Ray catches me staring. "I don't remember ever seeing that symbol before, in case you're wondering, even when I did my refresher research for this trip."

He lifts the mic from its cradle, his voice strong and deep, despite the crackling of the gondola's speakers. "Gente, you have now entered the fabled Boneyard Bayou, the lair of Los Biembiens."

Isabella aims her camera my way. "Quién? Spill, Ray."

"According to the legend, Los Biembiens originated in the Bahoruco mountains in the DR. In the 1700s, slaves escaped their Spanish captors and hid in the mountains, where they were transformed into wild, deformed creatures that communicated only with grunts, sacrificed humans to the gods, and feasted on their entrails. Unfortunately, the Biembien animatronics were damaged through years of neglect, so they won't be rising from the sea to make an appearance now."

I stick a finger in my mouth, pretending to gag. "Sounds like a colonizer's wet dream."

Sofia cranes her neck to get a better look at the water, then fixes Ray with a mischievous smile. "Hmmm. Too bad. The *communicating through grunts* part sounds like a creep I dated once."

The reminder that Sofia and Ray used to date rattles my already raw nerves, until I remind myself I have no right to be jealous, considering why I maneuvered Ray into returning here. Besides, in three days, none of it will matter anymore. My throat burns with bile.

Beyond the mist up ahead, there's a small tributary branching off to the left of the river, half hidden by shrubs and moss, which Ray explains is the service accessway for staff and crew to reach the hotel lodge without disturbing guests. My heart rate intensifies again as he steers the gondola toward this narrower offshoot, guiding it to the docking area and into the slip.

A solitary figure is waiting on the dock, a hulk of a man— mid-forties, tall, and broad-shouldered. His face is pale, eyes bloodshot, as if he hasn't gotten any sleep in a while, and judging by how wrinkled his uniform is, he was probably wearing it when he did.

Wait a minute. I recognize this guy. I've seen him before. At one of the ceremonies. What's he doing here, and why is he looking at me like that?

"Carlos!" Ray shuts off the engine and hops out to greet him, shaking his hand.

Carlos nods, dropping his gaze. "Senior Delvalle. Bienvenidos. Welcome."

Ray studies the foreman's face. "Are you feeling okay, amigo? Te ves mal."

He shrugs it off. "Comí algo que no me sentó bien."

Uh, food poisoning? I don't think so. His skin is so pale you can practically see the veins pulsating underneath. And what's with that B.O.? A cloying, sweet stench with a hint of something that's going bad. Those aren't symptoms of salmonella, and I'm an armchair expert on every disease imaginable. This is no coincidence. The coven sent him here. But why? To spy on me? To make sure I do the job?

As Carlos starts to unload our bags, Ray tries to wave him off, telling him he should go get some rest, but Carlos won't hear of it, mooring the boat to the posts and anchoring it, while the rest of us grab our packs and disembark. Once he's done securing the gondola, Carlos single-handedly loads our packs onto a dolly.

Ray taps him on the shoulder and asks him in Spanish where the rest of the crew is and why they aren't helping him.

He smiles broadly, but there's something forced and almost ghastly about the gesture. "No problem. I do alone."

Then he laughs, whistling an off-key tune as he rolls our stuff away and disappears.

Everything's eerily quiet. No birds. No insects. Just the incessant, mournful wailing of the wind and the occasional rumble in the sky.

Above the archway, a giant, sinister face glares down at us. A bald, scarred head, pale as bone, with sunken red-slit eyes and emaciated cheeks. It's Master Crawly—El Cucuy, the gruesome Majordomo and mascot of Malicia Theme Park—looming above, ready to devour each of us in that wide, fanged grin that reminds me of the expression on Carlos's face.

"Qué lo qué, pana? You okay?" Ray rests a hand on my shoulder.

I hug myself, rubbing my arms against a sudden gust of chilly ocean air.

"I'm good. Just a little seasick." I avoid his eyes and move away. The last thing I want is for Ray, of all people, to think I'm a little pendejo, especially since I really am.

Ray leads us all up the narrow steps toward the lodge. Then we cross an immense wooden drawbridge overlooking a surrounding moat filled with dark, swirling water.

He holds out his hands above his head and slowly revolves in a three-sixty, letting us take it all in. "Here it is, gente, The Conde's Keep, our humble accommodations for the duration of our stay. In its prime, this was the premiere guest hotel for park visitors interested in an even more immersive experience."

Isabella pans the scene with her camera. "Welcome to Mordor, bitches!"

The lodge is a medieval fortress, with towers and walls sprouting all over the place like insectile appendages. Two enormous oriel windows flank the building's upper story, jutting from the ancient stone, bulbous eyes filled with blackness, soulless and empty. Instead of traditional gargoyles, there are elaborately carved stone Chupacabras. The legendary blood-sucking creatures are hunched over, with a line of sharp spikes running down their backs, kangaroo hind legs, and short T-Rex arms, which end in razor-sharp claws. Their eyes are huge and elongated, but the centermost statue is missing one, creating a more chilling effect.

We follow Ray through the huge double doors and into

the Great Hall. Carlos has deposited our packs here, but both he and the dolly are gone. The inside of the castle's filled with flickering shadows, casting grotesque shapes across the walls and vaulted ceiling.

Ray drapes his arm around me and pulls me close. "Tengo una idea. After such a long day of travel, the Quisqueya Club deserves to relax in style. I'm sure I'm not the only one whose stomach is already growling louder than el huracán." His ear-to-ear grin lights up the entire room, eclipsing my anxiety.

I give him a playful shove. "You're always hungry."

"Hey, I have big muscles to feed." He flexes one of his enormous biceps, and we both crack up.

But inside, the familiar gnawing at my heart is almost unbearable now that we are actually here. How am I really going to do this? This is Ray—*my* Ray—and on Halloween night I have to get him to the top of that mountain and—I pull away from him.

Isabella sets her camera aside. "I'm due for a recharge anyway."

I'm not sure if she's talking about herself or her camera.

Ray picks up the heavy coolers with ease. "There should be a small staff kitchen area behind those doors where we can set up our spread. What did you say was in these, Sofia?"

"Joaquin and I packed a little welcome-to-Malicia meal in order to celebrate our arrival."

Ray hustles us into the kitchen, which, considering it's for the staff, is huge. He gives it a quick survey, testing the power, the faucets, and the oven. "It looks like the crew must have been using this, so everything's in working order."

While he and Isabella ransack the cupboards for plates and cutlery and set the table, Sofia and I remove the trays from the cooler and heat everything up in the oven before setting things out on the long banquet-style table. There's sancocho, mangú, arroz blanco con habichuelas, tostones, and yaniqueques.

Ray closes his eyes and takes a big whiff. "Oh my God, que rico! You guys made this all yourself, pana?"

I scoop the sancocho into a serving bowl. "Some of it. Sofia's abuela helped a little."

She chuckles, finally seeming to come around. "Just un poco."

I nod at Ray. "Make sure to try the meat stew and the mashed plaintains. I made those myself."

The last meal for a condemned man. Suddenly, I'm not hungry anymore.

Ray swallows a mouthful and clears his throat. "Now that we're here, I'd like to wish everyone a happy Halloween weekend and give mad props to the fierce foursome, who came together four years ago during freshman year at the first meeting of the Quisqueya Club—"

"Or as I like to call it," I cut in, "the Wayward Dominicans Club—"

"And became its charter members—"

"Its only members." I snort.

Ray grins at me. "And to commemorate, I'd like to propose un saludo."

"A toast?" Sofia asks. "You mean you've got booze, and you've been holding out on us?"

"Pana, can you take out that bottle of rum from the blue pack? There should be some cups, too."

"Aye, aye, Compay!" I rush over and pull the bottle out.

In seconds, everyone's crowded around me, waving their red Solo cups in my face as I fill each to the brim with Brugal.

Ray grins as he takes the Solo from me. "Here's to the Quisqueya Club! Tranquilo y tropical!" he announces.

Tropical tranquility, our club motto.

"Tranquilo y tropical!" we all reply in unison before we each chug our drinks and start chowing down.

The rum is definitely easing my anxiety. I turn to Ray, pouring him another cupful. "Remember that time Quisqueya Club went on that field trip to Punta Cana, and Isabella had one too many?"

Isabella chuckles and flings a scoop of plantain at me, which I duck and avoid. "It was more like ten too many."

Ray elbows me. "Estaba ajumada."

I poke him in the ribs. "So drunk that she spilled her drink on that chick with the big hair and almost got into a piña with her."

Sofia crosses her arms. "Because nothing says class like street fighting while on vacation."

Ray holds up his hands. "In all fairness, we were all wasted, even you, jevita."

He nudges Sofia and she reluctantly gives in and starts laughing as well.

I wrap my arms around Ray and Sofia. "If I hadn't hailed that concho and gotten us out of there, we would have all spent the night in a Dominican jail cell."

Ray shoots us his frat boy smile. "Good times."

Another loud gust of wind echoes through the complex,

freezing us in our tracks, but Ray's not having any of it. "We need something to drown that shit out. Izzy, you got any tunes?"

"Coming right up." Isabella plugs in her gear to a small portable speaker, and in seconds, the kitchen is filled with the sounds of Dominican music. She chuckles. "Now it's official. The Quisqueya Club's first meeting at Malicia is in session!"

We all crowd around the banquet table and dig in, hunger overriding fear for the moment.

For a couple of hours, everyone else seems able to forget about the stress of a potential hurricane hit, college acceptances, and their futures and just enjoy each other's company.

No amount of liquor can make me forget why I'm truly here. I fight the impulse to yell out at the top of my lungs that we should all leave now, while there's still a chance, before I do something there'll be no turning back from.

But I stay silent. My grandparents have conditioned me too well. Cults have a way of doing that.

Ray finally pushes his chair away from the table and rubs his belly. "Que hartura! I definitely overdid it. Going to have to double-up on workouts when we get back. But it was so worth it. Gracias, you two." He nods his chin toward Sofia and winks at me, his gaze lingering and making me feel all warm inside.

Isabella switches the ballads to some high energy merengue music. "Now's your chance to work it off. Baila conmigo!"

Before Ray can protest, she pulls him to his feet and the two of them dance, with Sofia and me cheering them on.

Ray grins and spins Izzy around and dips her, calling out to us, "C'mon! Let's see what you two got."

Another pang of anxiety. I shake my head. "I'm probably the only Dominican with two left feet."

Sofia nods. "And dancing is the one area where I can't lead."

"Que vaina! It's not that hard," Ray calls to me. "Let me show you."

He and Isabella dance right over to us, Ray grabbing my hand, and Isabella hauling Sofia to her feet.

Ray pulls me close to him and places his hand around my waist. "Just put one hand on my shoulder and hold my other hand like this." He wraps his other hand around mine, squeezing gently, but firmly.

I can feel the heat rising in my face as I look into Ray's eyes for a long moment and then we're off, spinning and twisting across the kitchen floor.

As we whirl, I can barely hear Isabella and Sofia laughing and giggling as they glide alongside us.

"You're really good at this!" Ray's laughter echoes through the room as he deftly maneuvers us across the makeshift dance floor.

I'm surprised at how effortlessly I'm following his lead. For the first time in a long time, something other than fear and guilt pumps the blood through my heart. How can I possibly go through with it? Ray would never look at me the same way if he knew who I really am.

The fast-paced merengue music has given way to the slow, romantic rhythms of a crooning bolero. Isabella and Sofia collapse into their chairs, exhausted.

I'm prepared to follow suit, but Ray holds on to me firmly. He looks deep into my eyes as we slowly sway to the music.

"Been worried about you."

"I'm good. Just a little anxiety about the storm. Nothing a swig of Brugal can't handle."

"Seguro?"

"I'm sure."

"You've got nothing to worry about, Joaquin. I'll always have your back."

If you only knew I had a knife in yours.

In that moment, I'm hyperaware of how closely our bodies are pressed together. So close, I can feel the heat radiating off him, his musky scent mixed with the remnants of his cologne.

Movement to our left. My head whips to find Isabella aiming her camera at us.

She giggles. "You two look like you're about to act out the climax in one of those cheesy, melodramatic telenovelas, where the one character is declaring their undying love before they . . . you know . . . sacrifice themselves and die and shit."

Before I can blast her with words, Ray dips me backwards and says, "No matter what happens, mi amor, always remember that I love you!"

"Kiss him!" Isabella squeals.

His lips move closer until they're just an inch away, and even though I know he's playing, part of me wonders what it would feel like if it were real, if I could just experience it one time before the end.

The loudest gust of wind yet rumbles through Malicia, and the entire complex vibrates. For a frightening moment, the lights flicker, and I'm not sure if I can hold it together if there's a blackout.

But it passes, and so does the moment between Ray and me. He gently lifts me back up and I slip out of his arms.

He pulls out his phone and dials. "I don't like the sound of that. I guess we should try and find out why Carlos hasn't come back yet and where the rest of the crew's at."

Ray tries for several more minutes until he finally hangs up. "Still nothing. And it's been hours. I don't think they're coming. Something's wrong."

My heart starts racing again. Something's definitely wrong, Ray. And it's me. And in three days, you'll be dead.

I take a deep breath and stand. "If they're not coming to us, then we go find them."

Ray sighs. "This park is huge. That's a lot of ground to cover. They could be anywhere."

My mind's working overtime. I knit my brows together, concentrating, thinking up all the logical scenarios. Then a thought hits me, and I look back up at Ray. "You said that sometimes the cell service is spotty here, correcto?"

"Sí."

"Wouldn't the crews have an alternate way of communicating with each other that was more reliable? Like SAT phones or—"

"An app!" His eyes light up. He checks his phone. "My cell's almost dead. Let me borrow yours."

I hand him mine and his fingers fly across the keyboard.

"I'm downloading Ouija onto your phone."

I narrow my eyes. "Never heard of it."

"It's a special app that was designed to be used only on Malicia through its private network server."

I take the phone back from him. "Hopefully, the work crews thought to set up a temporary network so they could communicate while the park was being prepped for demolition."

Ray kisses me on the forehead. "You're a genius."

I shrug. "I try."

I turn to Joaquin and Isabella. "It's a good thing you decided to charge our phones during the feast, just in case we get any power outages."

"Almost forgot." Joaquin gives back Isabella's phone and charger and tucks his into his pocket.

I can't help but notice how fidgety Isabella seems when she powers her phone on and begins checking her notifications.

"Don't worry, Izzy," I say. "It's only been a couple of hours. There's still a world out there."

"Not if Edgar has anything to say about it," Joaquin mutters. "The winds have strengthened. Can't you hear them?"

Isabella groans.

A few pings later, and the Ouija download is complete.

I examine the app's icon, modeled after a traditional Ouija board, except with an eye staring out through the circular glass of the tiny planchette.

I'm rolling my eyes when a notification, accompanied by the sound of a creaking door, startles me. . . . It says:

You Have a Request from the Great Beyond.

Without waiting for a response, I tap the notification.

A familiar purplish, decaying face appears, eyes opened wide and crimson from burst capillaries, vomit caked on slightly parted and cracking lips, a bloated tongue just visible beyond them.

It's my face. My dead face.

My eyes glaze over at the user profile name scrawled in red at the bottom of that face.

SofiaRIP.

"What the hell . . . ?" I whisper. I look back up at them accusingly. "This isn't funny. Which pendejo photoshopped my face?"

"What are you talking about?" Ray seems genuinely surprised. His voice is the epitome of calm and concern. "I didn't send you anything. All our phones are charging, remember?"

Joaquin moves closer. "What exactly do you think you saw?"

A pang of anger momentarily shoves aside my fear. "I don't *think* I saw anything. I *know* I did."

Ray slips between us. "Lemme see. Please."

While I resent being coddled, I hand him the phone.

Joaquin and Isabella crowd around him and study the screen.

Finally, Ray looks up at me. "It's just the generic welcome message. The same one everyone gets when they initially sign on."

I rip the phone from his hand. "I'm telling you it says—"

Master Crawly is dying to be your friend. Accept? Decline?

Accompanying this message is the Malicia logo with the decaying face of the grinning ghoul mascot.

Plastering a smile on my face, I manage to laugh. "I guess

this place is creeping me out more than I thought. Sorry. Didn't mean to jump down your throats."

Turning back to the phone, I decline Master Crawly's invitation, even though all I can think of is the original message, the one I know I saw.

What if Ray's playing one of his infamous practical jokes on me and enabled some kind of corpse filter on the app? I sigh. I wouldn't put it past him, or any of the others, for that matter. They can be such infants at times.

The phone pings again, and I see a red dot by the tracker tab labeled *Dearly Departed*. "It looks like at least one of the crew is online. I'm calling."

I press the screen and put the call on speaker. The rings echo through the chamber in a series of ascending bells that sound slightly out of tune, unnerving. Just as it looks like no one's going to answer, there's a click.

"Hello?" I mutter into the empty silence.

No response. Just something that sounds like a mixture of breathing and scratching.

"This is Sofia Montero. I'm with Raymundo Delvalle," I say, enunciating every syllable. "You guys were all supposed to meet us at the dock, make sure we were stocked with supplies. What's going on? Where are you? Adonde están? Carlos?"

Still no response.

Then there's another sound. Like a whisper, muttering something unintelligible, making my skin crawl.

But one phrase stands out.

". . . Serial Springs . . ." the voice whispers.

The call cuts out.

"What was that all about?" Isabella asks.

I dial again. But this time there's only ringing, until eventually that cuts out, too.

Raymundo averts my gaze, but I can still see how uncomfortable he is. "There's probably something wrong with the connection. That's all."

I'm still focused on the screen when it pings again. This time I see what looks to be some type of GPS system with a red flashing beacon in the form of a skull and crossbones. "I think I've got something."

They all crowd around me.

I hold up my phone so they can see. "I'm getting another signal from Ouija. On the GPS tracker. It looks like there's a user signal coming from the other direction. We should see who or what it leads to."

Isabella holds up her camera. "And maybe get some more sightseeing in along the way."

"Sorry for the poor lighting," Ray says through a mouthful of crispy fritter that he must have snatched from our banquet feast. "Though the electricity's been temporarily hooked up, many of these candle bulbs aren't working, especially in the west wing, so I suggest we use the flashlights we packed."

There's a bit of rustling as I join the others in rummaging through our respective packs and retrieving our flashlights. Soon the vast chamber is filled with creepy, crisscrossing beams of light, as the dying light bleeds through gunshot windows.

I shudder, despite the hall's humid stuffiness.

"It didn't happen here." Joaquin's words startle me, as if he has a backstage pass to my thoughts.

I purse my lips and nod, not wanting to ask the obvious question. Somehow, knowing exactly where the massacre took place isn't going to set my already frazzled nerves at ease. I check the tracker on the phone. "Por aquí. Follow me."

I lead the way, with Ray right behind me, followed by Joaquin, and finally Isabella.

Once I reach the end of the corridor, I check the phone. "We go left from here."

Isabella hurries ahead of me in order to turn and get footage of our approach. "You have to admit, what happened here was especially out there."

I pause and swallow hard, stopping to check the tracker again. "How so?"

Joaquin clears his throat. "The Malicia Massacre set the bar pretty high (or low, depending how much you value human life). In addition to having a much higher body count than all those other horrific tragedies, there's another distinct factor that sets it apart."

"The killer—or killers—have never been identified or caught," Ray finishes for him. "No police shoot-out. No murder-suicide. No bullying, mental illness. No viral videos taken by visitors during the attack. No terrorists to claim any credit. With all the park's surveillance mysteriously malfunctioning during the murders, the guilty just vanished without a proverbial trace, leaving behind a haunted legacy of hundreds of corpses to fuel the endless speculations of conspiracy theorists, twenty-four-hour news media outlets, and Internet message boards. Una vaina inexplicable."

I lead the way forward again, moving past a dilapidated

game room. "What about the families of the victims and that one kid who survived?" I ask through a dry mouth.

"What's through there?" Joaquin nudges me toward the two double doors directly ahead of us.

Ray marches over toward the doors back in full tour guide mode. "El Salón de Leyendas. The Hall of Legends."

He seizes both ornate door handles and pulls on them. It's a good thing Ray's strong, because the massive doors slowly creak apart with all his efforts. Joaquin jumps in, and between the two of them, they manage to open both doors and secure them to the wall.

I lead the way in as Ray hits the light switch. The glow from the generators gradually illuminates the hall, and I have to stifle a gasp.

ISABELLA

"¡Vacano!" I focus my camera.

I snap a series of photos from as many interesting angles as I can think of.

"Coño! This place is cool as shit!"

The domed Hall of Legends is the size of a large cathedral, except instead of dazed parishioners stuffed into pews, it's crammed with dark figures—row upon row of infamous movie monsters—glaring down from their oblong pedestals, sizing us up like a rival gang, as if they're trying to decide who to pounce on first.

I recognize every single one of these movie monstros, the only friends I had when I was little.

"It's them! The Malicia all-stars!" The words escape before I have a chance to check myself.

The flashes light up the gruesome silhouettes like lightning, as Edgar's feeder bands chant his approach through the shattered stained-glass windows.

"What the hell . . . ?" Sofia mutters as she holds her screen up closer.

"*Hell* pretty much sums it up." Joaquin looks at all the statues like he's going to piss himself.

"What is it?" Ray's eyes narrow as he examines Sofia's phone over her shoulder. "Getting anything else on that GPS?"

She shakes her head. "The signal's going all funky."

Ray crosses his arms. "If this is some kind of joke, it's not funny anymore."

Sofia glances away from her phone. "Let's have a look around."

Sofia leads Ray and Joaquin through the sea of macabre icons. While they're *ooh*ing and *aah*ing over their personal faves, I'm frozen in place, gaping at the figure towering directly over me.

"So awesome," I whisper.

The plaque on the pedestal reads Julia 'La Jupia.' She was the antagonist of the *Bloody Belly* movie franchise, inspired by the mythical Jupia of Dominican folklore. She's riding a black steed, draped in her signature crimson hood and robes, her piercing yellow eyes the only part of her face that's visible. Her body is practically naked, with not a hint of a navel on her abdomen, because according to the legend, La Jupia was not born of a woman. She's a spirit of the air that assumes human form at night, the better to seduce her human prey and slaughter them during the climax of their lovemaking by cutting a deep gash in her victims' belly buttons and ripping out their intestines through it.

I'm going to get massive hits with this one. I take more video of this badass bitch before rushing to catch up with the others. "Wait up!"

Ray's hamming it up again, hands raised as we weave in and about the lifelike statues.

"They're all here, gente. Real-life deranged serial killers, supernatural entities, man-made aberrations, alien parasites, prehistoric menaces. Every single nasty from TV, film, and real life that has kept you squirming in bed, lights on, covers over your head, afraid to look under the bed or behind the shower curtain. Malicia's massive collection of classic baddies at your service." His voice echoes through the musty, cavernous chamber.

I poke Joaquin in the ribs. "Remember when we all skipped class sophomore year to go see the premiere of *La Jupia Part VII: Barrio Bellies?*"

Joaquin lets out a chuckle. "And I pigged out on chocolemon curly fries and threw up during the climax?"

"Sí, but the worst part was you threw up on *me!*" Ray musses his hair. "I reeked like un zafacón."

"And your garbage can smell cleared the theater, allowing me to get a better seat." I take a few pics of Ray and Joaquin play wrestling.

Sofia looks up from her phone and rolls her eyes. "And I had to cover all your asses—yet again—with Mr. Salort, so you wouldn't get detention. It's always so much fun being the one who has to stay focused."

I scowl at her. "You need to lighten up, chica, and stop being a hypocrite and giving me flack for living on my phone when you can't tear your eyes away from yours right now." I shoot Ray a look. "Though I can't blame you for tuning his tour guide routine out."

This gets a laugh and a smile from Sofia.

Joaquin shakes his head. "Esto es increíble. This collection has to be priceless. I can't believe they just left it here to rot all these years."

Ray nods. "After the massacre, when my family's holdings in the company took a massive dump, this collection was one of the few things they held on to as a sort of insurance policy. Because of its size and what it would cost to transport and store it, they just kept everything here. The new owners paid a lot of money for all this stuff. So look, but don't touch."

I chuckle. "They'd probably shit if they knew a group of teenagers had the run of the place for the weekend."

Joaquin sighs. "Of course, Edgar might put a wrench in that plan."

Sofia's smile fades and she stares at her phone, all serious again, back in tracker mode.

My teeth dig into my lower lip as I retreat into documentarian role again. As much fun as this is, I really need to focus, like Sofia's doing. This docu-project is my key to getting into a good college. Sure, I can try and make it big as an influencer, and I've already built up a pretty decent following, but is it wrong to also want to be taken seriously? Getting into Northwestern can make that happen. I taste blood, which I quickly swallow. So, what if the others don't know that while Malicia is the subject of my doc, so is the Quisqueya Club? They're my friends. They'd want to help me. And not telling them they're a part of it keeps it all real. I don't really care about murders, massacres, or monsters. Yeah, that sells. But I'm more interested in the human element. Friendships. Relationships. That's the shit that's real. That's also what's going to set me apart from those that live to exploit tragedies. At least that's what I'm telling myself. Looking through the camera's viewfinder, I scan each of their faces.

Sofia, calm, in control, tracking the signal, and almost ignoring the statues all around us. She's trying too hard to act like she has it together, as usual. But my camera lens cuts through the B.S. as efficiently as La Jupia's sharpened claws.

Snap. Snap. Snap.

There. I caught it. The split second where Sofia lets her guard down, exposing the glassy, haunted eyes of an animal caught in a trap.

She's afraid, no matter how in control she likes to pretend to be.

Cameras are the ultimate lie detectors.

I aim the lens at Ray. The classic "pretty muscle boy" who may as well be wearing a T-shirt that says, "Don't hate me 'cause I'm a rich papichulo."

Maybe it's the flickering of the shadows, but I swear there's something lurking just under the surface as far as Ray is concerned. It's like his skin is una máscara, a bright and shiny disguise, like a mortician's work of art covering up disease and decay. Hay algo mal. No matter how good they are at their job or how hard they try to cover things up, the person always looks dead. There's another reason Ray dragged us all back with him to Malicia. A real reason. And it's not just to play tour guide.

"Here we have the infamous El Galipote," he says, gesturing toward a towering figure with the muscular torso of a man but sprouting grisly appendages, including tentacles, misshapen wings, canine paws, and razor-sharp teeth. "There's a reason this dude is the star of one of the biggest grossing sci-fi horror franchises since *Alien*. Terrifying, right?"

My throat goes completely dry, and I can barely speak. I'm feeling numb and tingly all over. "My cousin used to scare the crap out of me with this guy when she babysat me, telling me that if I misbehaved, El Galipote would take the shape of a wolf, crawl into my bedroom window, and suck the blood out of me, kind of like a cross between a vampire and a werewolf. I couldn't sleep for years. If memory serves, the only way to kill the wolf is by fashioning a wooden cross out of a branch that was cut on Good Friday."

Ray elevator eyes the effigy. "They say a machete or some sort of knife or dagger will do the trick, as long as they've been blessed with salt and water."

"What's all this talk about a wolf?" Joaquin frowns. "My family always said El Galipote could take the form of a nocturnal bird"—he pauses and cocks his head—"un Zangano, I think it was called."

Ray laughs. "Birds, wolves. The way my folks used to tell it, El Galipote could change into inanimate objects, or even become invisible, so behave or else."

Joaquin elbows him. "Kind of like a demonic Elf on the Shelf."

Ray shakes his head. "Nothing's more demonic than *that* thing."

Everyone laughs except me.

I look away from them and squeeze my eyes shut for a moment before opening them again.

Sofia stifles a yawn.

I shake my head at her. "Doesn't anything scare you, Sofia?"

"What do you mean?"

"I was traumatized by El Galipote movies as a child. The way Joaquin was eyeing that marquee of Master Crawly when we arrived, it was obvious it scared him shitless."

Before Joaquin can protest, I cut him off.

"Ray puts on a good show, but he's obviously overcompensating," I continue, ignoring Ray's chuckles. "What monster are you scared of?"

Sofia tilts her head and furrows her brow for a moment. Then her eyes open wide with mock excitement. "Oh! I know. Medical malpractice."

I groan and plaster a smile on my face, aiming the camera at them. "Everybody smile and say 'El Galipote!'"

They all turn my way and grin.

I take some video, then snap a series of photos.

I'm doing my best to hold it together and not let them see how disturbing the figure of El Galipote really is to me. But my heart's thundering in my ears, drowning out their voices.

Ray and Joaquin are roughhousing for the camera again, laughing and pawing at each other, and for a split second it looks like they've got tentacles instead of arms.

"Hola. What are you staring at, Iz?" Joaquin's voice snaps me back like a bungee cord.

Shields up. I wave a hand to indicate the sea of rogues looming over us. "I've just never seen so many spooks in one place."

"So, you have seen actual spooks before?" Joaquin's face is deadpan.

I curse myself for letting my guard down, replacing it with a mask of sarcasm and boredom instead.

"*You're* the scariest thing I've seen in a while, Joaquin."

"Gracias. Do I look *that* bad?"

I burst out into a perfectly timed giggle, breaking the tension. "I'm just playing with you. You should see the look on your face."

Despite his protests, I aim the camera at him and fire off a rapid series of shots.

He holds his hands up to cover his face, unable to control his own laughter.

"You guys sound like you're having way too much fun." Sofia moves into view, with Ray in tow.

"No respect for las leyendas," Ray says with mock concern, his words echoing through the vastness around us.

They're all laughing now, poking and prodding each other, making faces as I take photos, imprisoning a fragment of their souls with each shot, finding out what makes *them* tick for my documentary.

Sofia's phone bleeps like the sound a heart rate monitor makes.

"I'm getting that signal again," Sofia says, her voice filled with excitement as she assumes command and control once again.

I zoom out to wide angle and pan. My finger jams down on the shutter button and freezes, as we all huddle around Sofia, following her into the dark shadows.

Snapsnapsnapsnapsnapsnapsnapsnapsnapsnapsnap . . . The sound bores through my head like the sound of a thousand snapping bones. There goes a dislocated shoulder. A cracked neck. A severed spinal cord.

"Look over there," I hear myself say. I aim the camera toward a small object lying on the floor in a corner.

It's a cell phone. And it's bleeping. Before Ray can intercept, I let the camera hang around my neck and pick up the phone. It's wet, sticky. Blood?

I gasp, letting go, as if I've been burned. It falls to the floor with a sharp cracking sound, like brittle bones splintering in the dark.

Sofia hunches down and examines the phone. From the expression on her face, she's noticed the blood, too.

"What is it?" Ray asks.

She hands it to him to examine. "One of your crew must have dropped it."

He locks eyes with Sofia. "But why did he bleed on it first?"

A loud crash jumpstarts my muscles.

"What the hell was *that*?" Joaquin's body twitches as he scans the gloom.

El Salón de Leyendas has worn out its welcome. None of us seem amused anymore. I slowly turn away, avoiding the eyes of those statues, standing perfectly still on their pedestals, sizing us up. Judging us.

For a second, I could swear one of them moves, way down the other side of the room. It's just a shadow. Has to be. But something about that silhouette reminds me of El Galipote. I snap a few pictures, before the shadow fades, then look away quickly. I need to get a grip. The supernatural is all bullshit. You can't trust your eyes. They may be windows to the soul as some people say, but eyes lie. Cameras are all about facts and truth.

We all stand still, listening. But there aren't any other loud crashes, only the wailing wind, whistling through the wooden planks covering the shattered windows and broken doors, creating a chilly draft that pierces my skin like a thousand tiny projectiles. I can't even imagine what the bullets and shrapnel must have felt like when they tore through this place.

Joaquin clears his throat. "You guys listening? Are those feeder bands courtesy of Edgar? What if he's changed course and is heading in this direction?"

Ray wraps an arm around his shoulder. "It's cool, pana. Scared me, too. But this is an old place. Maintenance guys probably moved stuff around. Or some rotting furniture could have toppled over in the wind. I'm sure it's nothing."

"Isn't that what they always say in horror movies before it turns out to be something?" I check the gauges on my camera, almost as if on remote. That always helps to keep me focused, pun intended. Looking through the viewfinder, I scan the video and pictures I've been taking, especially the one with that shadow I thought I saw in the Hall of Legends.

My insides threaten to let loose.

There's no mistake. There was a figure darting about in the shadows, one not visible to the naked eye.

Eyes lie. But cameras tell the truth.

My hand reflexively goes to the little wooden cross I've worn around my neck since childhood. The one carved on a Good Friday. The one blessed with water and salt for good measure.

RAYMUNDO

ofia's phone is really acting up now. Her eyes grow wide. "The signal's much stronger now. Coming from the room next door. Could be the entire crew. Let's check it out."

"The Quisqueya Club is on the case." I rush over to the far side of the room. With everyone in tow, I push the doors leading from El Salón de Leyendas into the mammoth banquet hall wide open—

Qué vaina! I almost gag. What the hell is that stench?

The once lush drapes my brother Rudy and I used to hide behind hang in ghostly tatters. Splinters of glass from shattered gilded mirrors lie everywhere, reflecting dismembered glimpses back at us as we make our way across the debris-strewn broken marble.

The signal on Sofia's phone is bleeping harder and faster.

The sound of other loud bleeps surrounds us then, like

lambs bleating in a slaughterhouse. Flashes of light cut through the shadows.

Someone screams. I can't tell if it's Sofia or Isabella.

Hell. Maybe it's me.

The mystery of the missing work crew is no more. They're here, engulfed by a foul cloud of stink and flies. Cell phones are strewn all about the bodies, flashing with calls and messages that'll never be answered. Heads have been removed, replaced by the ghoulish effigies of Malicia Theme Park icons. But their work uniforms are intact, complete with blood-stained name tags.

There's 'Jose' over there. And over there. And over there.

Everything's suddenly muffled. Is that Sofia barking orders? Joaquin's fingers digging into my arm?

Warm droplets hit my forehead, like an insistent finger, tap tap tapping.

I scoop up one of the droplets with my finger. It's dark. There's something familiar about that smell, but I can't quite place it.

I crane my head up, vaguely aware that the others are doing the same. Pointing. Screaming.

What the hell is that? Someone shouts.

Strange cables dangle from the rafters, swaying in the wind streaming through shattered windows.

Drip. Drip. Drip.

I swipe more dark gook from my eyes. What are those? Hydraulic cables from some animatronic exhibit? I don't remember ever seeing—

There's someone repeating *DiosMioDiosMioDiosMio....*

My God indeed.

Joaquin's having a meltdown. He's clutching Sofia. Crying. Sobbing. I should go to him. To all of them. I need to make sure everyone's safe. But I can't move.

Isabella may as well be an exhibit at the Salón de Leyendas. Paralyzed. Expressionless. Staring at the carnage through her camera, recording everything.

More warm droplets pelt me. I don't bother trying to wipe them away. They ooze down my cheeks, mixing with the sudden tears streaming down my face.

Blood.

Those aren't cables dangling from above. They're organs. Intestines. Ripped from the bodies of the maintenance workers.

I turn to face everyone. They look like frightened children in the gloom, except for Sofia.

"Get to the boat. Now!" My breathing's competing with my racing heart as I herd them away, leading them out of the lodge, across the moat, down the narrow steps.

The dock's getting closer. I can see the gargoyle masthead and wooden facade of the gondola now. In a few minutes, we'll be safely aboard, heaving huge sighs of relief as we gun the engines and blow this place, taking our chances with the hurricane.

Unfortunately, that means I won't be able to complete the ritual I brought everyone here for, discover the truth of the ugly weight that's been crushing me ever since I can remember.

I can't think about that now. I grab Joaquin's and Isabella's hands, running faster and faster.

A large figure steps off the gondola, directly in our path.

"Stay back," I call to the others, but there's no need.

The figure is tall and stocky, a middle-aged guy. The tattered remnants of a once white poloché flutter like crimson streamers, the shirt dripping blood and God knows what else down his soiled jeans and tattered work boot. The other foot is bare and more like a swollen, purplish, festering stump. His exposed arms hang apelike at his sides, also coated in gore and open wounds, which look like symbols carved into his skin, the same symbols carved into those trees in Boneyard Bayou.

It's the face of nightmares, covered in blood and pulsating veins, the eyes emotionless black mirrors. A grin forms on torn lips, spreading wider.

It's Carlos's face. Dios mio. What the hell happened to him in a matter of hours?

"Are you injured?" Sofia calls to him.

I shake my head in disbelief. "Is *he* hurt? Have you lost it? Didn't you see those bodies back there? Quién carajo do you think did that?"

She whirls on me. "You don't know! Maybe Carlos was also hurt by whoever did that. If that's the case, then we need to help him. He obviously needs a doctor."

I push past them, stopping a few feet from Carlos. "What's happened to you? Qué te pasó?"

He just grunts some more.

The loud bleep from my phone almost gives me a heart attack. I glance at the screen. "Great. The latest advisory's in. El huracán's heading right toward us."

Isabella takes a few steps back toward the lodge, still recording. "There's got to be another way off this island that doesn't involve crossing paths with a potential homicidal maniac."

I sigh. "The boat's the only way off this island, and if we want to leave before Edgar pays a visit, we have to go through him." I nudge my chin toward the blood-soaked figure.

Joaquin shakes his head. Actually, his whole body's shaking, and I reach out to steady him. "No! We can't leave!"

He registers my shocked face and shakes his head. "I mean, if this guy is a killer, it's not worth the risk. We have to get back inside, tiguere."

"No gracias." Isabella shoots me a look. "Why can't we just . . . swim?"

"It's too deep to swim, the current's too strong, the mainland's too far, and there are sharks in these waters," I answer, anticipating every one of their counterarguments.

Joaquin's eyes bulge as he stares past me. "Oh, my god. It's—he's—moving."

Carlos grins, dark liquid oozing from the corners of his cracked lips, dribbling down his chin and onto the dock.

"Do you smell that?" Joaquin asks.

Now that the wind's picked up, I can smell it, too. "Gasolina."

Isabella jabs a finger in Carlos's direction. "He's covered in gasoline."

"So's the dock." Sofia points at the trail leading from the puddle underneath Carlos, spattered back toward the boat.

Carlos's eyes fixate on me, totally draining my resolve. The silent giant reaches into his pocket—

And pulls out a lighter, which glints in his bloodied fingers.

"Nadie debe sobrevivir," he croaks.

No one must survive.

His thumb fumbles, flicking the lighter, once, twice—
"Puta madre!" I only have time to shove Joaquin, Sofia, and
Isabella into the water before the dock ignites like a fiery sun.

JOAQUIN

I'm going to die.

Can't see. Can't breathe. Ice-cold fingers tear across my skin.

I'm drowning.

Can't let go of Sofia. Have to get back to the surface.

This is all my fault. What happened to Carlos was no accident. It got to him. Made him kill the other members of the crew and blow up the dock to trap us on this island. But if Ray's already dead . . .

A fresh wave of panic surges through me. I fumble for Sofia's hand, almost losing it, along with my sanity. Izzy's gone. Not sure where. Something else is here. In the dark murky depths.

El Bacá's coming. *Coming for you, Joaquincito.*

I'm choking. Can't breathe. Something clutches my paddling legs. I wrench them free. It has to be seaweed. That's all it is. It's okay. It can't hurt you, Joaquin.

Oh, but it can. . . .

A deep orange glow swirls above, growing brighter and brighter. Sofia and I break the surface with a big splash. Then I'm gasping for air, trying to hold up Sofia's head. Only she's not breathing. Her eyes are closed. No. It can't be. She can't be dead. That wasn't part of the deal. Sofia and Isabella have nothing to do with any of this.

"Hang on, Sofia!" I yell.

Chunks of the wooden deck and debris litter the water in every direction. What's left of the structure is engulfed in flames. The gondola is nothing but a burning pyre, half sunk beneath the waves.

"Raymundo!" I cry at the top of my lungs. "Izzy!"

It's tough going trying to swim to shore with Sofia in tow. She's dead weight, an anchor, threatening to drag us both down into the dark depths, where something much worse than sharks waits for us.

I whip my head from left to right, spitting out the salty sea flooding my lungs.

Where the hell is Ray?

He was right at the apex of the explosion when Carlos set things off.

"Stay . . . with . . . me . . . Sofia. . . ."

The adrenaline rush is starting to wear off. Lungs and muscles straining with the effort. Something bumps into me, and I almost let out a shriek.

It's a large chunk of dock. I heave myself onto the section of torn plank beside Sofia. For a few tense seconds, the makeshift floatation device teeters and almost flips, then we settle into the water. Wasting no time, I'm paddling away with my hands and feet, trying not to think about the sharks or El Bacá waiting below every time I plunge my limbs into the icy waters.

The dock entrance looms closer.

"Don't worry, Sofia. We're almost there. You're going to be okay. Trust me."

Who am I fooling? I can't be trusted. I've betrayed them all. Of course, Sofia's dead. Just like all the others, including Izzy and Ray.

Ray.

He wasn't supposed to die yet—at least not like that. The anxiety's really hitting hard now. The whole time I was planting the seeds, maneuvering him to come back to Malicia, making sure he found that book of rituals to compel him to come back here—through all of it—it never truly hit me what it would be like once we were here and I had to actually go through with it. And now he's probably dead already, and all I can think about is if that lets me off the hook of having to do it myself, or have I botched the only chance to save my own ass?

The way my heart's headbutting my chest, and the way I can barely take in any more air, it won't make much difference. I'm going to die. Heart attack. Stroke. Drowning. Any second now, and it'll feel like an elephant sat on my chest, crushing it, puncturing my ribs, rupturing my arteries, cutting off the blood supply to my heart, my brain.

The dock entrance is only a few feet ahead. No way I'm going to make it.

"Lo siento, Sofia." I spit out more water. Sorry doesn't cover it.

Just a few feet away. But my strength is almost completely gone.

Something floats into my peripheral vision. Something dark. Something bloody. It's an arm.

I shriek, swallowing more water and retching it up just as fast, thinking of all the blood and gore surrounding us.

Something grabs me and won't let go.

El Bacá's come for me. I've failed him. And now it's time for my soul to pay.

ow the hell is all this happening, and I didn't get it all
on camera? Another mass killing? Check. The killer
still lurking on the island? Check. Everyone else maybe
blown to smithereens in that fireball that took out the boat?
Check.

Que carajo! Here I am trying to focus on a quiet and serious documentary about friendships and relationships instead of
sensationalism, and the makings of a viral video land in my lap.

The first thing I do after swimming back to shore is check
the camera to make sure the waterproof casing is still intact. It
is, but the battery light on the power indicator is weak, barely
a blip. But it's something. I might be able to salvage this fiasco
after all. I can focus on the aftermath, how we're helping each
other make it through this, rather than on the event itself. That's
less exploitative, right?

Coño. Looks like we won't be leaving anytime soon, judging by what's left of the boat that brought us here. Patches of flaming debris litter the water, floating like molten lava oozing out of a volcano, contrasting against the darkening gloom. If I were live-streaming this shit, the number of clicks would be off the charts. Are those body parts, strewn across the surface? It's hard to tell who they belong to, even by zooming in.

My hand reflexively clutches my throat. The little wooden cross is still there.

I take in a deep breath of salty sea air, mixed with burning debris. The sound of crackling flames surround-sounds all around me, accompanied by the waves lapping up against the remnants of the dock.

Nippy wind claws at me. Cupping my hands, I call out to sea. "Sofia! Ray! Joaquin! Can you hear me?"

No answer. Everyone is gone.

Shit. Shit. Shit. The emotions start to seep through my armor and I shake them away. My body jerks as I fight the sobs. The Quisqueya Club can't be gone. Something splashes in the water ahead. There's a muffled cry.

El Galipote is coming. That movie monster that traumatized me as a kid during a sleepover with my cousins at Tia Josefina's house. That was him the camera picked up in El Salon de Leyendas. Cameras don't lie. He's real. No. That doesn't make sense. The supernatural is all just bullshit. The real world is what's scary, not some ghostly boogeyman shit.

I turn quickly away. I won't look. I can't, especially through the camera lens, the lens that shows the raw, unfiltered truth.

Whatever is making its way through that bloody water and

moving toward me is not something I want to come face to face with. I run in the opposite direction of the shoreline, ignoring the cry sounding over and over.

Isabella. Isabella.

ISABELLA.

I slip and land flat on my face, hitting my chin. There's blood on my tongue. But I don't care. I just want to get away from that approaching nightmare. But when I look up, it's staring me right in the eyes.

I can't stop screaming.

JOAQUIN

"I tried to do what you wanted!" I shout at the blurred shape, beating at it with my fists.

It takes me a few seconds to realize it hasn't started to eat me yet. No razor-sharp fangs ripping open my gut, pouring my insides out into the bloody sea.

"Pana, it's me!"

The voice sounds like it's coming from a deep well. Then there's a lot of thrashing and splashing. The next thing I know, I'm being dragged the rest of the way to shore. I panic. Where's Sofia?

But I feel her cold hand still gripped in mine, and I get an absurd thought, like when you're using your cell phone flashlight to try and find it.

I chuckle. My body smacks down on the sand with a thud. A dull chant assaults my ears.

"Sofia. Oh, god. Please be okay. . . ."

The voice grounds me, pulls me back from the void. I shake the sea from me. Rub my eyes. Focus. Ray is huddled on the ground next to me with Sofia.

"You're alive, tiguere . . . " my voice peters out. I'm not sure why I'm feeling such a surge of relief to see him. It doesn't matter. He's too distracted to hear me. That familiar dread floods my soul. Once again, the impossible burden has been thrust into my lap. No relying on accidents here. Ray has to die. In three days. And I'm the one that has to do it.

Ray's shirtless, every muscle in his broad back and arms glistens with wetness, his long hair loose and cascading down his shoulders as his body heaves over Sofia.

He lifts his mouth from hers, replacing his hands on her chest. "C'mon Sofia, breathe," he mutters. "Por favor . . . you can do it. Respira."

Then he's back to giving her mouth to mouth, his tears spilling onto her cheeks.

Anxiety carves into my chest, deep. What if he can't see me because El Bacá has already claimed me? My body recoils. I'm shaking. Pressure fills my chest, as if a huge foot presses down on an accelerator, speeding up my heartbeat, making it difficult to breathe . . .

Stop. It.

My eyes spring open and I'm at Ray's side. "What can I do?"

I don't know how many minutes we work on Sofia, me giving her compressions, him tilting her neck back and administering artificial respiration.

What if she doesn't make it? What if she dies? What if—

Sofia coughs up a burst of sea water.

"We did it, pana!" Ray's laughing, crying, hugging her close.

Then he turns to me with a big grin and takes me into his arms, pulling me tight against his chest. As much as I feel at home there, it's all I can do to not recoil from his touch.

Until the screaming starts.

ISABELLA

Staring down at me, it's El Galipote, like I've never seen him in any of the movies before.

Tall, dark, and standing in a puddle of oozing darkness, the stink of blood and charred skin choking the shit out of me. It reaches those fingers toward me, a deep gurgle busting loose from its throat—

I scream, backing away. But the figure keeps shambling toward me, arms outstretched, fingers reaching, almost as if it's begging.

Fear turns to anger. What the hell is wrong with me? I am not going down like some weak-ass punk. I stop screaming now, grabbing my camera as a shield. As a weapon.

"Hijo de la gran puta," I swear at him, tensing my muscles.

I snap a series of pictures right in his face. Something's . . . different. He's not as scary as he was before, in the movies, or en El Salón de Leyendas. In fact, he looks pathetic now, barely able to stand straight, teetering as he tries to come closer to me. He drops to his knees, grunting.

Looks like El Galipote is having a rough day. He's crawling, leaving a trail of blood behind him. Now's my chance. I may not get another one. I take a deep breath and stand my ground.

In the waning light, he's not so scary. I raise my camera high over my head trying not to flinch as I imagine the impact against his skull, crushing it, his brains leaking out from his ears.

"Izzy, what the hell are you doing? You can't kill him!" Ray shouts, just as my arms arc downward.

RAYMUNDO

I grab Isabella's arms just before she can slam the camera she's holding like a rock over the poor guy's head.

Carlos—at least what's left of him.

Damn. Carlos looks ten times worse than he did before, his burnt flesh hanging in tatters like a gruesome scarecrow. But the worst is the stench. The right half of his upper torso is badly burned, the raw, exposed flesh red and pulsing. One of his arms is just a ragged stump.

I fight the urge to gag, even as I'm struggling to control the hysterical Izzy, twisting in my grasp like a slippery snake.

"Let go! Now's my only chance to get rid of this asshole!"

I grab both her shoulders. "What's wrong with you? You're not a killer. He may have tried to blow the shit out of us, but he's not a threat anymore. Can't you see he's badly hurt?"

She shoves me aside, staring down at the hunched figure,

collapsed on one knee, struggling to remain upright. She's in shock. Understandable.

Then it's like a switch gets turned on. She blinks a few times, her eyes growing wide as she finally recognizes who it is. She drops the camera on the sand and cups her mouth with her other hand. She shakes her head.

"I didn't know . . . no sabía . . . I . . . thought it was . . ."

Carlos finally falls prostrate a few feet away.

Running steps behind me. I turn and come face to face with a very out of breath Joaquin.

"Qué lo wha—?" He looks past Isabella and me and takes in the awful sight of Carlos.

He almost seems relieved as he moves a little closer to Carlos, cupping a hand over his own mouth and nose because of the stench, and looks him over. He finally stares up at me, eyes glistening. "I don't think he's going to make it."

I tilt my head back where he came from. "What's going on with Sofia?"

"She's better. Weak. And pissed that I left her behind."

I grab Isabella's arm and point in the direction we left Sofia. "Go get Sofia. Make sure she's okay. Por favor."

Izzy doesn't say anything, just nods. Then she scoops up her camera and continues down the path.

I rush to where Joaquin is crouched close to Carlos. "This guy's been a friend of our family for years. I don't know what happened at that dock, but he's no killer. We need to keep him alive, at least long enough to find out what's going on here."

"This is really bad . . . I don't think there's any way he's going to make it. Maybe Sofia can help him better than we can."

I nod. "There are some first aid supplies back by the concierge area at the hotel. Sofia can use her Bach skills to patch him up. Or at least ease the pain."

Joaquin glances in the direction of the hotel, then back. "How are we going to get him back there? He's in too much pain, and if we try to carry him—"

Carlos lets out an agonizing moan, and I can't help but feel for him as a fellow human being, despite the fact that something made him try to kill us. Especially since it's all my fault for bringing everyone here.

I scan our surroundings, desperate, seeing nothing except—

"There!" I point.

Half-buried in the shrubs is a long-forgotten deck chair. Despite the pain, I sprint for it, dragging it back.

"Help me."

It takes a few minutes for Joaquin and me to carefully maneuver Carlos onto the remnants of the chair without causing too much additional pain.

I wipe the sweat from my brow. "Okay, I'll take the back. You take the front."

"On the count of three," he says. "Uno. Dos. Tres . . ."

We lift the chair, huffing and puffing our way along the shoreline with the heavy weight of Carlos's body.

"Hold it steady," I say through the strain.

Flashes of bodies being zipped into bags on this very beach kaleidoscope in my mind's eye, some like grainy newsreel footage, the others in vivid color.

Zip. Zip. Zippppppppppppppppppppppppppp.

How does it feel to lose your mother and brother in such an awful tragedy, Raymundo? The wind seems to whisper, mocking me.

No. This is different. Carlos isn't a body. He's still alive. In some ways, another victim of Malicia.

We finally make it up the steps, bursting through the service doors and into the concierge offices, depositing Carlos on the floor as gently as we can, despite our trembling muscles.

"Look in there." I point past Joaquin's head. "I'll check these supply drawers over here."

We ransack the room, finding bandages, gauze, N95 masks, anti-bacterial ointments.

Joaquin rips open a pack of masks, dons one, and hands one to me to do the same. "It's lucky you still have these things in stock after all these years."

"The company keeps them on hand in case one of the work crew gets injured. Not much left. Must be clearing things out in preparation for the shut down."

I swallow hard. "Listen. We need to get Sofia and Isabella—"

"No need," Sofia says.

We turn to find both girls staring at us from the doorway, disheveled and ashen, just like the two of us.

I nod. "You guys holding up? We were just on our way to find you."

Sofia runs a hand through her soaked hair. "We're fine. I mean, under the circumstances."

"How did you find—?"

"I told her about . . ." Isabella hesitates, glancing at Carlos, "him."

Sofia purses her lips. "We figured you'd try to find some

way to patch him up, so took our chances that you'd bring him here."

I smile. "Smart thinking, as always."

"It sure beats the hell out of waiting out there for you to find us." Isabella aims her camera around the room, back in full documentary mode after her meltdown.

Joaquin offers them the box of N95s. "You may want to wear these. Just in case. Maybe he got infected with something that made him completely lose it. We shouldn't take any chances just in case it's contagious."

"Agreed. How's he doing?" Sofia dons her mask and kneels by Carlos, running her palm across his forehead.

"Pretty bad," Joaquin replies.

I watch as Sofia carefully administers the ointments and bandages the skin with the skill of a paramedic.

"Columbia is going to be lucky to have you in their program, doctora," I say.

She continues to work without looking up at us. "Gracias. Can you see if there's anything in that cabinet for pain?"

I rifle through a bunch of bottles, rattling off half a dozen.

She motions to the third bottle on my list. "Those seem like the best option. Now, if you can get me some water, we're golden."

The rest of my search yields a case of lukewarm but unopened bottled water. I quickly pull one out and twist off the cap.

Sofia's cradling Carlos's head in her lap without even a hint of squeamishness, lifting him and slipping a couple of pills into his mouth.

"Carlos, you're going to be okay." Sofia tilts the bottle

against his lips. "Drink this." A lot of the water dribbles down his chin and throat, soaking his chest, but eventually he swallows the pills and Sofia lays his head back down, propping a small pillow we found underneath it.

We stare at him, listening to his raspy breathing becoming slower and slower, until it appears he's fallen asleep.

"There's not much else we can do." Sofia breaks the silence. "I mean, we bandaged him up and loaded him up with antibiotics and pain meds, but that's not going to be enough. We have to get him to a hospital. He needs to be in a burn unit."

Joaquin shakes his head. "And we need to be in quarantine."

I squeeze my chin, trying to think. "The gondola's totaled. We lost our ride back to the mainland, doctora."

"What about the work crew?" Joaquin asks, his face lighting up. "They must have a way in and out of here."

I look away from him, unable to confront the desperation in his eyes. "I don't think anyone's coming. And with all our phones taking a dip in the Caribbean Sea with us, there's no way of contacting the outside world."

Sofia clears her throat. "I hate to be Captain Obvious here, but are we forgetting all of those working cell phones lying around in the banquet hall?"

Joaquin's cinnamon eyes saucer. "Where all those dead bodies are?"

I wrap my arm around his shoulders and squeeze him closer. "La doctora is right. All we need is one phone and we're home free. I'll go."

He turns, grips my arms, and looks up at me pleadingly. "No way, tiguere. You can't go alone. It's not safe."

Isabella looks up from her viewfinder. "Joaquin's right. This is a job for the entire Quisqueya Club. We all go."

I wonder what's motivating Izzy more? The need to get a phone? Or the obsession with getting more gruesome footage of the crime scene?

"I'll lead," Sofia says, and before anyone can respond, she marches off, leaving the rest of us scrambling to keep up.

The wind has picked up, creating a mournful howling that echoes down the corridors and penetrates the dank, musty halls with chilly, salty air.

Joaquin looks like he's on the verge of a panic attack. I fight the urge to squeeze his hand "You don't have to go inside."

He looks up and shakes his head. "We're all in this together."

Sofia stops at the entrance to the banquet hall and puts on her N95 mask. The rest of us follow suit.

I brush past Joaquin and join her. "Let's make this quick, doctora."

She sighs. "I can handle the sight of blood. Just make sure you don't pass out on me. I have limited supplies to deal with multiple patients."

Before I can think of a snarky comeback, she pushes the door open.

Once again, we're hit with a wave of foulness that penetrates our masks. Sofia wastes no time hunching down and rummaging through the bodies for a cell. I join her, while Izzy captures the whole thing on video. We all make sure to avoid the steady dripping of blood from the organs still dangling above us.

I catch a glimpse of Joaquin, eyes wide, body rigid. While I care very much about the others, Sofia is stronger than the rest of us put together, while Izzy is coping through her camera. Joaquin seems terrified, and it's all I can do not to take him in my arms and shield him from all this horror.

Sofia's shaking her head and holds it up for all of us to see. The screen is shattered and it's dead. She picks up another cell, examines its smashed casing, before tossing it aside on the growing pile that's beginning to resemble Malicia Mountain itself. All of these phones were working just a little while ago. We saw them flashing and heard them bleeping, and now they've all been destroyed, just like their owners? It doesn't make any sense.

I pick up another cell, clutched in a severed hand. Damn. This shit is so gross. I push a few buttons, then fling it away. "Looks like Carlos had a little party."

Sofia shakes her head. "It couldn't have been Carlos. We encountered him outside by the dock right after we first came in here and fled. He wouldn't have been able to double back and destroy the phones before blowing up the dock."

"If Carlos didn't do it, doctora, then who did?"

Isabella pans each of our faces with her camera. "Unless there's someone else on this island that we don't know about, it must have been one of us."

Joaquin's jaw drops and he stares directly into her camera. "Que vaina. That doesn't make any sense. When would any of us have had the opportunity to destroy these phones?"

"And more importantly, why would we?" Sofia asks.

"I'm not sure about the why, but after the dock blew," Isabella replies, "everything was in a state of chaos. Ray was off by himself before finding Joaquin and a passed-out Sofia, who was then left alone when Joaquin went off by himself to follow Ray—"

"Where I found you and a badly injured Carlos," I say, playing her game. "You were also alone when I sent you back to find Sofia. You could have taken a little detour here, destroyed the phones, and then met up with her, just like you're accusing the rest of us of."

Isabella chuckles. "Oye. Don't get so defensive, Ray. I'm just putting the possibilities out there. Because if it wasn't Carlos, or any of us, what does that leave? Ghosts? You know I don't believe in supernatural bullshit."

"What a minute! What's that?" Joaquin hunches down and plucks a phone from a severed hand, trying hard not to gag as he does so. Everyone crowds around as he fumbles with the gore-soaked screen, which is frozen on a single phrase in a text message.

Serial Springs

The cracked screen cuts off and goes black.

Dead. Like everything else in this room besides the Quisqueya Club.

"Serial Springs?" Sofia asks. "Isn't that one of the regions of the park?"

I nod. "Maybe that text was sent by another member of the crew that's stationed there."

"We'll just have to assume that there's someone else on the island that's responsible for sabotaging those phones and sending that text. It's the only logical explanation."

"Is it?" Isabella mutters, taking one final shot of the pile of phones.

"All these cells are shot. Let's get out of this awful place," Joaquin says.

He takes my hand and hauls me to my feet, giving it a squeeze before letting go.

This time I lead the way, trudging back in silence to where we left Carlos. Once there, we pass around the sanitizers and wipes, but the stench of death still lingers.

Sofia presses her palms against her forehead. "With no way to call out, it looks like we're on our own then. At least none of us was badly hurt."

Isabella pans the room. "For the moment."

Now she's starting to piss me off. "Sorry for getting you guys into this mess."

Joaquin shakes his head. He looks worn. "You don't have to apologize. None of this is your fault."

"Gracias." I'm about to move in for a hug but he turns away.

Isabella tilts her camera toward Carlos. "And now we get to face a hurricane without any supplies."

I kick the chair nearest me, sending it sliding across the room. "Fuck!"

Sofia rests her hand on my shoulder. "If it's any consolation, there's still some leftover sancocho, tostones, and white rice in that cooler we brought with us. It should be enough to help us ride out the storm if we ration it properly."

"But there's no guarantee anyone will come for us for quite a while," Isabella says. "An abandoned theme park isn't exactly going to be high priority after a storm. What are we going to do without any power? I need a functioning camera!"

My mind's racing. "There are several generator stations

located around the island. We just have to find one that has enough fuel—"

"Looks like somebody's already found another use for that fuel." Joaquin's staring at Carlos, his voice monotone.

Sofia takes a step forward, blocking Carlos's prone form from view. "Ray, you know this island better than any of us. What about that tunnel you mentioned on your tour where we could ride out the storm?"

"I'll show you." I rummage through one of the larger drawers in the office and pull out a long tube. After I snap it open, I unfurl a schematic over the desk, displaying an entire map of the park.

"We're here." I point to a blip on the map. "See this?"

Everyone scoots in closer to focus on where my finger is poised on the outskirts of an enormous maze that encompasses the entire island.

"Here's the entrance to the underground transit system I told you about before, known as El Nido," I continue.

Joaquin shoots me a look. "Nido? A 'nest' for what?"

"There's an entire community hidden from view just below the park to allow maintenance, hospitality, food and beverage services, etc. to get around to each of the park's four sections without having to interact with guests and interfere with their Malicia experience. In addition to personnel offices, creature costume areas, and maintenance systems, there's also the operational system that controls all the park's animatronics and special effects. The entire labyrinth is basically a secure bunker network. No windows. No glass. You get the idea."

Sofia nods. "What about supplies? Where are they located?"

My index finger traces a pathway along the spiderweb-looking maze, stopping at a central hub that branches into five distinct directions. "This is command central. From here, you get direct access to each of Malicia's four lands: Serial Springs, Creature Canyon, Paranormal Place, Angel Falls, as well as Malicia Mountain itself. This is where cast members don costumes, the undead procession parade is staged, basically the heart of the mountain, so to speak."

"Now you sound like you're in full tour guide persona again." Joaquin gives me a tentative smile.

I smile back. "Makes sense, considering how many times I snuck around this entire map as a kid. My brother, Rudy, and I used to play hide-and-seek in this maze after the park closed, dodging the skeleton crew, who usually pretended not to see us. . . ."

My voice deflates like a dying balloon at the memory.

It was in that maze that I found that book. And less than a week later, Rudy, my mother, and all those people in the park were dead. Since we're all trapped here now, is it still wrong that I want to lead them to Paranormal Place and conduct the ritual? Or am I just a self-centered asshole?

Something touches my shoulder and I flinch. I exhale when I realize it's Sofia.

"You okay, Raymundo?"

"Yep. Just concentrating on the layout of this place, in case I missed something."

"How do we reach the tunnel?" Joaquin asks.

"There should be a service elevator down this corridor behind the concierge desk."

Joaquin's eyes widen. "Un elevador? Is that a good idea?

I mean, what if there's a power failure? What if we get stuck between floors? There's no one to respond to any type of alarm. What if we get trapped in that cramped—"

"Relax. The elevator's more like a freight lift. It's pretty big, used to transport supplies and stuff. Besides, we should be fine if we get down there now. And I'll check the emergency generator to make sure it has enough fuel to power the elevator before we use it. Sound good?"

Joaquin's stern nod tells me he's not convinced and there's nothing good about any of this.

"Not to be a pessimist," Isabella hikes a finger at Carlos, "but how are we going to get him down there, Ray?"

"Been thinking about that. He's too hurt to carry without causing further damage. Maybe this will work. Wait here."

Before they can ask any questions, I dart through one of the doors leading into a storage room, hoping there's still one left I can use. Luckily, there are a couple. I grab the wheelchair that looks the most intact and roll it into the outer room.

It takes all four of us to haul Carlos onto the chair without jostling his body too much. Still, there are couple of times when he grunts and whimpers, and I wince with guilt at each sound. Finally, he's settled into the chair, his feet dangling off the foot pads.

"Un momento." I grab the roll of bandages and carefully bind Carlos's limbs to the chair, tugging to make sure he's immobile.

Isabella's been recording most of the procedure and finally looks up from her camera. "You really expect him to just get up and try and finish what he started in his condition?"

I look up at all their anxious faces. "I don't believe in taking chances."

Isabella sighs. "I'm telling you. There's someone else on this island. Carlos didn't destroy those cell phones. Unless he has an accomplice."

Sofia turns to a fidgeting Joaquin. "Why don't you give me a hand grabbing those leftovers to bring down to El Nido with us?"

"Sí . . . sure thing."

By the time Sofia and Joaquin get back with the cooler, I'm done making sure Carlos can't possibly go anywhere, no matter what his condition is.

There's a loud crash which makes us all jump.

Isabella grabs her camera again. "What now?"

I race out into the lobby area, the three of them at my heels.

The lobby doors are wide open, and it only takes a moment to register that they've been blown open by the cold gust of wind weaving through the space, ruffling stray papers, rattling the debris littering the room. Slowly, we make our way to the entrance, glancing at the scene before us.

The ocean is a choppy stew of swirling whitecaps, contrasted against a horizon crowded with bulging, dark clouds. The roar of the waves crashes through my ears. The cold, salty sea air stings my nostrils.

Joaquin wraps an arm around my shoulders. "Looks like the first of Edgar's feeder bands."

Shit. "Edgar's closer than we realized."

Isabella pans her camera around the lobby. "With all the crap and broken glass in this room, it'll be a death trap in here."

"We should all go down to El Nido." Sofia's tone makes it clear the topic is not up for debate.

"Let's do it." I lead the way to the concierge area.

I grab hold of the wheelchair, push Carlos over to the service elevator, and load him in, while Joaquin and Sofia make sure the cooler and med supplies are on board, and Isabella records the whole thing.

As the doors slide shut and the elevator lurches downward, I can't help but shudder at the thought of what's waiting down below in the darkness of the nest.

JOAQUIN

When we first descended into the depths of El Nido, there were so many things to focus on, it kept my anxiety at bay like a cross to un vampiro. The four of us pitched in checking supplies, scouting for more first aid kits, not just for Carlos, but to have handy in case one of us suffered an accident or the consequences of Edgar's wrath.

The added bonus was that it's kept their focus off what happened with those phones, and distracted me from Ray's impending fate at my hands. I have to figure out a way to get him alone on that mountaintop by Sunday night. At first, I was going to make it a fun little adventure for the two of us to wander off during the weekend in the guise of a private tour. But the hurricane has changed everything. I need to think of another pretext fast before time runs out.

Earlier, Sofia suggested we thoroughly check the surrounding tunnels to make sure there weren't any other locos lurking around before sealing all the doors leading in and out, once we made sure it was only the Quisqueya Club and Carlos down here. Though it was a logical suggestion from Sofia as usual, it didn't take into account that the danger might already be down here among us.

And what's the deal with Carlos, anyway? Ray obviously has no idea that his father's trusted employee is part of a coven of dark witches, my grandparents' coven in fact. I get Carlos wanting to trap us on the island. But why risk killing us all in that explosion, especially Ray, who's the key to everything. He said *No one must survive* before he did it. Did he have a change of heart? Has he betrayed the coven?

Now that we're all huddled together in a small employee break room with nothing else to do, there isn't anything to calm the emotional cyclone inside me. My adrenaline turns on me and starts working overtime. The howling wind outside is growing louder, echoing throughout the tunnels like a pissed off bruja. My heart's pounding. Fingers of icy-cold sweat trace a path down my forehead. It feels like I'm buried alive down here. Carajo. I've got to get the hell out of here—I can't breathe. . . .

Something warm and strong clamps down on my shoulder. I whirl to find Ray's eyes staring deeply into mine. "You okay, pana?" he asks softly.

The dim light accentuates his chiseled face, which is filled with concern. His mane of wavy, shiny jet-black hair is hanging loose about his broad shoulders, which are straining to burst out of his fresh Malicia T-shirt. Isabella was right. He really is un papichulo. He doesn't deserve to die in his prime, at the hands of someone he trusts. Someone who . . . trusts him, too.

A wave of dizziness hits me, and I grip one of his massive biceps to steady myself. "I'm fine. The storm's kinda freakin' me out."

"You're not the only one," Isabella chimes in from the other side of the room.

A gust of wind roars like a freight train through the complex, and I just want to bury my face in my hands.

Sofia stands up. "I'll take first watch on Carlos duty."

We'd previously drawn straws and come up with a shift rotation to monitor Carlos's condition. First Sofia, then me, followed by Isabella, and finally Ray.

"See you guys in a bit," I mumble, heading out of the kitchen and into the small office that's doubling as a bunkhouse. We've set up makeshift cots in several adjoining offices to sleep in. They're not the most comfortable bedding, but definitely better than the cold, hard floor. With everything weighing on my mind, sleep may as well be the Holy Grail. I'd be grateful to just stop the ache inside of me, if only for a little bit.

Ray follows me inside and plops himself down on the cot right next to mine, slipping his T-shirt over his smooth rippled torso like a python shedding its skin.

As I sink into my own cot, Ray grips my shoulder. "Rest up, pana. I'm here if you need anything."

I reach back and fist bump him. "Just you being here with me at Malicia is all that I need."

I'm crying, running through a dark maze.

A horrible giggle drowns out everything else. It sounds as if its owner's mouth is filled with slugs slithering in and out.

It calls out to me: *You can wriggle, but you can't hide from me, little worm. Sooner or later, I'm going to find you. . . .*

I trip and crash to the ground. A dark shadow falls over me. I'm bawling, as I roll over and see it looming over me, Master Crawly, El Bacá, the sinister Majordomo and mascot of Malicia Park. . . .

I bolt upright from the nightmare, bathed in a cold sweat that plasters my T-shirt to my skin.

Deep breath. Exhale.

Ray's cot is empty. He said he would stay with me. Maybe he's figured out that I've been lying—

The office door swings open, and in comes Ray, bearing a steaming cup of heaven.

I take a long whiff. "Is that what I think it is?"

He smiles and hands me the cup. "One café con leche at your service, sir. I already gave Sofia and Isabella theirs. You were still sound asleep when I stopped by earlier. I figured it was almost time for your shift so I wanted you to wake up in style. Careful, it's piping hot."

I blow on it for a bit before taking a sip. "Qué rico! Where did you find non-expired milk on this island?"

"I actually used a can of condensed milk, but it'll do the trick. My mother used to make this special recipe for me when I was little kid and had bad dreams."

"I don't mind sharing." I muster a smile and offer him a sip.

We sit cross-legged across from each other, not saying a word, sharing the best cup of café con leche I've ever had. If only my feelings, the camaraderie we've shared for years now, weren't based on a deadly lie.

The lights flicker again. He sighs and gets up. "I need to go check on the emergency gennies. The last thing we need is to get caught in pitch black down here." He notices my expression and quickly adds, "But you have nothing to worry about. There's enough fuel to power them until after the storm's passed. Promise."

"Oh, I'm not worried about that. I should go relieve Sofia of Carlos duty, so I'll follow you out."

As the howling wind echoes down the corridors, we nod and set off in opposite directions.

Sofia's grateful to see me and makes me promise to get her if there's any change to Carlos's condition before she leaves.

Carlos is sprawled out on a cot. Earlier, we all helped Ray carefully transfer him from the wheelchair into the small bed. After doing so, Ray made sure to use bandages to secure him to the cot, not that Carlos was in any condition to go anywhere, but Ray wasn't taking any chances.

I try to settle into my new surroundings but am definitely not feeling it. I twist my body, but it's impossible to find a comfortable sitting position on El Nido's ice-cold floor, which I imagine is as close to a graveyard slab as you can get. The lights have been flickering on and off for the past half hour, and every time they do, my heart skips a beat. I know Ray said I shouldn't be concerned, but he has no idea what it is that's really troubling me. Knowing Ray, he probably doesn't want to worry me. Wants me to feel safe. This whole thing would have been so much easier if he were an asshole. But he had to go and actually be one of the good guys and make it that much harder on me.

In some ways, I think I did my job of befriending him and getting him to trust me too well. He actually cares about me. I've seen it more and more each day, especially as we prepared to come to Malicia. While becoming part of his inner circle definitely made my mission easier, it's become a double-edged sword that I have to be very careful to maneuver around without running the risk of getting impaled myself.

Hours later, I glance at Carlos for what must be the millionth time, lying across the room.

"Why did you try to kill us?" I whisper.

It's unnerving to listen to his grunts and wheezes, but I've positioned myself as close to the exit door as possible so I can scramble out of there if I have to. I wonder if he knew what he was in store for when the others planted him in the work crew to make the initial sacrifices and begin the preparatory rituals? Did he volunteer willingly or was he ordered to do his duty by the rest of the Brujas? Something must have happened to make him change his mind and try to kill us all.

Whereas before he looked menacing, now he's burned and feeble, the life draining out of him with every struggling breath.

Part of me wants to run as far away from him as possible, even if it means getting lost in El Nido, this terrible maze, a latticework of spiderwebbed steel lining the ceilings, casting eerie shadows down the constantly curving corridors. But I can't. Even if I could get off this island and as far away from Malicia as possible, It would find me. That's the one thing my abuelos consistently drilled into me since the massacre, during the ceremonies in that terrible attic room. The room with the horrible symbols carved into the door, like in Boneyard Bayou, and the rancid stench and guttural sounds oozing from under it.

El Bacá will find you wherever you go, Joaquin. And you'll be forced to pay for Mami and Papi's sins. . . .

Lying here now like a barely living corpse, Carlos is a reminder of everything I fear, my every nightmare come true, the shroud that has bound my existence ever since I can remember.

I can't leave him. We all promised to keep watch on him, and it's currently my turn. If I were to abandon my post, it would do nothing but arouse more suspicions, especially from Isabella. She was spot on about those destroyed cell phones. I'll have to watch her more closely and deal with her if she becomes a problem. Nothing can go wrong now. Not when I'm so close.

Securing one of the N95 masks around my face, I force myself to get a closer look at Carlos. He looks much worse. In the short time it took to find the pills, his visible skin has gone several shades paler, his skin ice-cold but dripping in sweat. The moaning and writhing have increased. But most alarming are the darkening splotches on the bandages. They look too dark to be blood.

I move in closer to get a better look and smell it.

I can't pinpoint exactly what it is, but it reminds me of un zafacón filled with rotting garbage on a hot, humid day, waiting on the curb for trash pickup. Whenever Carlos lets go of another raspy breath, that sickening stench clogs my nose.

I crane my neck to get a better look. One of the bandages

on his shoulder has come loose, and when I reach down to fix it, I notice the familiar brand carved into his flesh, a circular symbol with what looks like the letter V intersecting it, giving it the appearance of a horned animal, similar to the zodiac symbol for Taurus. It's a brand I'm all too familiar with.

A slight sigh escapes his lips, followed by words I can't make out, barely a whisper.

I hunch closer, murmuring in his ear. "Don't worry. You're going to be fine." I repeat it in Spanish, not that it matters. He's toast. Literally.

"B-b-acá . . ." he mutters.

The name of the Malicia mascot. The nightmare that's stalked me my whole life. My hand immediately goes to the scar on my hip. The remnants of a stray bullet that grazed my skin as a small child. But it's not just any scar. As I got older, it seemed to change, take the form of a symbol, the same symbol carved into Carlos's flesh.

The arcane mark of Dominican mythological symbols and the legend of the demon, El Bacá.

My muscles tense. "Why did you say that name? Is It here? Has It come for me? I still have three days!"

More grunting and spewing of bile.

"Tell me! I need answers!"

Something tiny and slimy slithers out of the birthmark. It's wormlike, with small tentacles. Pincers maybe. It disappears into Carlos's left nostril. I've seen this before, during the rituals in my grandparents' attic. A physical manifestation of El Bacá possessing a host body. It's infected Carlos, controlling his actions. Is that what Carlos was fighting on the dock? Is that why he tried to kill us all rather than become possessed?

I recoil, bumping into the stockpile of meds and scattering them every which way.

The door opens. It's Sofia. "What are you doing back here?" I ask her defensively. "I thought Izzy's shift was up next?"

She dismisses me with the shake of her head. "I couldn't sleep so she may as well get hers. Qué pasa? I thought I heard raised voices?"

Sofia can read me too well. I avoid eye contact. "Nada. I just hit my knee against the table when I was checking on him like an idiot. Still no change in his condition."

I hope she doesn't see the parasite infecting Carlos. It will just make her curious, and that's the last thing I need right now. Isabella is already a problem. I never meant for Sofia and Isabella to become a part of any of this. But I couldn't stop Ray from inviting them without looking too obvious. Hopefully, they'll stay out of the way and not try to interfere. Because if they do, I can't guarantee their safety.

Sofia dons a fresh mask from the box on the table beside Carlos's cot and leans in close to examine him, taking his pulse. She shakes her head. Then she inspects the bandages, lifting one to get a better look at his wounds. Even with a mask on, the stench is gag-worthy.

"Can you hand me some fresh bandages? These need to be changed."

I watch and assist as she removes the gore-sodden wrapping, disinfects the wounds as best she can, and applies fresh bandages, careful not to disturb the bonds Ray used to secure Carlos to the cot.

"You're really good at this." I smile through my mask. "Ray's right. You are going to make a great doctor. You know, he really still has strong feelings for you. . . ."

She smooths the tape sealed, peels off her gloves, and looks up. "Yes. But not like that. We're ancient history. More like brother and sister now." She squeezes my hand and smiles. "Besides. It's not my place to say, but I have the feeling Ray has completely moved on and has other romantic interests now."

I can feel my face turning red and a different form of panic settling in. "Ray needs to work on his family trauma issues before getting involved with anyone. Trust me, I know a thing or two about losing loved ones."

Sofia fixes her gaze on me. "Losing your parents in an accident must have been hell. You know you can share whenever you need to. No judgments here. I'm a very good listener, and if talking about it helps with your anxiety—"

"Please don't diagnose me."

"Sorry. I didn't mean to pry—"

Carlos lets out a loud groan.

"Maybe you should give him another dose of those pain-killers," I mumble to Sofia, grasping at anything to take the spotlight off me.

"Too many pills can kill him."

"What are we supposed to do? Let him suffer?" I snap. My eyes burn hot and wet. "Forgive me. I didn't mean to . . ."

She hugs me tightly.

"I get it. I'm scared, too." She finally lets go. "Maybe we can find something that won't interact adversely with what we've already given him. Let's look."

We sift through the dwindling painkillers until we find some that won't screw with the antibiotics.

Sofia smiles. "I might be pre-med, but you seem to know your medications pretty well."

I chuckle. "I've put in more than enough hours researching every possible illness known to humankind."

There. It's out there. My way of acknowledging that she was right about my anxiety disorder, if not the root cause.

Who needs WebMD when you have Joaquin?

Sofia pats me on the back and asks me to hand her a bottle of pills. "I'll wait at least thirty minutes before giving him one more of these. If you'd like, you can go check on Ray and Izzy before going back to bed." She smiles at me. "You've been a great help, Joaquin. I really appreciate it. Gracias."

"No problem, Sofia."

"You should have a real long talk with Ray. Life's too short, Joaquin."

You have no idea, Sofia. Without saying a word, I turn and open the door, heading down the corridor.

A loud shriek from somewhere deep in the complex curdles my blood, followed by running footfalls.

Then the tunnels are plunged into pitch black.

ISABELLA

What the hell's going on?

I press my ear against the office I've been hunkered down in, some kind of security station, after pretending to be tired and wanting to get some rest.

Everything goes dark.

Running footsteps echo down the corridor. I can just make them out through the sounds of Edgar's growing hissy fit. Then nothing else.

Was it Raymundo? Sofia? Joaquin?

When I threw out that bone about one of us tampering with the phones it really rattled their cages. And just what's in that backpack that Ray won't leave out of his sight? Joaquin's had increased panic attacks, but he also doesn't hesitate to grab a phone out of a severed hand? Not buying it. And out of all of us, Sofia was the one with the most "alone" time when she was supposedly passed out on the beach after Ray and Joaquin left her. Yet when I got to her, she didn't seem that out of it to me. Then Ray tries to turn things around and make it look like I'm the one hiding something?

No. Stop sensationalizing. Enough with the viral video shit. These are my friends. I love them. Why the hell would any of them sabotage phones to keep us trapped here? Give it a rest. They're all just as scared as I am. What I should be doing is talking to each of them right now, finding out how they're feeling, how they're coping. That's the kind of elevated journalism that's going to get me into Northwestern and taken seriously. Not the conspiracy theory crap that everyone else is doing.

Luckily, I charged all my camera batteries before the outage. Still, I have to be conservative, just in case something noteworthy pops up unexpectedly. I switch to infrared so I can see despite the blackout, carefully open the door, poke my head out, and glance both ways down the corridor.

Nothing. Nada. Zip.

As I creep into the open, I scan the left for any signs of life. I can't be sure if I hear voices coming from that direction because of the roaring wind drowning everything out. The light of the infrared casts everything in a sickly shade of green, like rotting fruit. I reach the next hallway and hang a left. Oh shit. Am I lost in the dark? Do I make a right at this hallway? No, it's left. I slink past a few more doors and my heart struts when I spot the nameplate above the door.

RECURSOS INHUMANOS. Inhuman Resources. Pendejos.

I bet whoever thought of the name considered themselves pretty clever.

I'm about to continue on my way back toward the others, but a thought hits me. This place will probably have some records about Malicia that could shed some light on what's actually going on here. Facts. Not fiction. It's too tempting to resist.

Of course, the door is locked, but nothing the crowbar I stashed in case any more psychos are running loose can't fix, just one of the many skills I picked up during my brief stint in juvie. With Edgar's fury to mask the sounds, I make quick work of the lock and jimmy the door open. If there were ever any alarms, they've obviously been disabled, unless they were of the silent variety. But even if they were still active, so what? No one's coming in that mess outside anyway.

I slip inside, closing the door behind me again in case someone unexpected comes calling.

The room's a little bigger inside than it appears from the outside. Rows and rows of cubicle workstations flank a central corridor that extends far into the greenish darkness, pulling off the creepy unholy church thing in spades.

As I walk up the aisle, I glance at the sea of dark computer screens staring back at me like unsettling eyes. It would be so much faster if I could access these terminals, but Edgar's thrown a wrench into that plan. I press the on button on the nearest one. Nada. Black screen. Guess Ray's generators are bypassing this wing.

I can't believe Malicia had gone totally paperless before the massacre happened. I rummage through the room, pulling drawers open, rifling through cabinets, nothing except old invoices, lunch menus, stationery, office supply order forms, etc. There has to be some hard evidence somewhere that I can use for my doc. Who needs some exploitative livestream or a podcast, when I can deliver a fact-based, behind the scenes account from one of the most notorious, yet impossible to access crime scenes ever, weaving it into the interpersonal relationships of the Quisqueya Club? That will give me serious cred. Make them notice me.

Every theme park, even the wholesome family ones, has some kind of body count, deaths that have occurred on the premises that most of the happy-go-lucky visitors never hear about. They might not be weapon yielding assassins unloading on multiple victims at once, but patrons who have gotten killed on rides, been assaulted on the premises, and sabe dios what else.

The loud roar that sounds like a locomotive rattles through my ears. Bangs, crashes, and the shattering of glass follow. What the hell is Edgar doing up there? One thing's for sure, it won't be very scenic when we return topside.

I spot the door to the Director de Recursos Inhumanos office. I smash through the panel of glass on the door, reach in, unlock it, and kick it open.

It takes a while, but I finally find something, tucked behind a false panel in the desk.

A file marked MMX, which includes a list and a USB drive.

After powering up my laptop, I plug in the drive and immerse myself in Malicia's sordid history, toggling through pages and pages of personnel bios, old photographs, property records, and news articles. Seems like the PR director was burning the midnight oil, going above her job description and pay grade to research the park's history. In addition to suicides and other tragedies befalling personnel, there's a piece on the land itself, how centuries ago settlers were besieged by plagues and mysterious disappearances, originally attributed to witchcraft and the native inhabitants. Claro, blame it on BIPOC folks as usual.

Some of the news stories detail the efforts of a Dominican archaeological team who went poking around here and uncovered who knows what before succumbing to illness and madness. The before and after images are jarring. A six-person team filled with smiling and hopeful faces in all their grainy black and white glory, juxtaposed next to shots of the expedition site weeks later, equipment scattered, several dead bodies covered in sheets, the expedition leader being led out by authorities, bulging, crazed eyes staring into the camera.

I can't help comparing the similarities of what happened to them to that loony Carlos on the dock and the carnage in the hotel lobby.

As I scroll through another file, I finally hit the jackpot, a treasure trove of photos and video clips from the Malicia Massacre. Over the years, I've seen some of this stuff while channel surfing and coming across a documentary or two. But as I was too young when it happened, I never paid much attention to it, even when that streaming channel did that smash miniseries a couple of years ago on the tenth anniversary. Until now.

Coño. It's a photo of Ray with his father, watching from a distance as the authorities cordon off the docks, a flock of choppers surveying the island in the distance. He's so young, tan inocente. There's a sidebar with a photo of his mother and older brother, a child himself, accompanied by a short blurb about how they had stayed behind on the island, and it was only a fluke that Ray and his father hadn't been there when the tragedy occurred. I can't help but feel sorry for Ray, or at least for the scared and innocent little boy he used to be.

Then I come across the next series of pictures, and my eyes nearly bug out of my skull. I slump against the chair, sitting stunned for a few minutes, trying to process this unbelievable revelation. Not what I was expecting at all. And it raises so many questions. Sofia. She's the only one I can confide in about this. She's logical and methodical. She'll know what to do. I power off the computer, scurry out of the office, and dart back through the moaning corridors and into the makeshift med center, where Sofia is waiting, her back to me as she's leaning over to check on her creepy patient.

She turns toward me. "Izzy, thank God you're okay!"

Something's up with her. She looks tired. Sure we all are, but this is more like a mental tired, like she's checked out and is somewhere far away from Malicia. And what the hell happened to her right hand? It's covered in a dark-stained bandage.

Before I can get a word out, she wraps me in a fierce hug, clinging to me like a life preserver.

I finally break away. "Ay niña, qué te pasa? Are you okay? What happened to your hand?"

She shakes her head. "I'm fine. When the lights went out, my patient kind of freaked, must have had a spasm or something. . . ."

My eyes bug. "Don't tell me he bit you?" I reach for her hand but she pulls it away.

"I'm fine, Izzy. No need to worry about me."

"I'm always going to worry about you, girl you know that."

She manages a tired smile. "Hey, I'm supposed to be den mother, remember?"

I return the smile before that rush of adrenaline hits me again. I set down my gear. "Where are Ray and Joaquin?"

"No idea. I wanted to go look for them but my flashlight gave out, and I didn't want to leave my patient alone and stumble around in the dark. Now that you're here, though, we can both go—"

"Hang on a sec, niña. I want to talk to you alone." I shoot a glance at that creepy Carlos's prone body, feeling self-conscious that we don't really have any privacy.

She nods. "It's about Ray and Joaquin, isn't it. Something's going on with them."

I let out a relieved sigh. "Cool. So it's not just me. You've figured it out, too? Damn you are smart, girl."

"You'd have to be blind not to notice. I just think they're both idiots for wasting all this time. At least they're going to the same college. They should just tell each other how they feel and be done with it." She shakes her head and chuckles.

"Qué lo que? Are we on the same page here? What are you talking about?"

Now it's her turn to look confused. "You were talking about how they both have the hots for each other but are too afraid of rejection to say anything, right?"

I shake my head. "No—I mean—yes, I know they have the

secret hots for each other even if they're both too pendejo to do anything about it, but that's not what I'm talking about."

She leads me to a bench in the corner where we both sit. "Cuéntame. What's going on?"

"Maybe it's better if I just show you, but before I do, I want you to promise not to get mad at me."

Sofia rolls her eyes. "Ay, Izzy. What did you go poking around in now? You said you were going to lay off the trashy tabloid-style vids for clicks. Remember? *I'm turning over a new leaf, going to Northwestern, becoming a respectable journalist? Ring a bell?*"

I shake my head and power up my computer. "This isn't just gossip rag stuff. Take a look and tell me what you think."

As I tab and scroll through the files, she leans in closer to the screen to get a better look.

I scroll and click my way through endless pics and videos, until I find what I'm looking for, once again not believing what I'm seeing.

"There it is," I say to Sofia. "One of the only known shots of the lone survivor of the Malicia Massacre."

She stares at the image of a dark-haired little boy with olive skin, bundled in a blanket as he's being airlifted from the crime scene on his way to the hospital. It looks like he was turning his face when the footage was taken, creating a blur effect and making his features indistinguishable.

She slides the keyboard over to her and skims through a few articles regarding this survivor, face deep in research mode, just like the Sofia I've known for years, analyzing every detail. She pauses and gives me a pointed look. "Seems like his parents were killed in the massacre and he went to live with relatives, who quickly moved and changed his name to avoid the barrage of publicity aimed their way. I can't blame them. I mean, the kid was traumatized and was entitled to grow up without any of the baggage following him around."

I swallow hard. "Don't you think it's kind of a cop-out to do that to a kid, I mean preventing him from actually dealing and moving on, rather than repressing that crap, which only screws you up even more? Trust me, I know."

Sofia rests her uninjured hand on mine. "I know you've had it rough, and so did this kid. But what does any of this have to do with Joaquin and Ray?"

"Observe." I tap a few keys and play the clip over and over, magnifying the image, searching for the detail that clinched it for me. The wound caused by a bullet grazing the kid's skin, visible just above where his shirt is hiked up. It's in the exact same position as another scar Sofia and I have both seen many times, as recently as earlier this afternoon, on the boat to the island.

Sofia's eyes grow wider as she begins to make the same connection I did. "Are you saying—"

I nod. "That scar, combined with the kid's age, his dark hair, olive complexion . . . it's not just a coincidence."

Sofia slumps against my shoulder. "But why has he been keeping it a secret from us this whole time? Especially from Ray?"

"No lo sé," I finally say. "But it's him. The same boy. Joaquin is the sole survivor of the Malicia Massacre."

RAYMUNDO

Right now, I'm barely a one out of ten. There's a fire in the back of my neck, and I'm lying on my stomach, barely able to move. My arms are splayed out in front of me as I grope for my flashlight. But my fingers find wet stickiness instead. The darkness all around me is disorienting.

What the hell happened?

It starts coming back to me like a jigsaw puzzle, piece by piece, one wrong segment that doesn't fit quickly replaced by another, tumbling through my mind.

I remember coming down here after making sure Joaquin was all set for his shift, checking the last of the generators after the others had settled in for what promised to be the night from hell.

At first, everything was going fine during my system check. Generator one was online and fueled up. Followed by generator two. It was during my check of generator three that everything went to shit.

Another jolt of pain strikes the back of my head, shooting down into the right side of my neck and shoulder.

The first detail that hinted something was off was the sound of high-pitched laughter. The laughter of a child. What the hell was un niño doing down here?

A horrifying thought hit me. What if one (or more) of the work crew had bucked the strict rules and brought kids to the park? And somehow one of those children had survived Carlos's bloodbath?

Another childish laugh petrified every single hair fiber on my body. What was it that was so unnerving about the combo of faceless, chuckling toddlers, being alone, and dim lighting?

"Hola," I called. "It's okay. You don't have to hide. Come out where I can see you."

It sounded like it was coming from the other side of the room.

It had to be a rat darting around the generator room, making high-pitched squeaky noises that my fogged-out brain was only interpreting as the sound of gleeful, unseen tots running amok on a restricted island. I mean, it's not like this place had been getting regular visits from the neighborhood pest control for quite some time now.

I whirled, catching a fleeting glimpse of something small, fast, and dark disappearing around the next corner. If that was a rat, it was the biggest mother I've ever seen. And that idea was just as unsettling as the prospect of kids playing hide-and-seek at the scene of one of the grisliest mass murders in history.

I raced after it. "Don't be afraid. I'm here to help you find your mai and pai."

More laughter froze me in place, assaulting me from all

directions now. Not just one kid. More like half a dozen, the high-pitched laughter prickling every hair on my body, getting louder and louder in blaring multichannel surround.

"Stop it!" I yelled at the top of my lungs.

The laughing stopped, followed by a loud creak.

Before I knew it, something toppled from above and slammed into the back of my head, sending me reeling headfirst to the ground. I landed with a thud, the flashlight skittering away from my grip. I let out a loud yell. Then all the lights snuffed out, smothering me in blackness.

Not sure how long I've been lying in the dark, listening to the sounds of Edgar. But Edgar can't drown out the persistent thud of my heart banging against my rib cage, sending pulsating vibrations through my ears.

Something warm and sticky pools around my body. Blood? That's not possible. I couldn't have been hurt badly enough to make me bleed. But maybe the bump on my head is a lot more serious than I thought.

The sound of soft shuffling approaches.

Holy shit. What is that?

I can't place it at first, especially in the disorienting dark. Then it hits me like a lead pipe.

The sound of little feet clad in tiny sneakers. My blood congeals. The footsteps are all around me. How the hell can they see me in the dark? Maybe they don't need their eyes. Maybe they don't have any.

"What do you want?" My voice sounds hoarse.

Another chorus of laughter echoes through the room and nearly makes me lose my shit. There's another sound, something rolling across the floor, grazing my fingertips.

I slowly feel around it, forming a mental image. Cold. Metal. It's my flashlight.

More laughing. Despite the pain, I shift to my knees, fingers paralyzed on the 'on' switch. I hesitate.

Carajitoooooooooooooooooooooo

Was that the sound of the wind? It has to be. Because the only person who would ever call me 'carajito' is dead.

"Rudolfo, is that you? Rudy?"

I flick the switch on. There's another face staring at me, just inches from my own. My heart skips a few beats and almost comes to a complete stop before I recognize the face.

"Joaquin!" I wrap my arms around him, hugging him fiercely, practically laughing and crying from the relief.

"Tiguere, are you okay? The lights went out, then I heard you yell, and that loud crash . . . I imagined the worst."

I reluctantly pull away from him and scan the room with my flashlight, making sure I shield him with my body. Behind me, there's a huge chunk of generator that's somehow dislodged from its perch. What's left is a mangled heap of metal.

"You're bleeding!" Joaquin touches the back of my head.

I can't help but wince. "I'm okay. That generator came loose and just missed crushing my skull by a hair."

Joaquin stares at the generator in horror. "You're lucky to be alive. As it stands, you may have a bad concussion. Any confusion? Blurry vision? Headache? Dizziness? Nausea?"

"You're beginning to sound like Sofia."

"Oh, hell no." He chuckles.

He reaches for my head again, and I give in to his

examination. "You don't have to worry about me," I say. "It's nothing, really. Are you sure you're okay? Did you get hurt in the dark?"

"I'm fine. But Carlos isn't. He's critical. I don't think he's going to make it."

"After what he tried to do, I don't know if I should feel bad he's probably going to die, or celebrate. Either way, his family doesn't deserve this."

I peer over Joaquin's shoulder at the flashlight's beam, searching for any sign of the intruders and finding none. Except—

I move away from Joaquin and bend down to get a better look. It's the remnants of a black balloon, tangled up with a tiny, frayed, and torn T-shirt. The kind the kids wore on—

"Tykes of Terror," Joaquin reads the logo on the shirt over my shoulder. His face grows really pale, and I can see that he's trembling. I put my arm around him and pull him close.

I swallow hard, battling against the nausea that's churning in my stomach as I hold the little T-shirt in my hands. The same type of T-shirt my brother Rudy wore that day. His last day on earth.

Clearing my throat, I lose myself in Joaquin's eyes. "Tykes of Terror. That was the name of the event going on here at Malicia on the day the . . . when the murders . . ." the rest logjams in my throat. "It was a special event. Hundreds of lucky visitors selected to inaugurate the first kid-friendly section of the park."

Those kids, the ones I heard laughing. That must have been what they sounded like just before they were mowed down. Just like Rudy. I slump to a sitting position on the floor. Hot tears pelt the T-shirt and I ball it up in my fist, wiping the rest away.

Joaquin nuzzles beside me, tilting my head against his, stroking my hair. "I'm so sorry. I know how hard this is for you. Losing your brother . . ."

"It wasn't just Rudy. My mother was killed during the massacre here, too. Mai was supposed to accompany mi pai off the island on the day of the massacre. I should have been the one who stayed behind and got killed with Rudy, not my mother."

"Don't say that."

"It's true. I'd just gotten over a case of—what was it? Chicken pox? Measles? Courtesy of an unvaccinated park visitor? In any case, I'd passed it along to my mother. Since she was ill, she stayed behind at the family resort on the island to recuperate, and my father insisted I take her place on his trip. When Mai was murdered, Pai lost his other half, just like I lost Rudy. He never forgave me. Only spoke to me when necessary."

"What an awful burden to place on a child."

"If you knew my father, you'd understand."

Joaquin shakes his head and takes my hands in his. "Sometimes sharing blood leads to awful things."

Every memory of Rudy and my mother's death has burst through the dam, mixed with all those hurt feelings of a lifetime of my father's disdain and rejection. Can I really blame him? I don't really know.

For a minute, I lose it, face buried in Joaquin's shoulder as silent tears spill from my eyes. He holds me close, stroking my hair.

Joaquin's fingers gently tilt my head until our eyes meet. "You know the Quisqueya Club always has your back, siempre.

I wish things could have been different for you. I really do. You don't deserve any of it." He pulls away.

I swipe the tears away with the crook of my elbow. "Did you hear anything else when you came down here?"

He shakes his head. "What do you mean? Like the storm?"

"No. I mean like anyone else prowling around down here."

"All I heard was you calling out for your brother, Rudy. What was that about?"

"Maybe it's easier if I show you."

I retrieve my backpack and pull out the Malicia souvenir I brought back with me, careful to keep the other contents hidden from view.

Joaquin's eyes narrow as he examines it. "What is this thing?"

"After you gave me that book on occult rituals to help unlock my writer's block with screenplay ideas, it got me thinking about some props and relics we had stashed in the attic back home. I went digging and found this. It's a limited edition souvenir Malicia Crawly Talkie that Rudy gave me just before he and the others were murdered."

He takes the lime green device from me and looks at the screen. Then back up at me, confused. "There's a message on here."

"That's the bizarre part. According to the time stamp, that new message shouldn't—couldn't—really be there, except that it is."

Swallowing hard, I take the Crawly Talkie back and read aloud the message that appeared on its screen the moment I found it again.

"I'm waiting for you, carajito. Time to come home."

"There's got to be a logical explanation . . ." Joaquin's voice fades into the darkness. "You don't think Izzy is staging any of this, do you?"

"You mean a prank?"

"I mean she'll do anything to get a genuine scare out of us for her documentary. She probably set this whole thing up."

"You really think so? But what about the cell phones? She wouldn't have sabotaged those. They were our only way to call for help and get off this island."

"Who knows? Maybe she wants to get a reaction out of us, you know, genuine fear and all, and she secretly has a phone stashed away in case there's an emergency. I wouldn't put it past her."

I shake my head. "I don't know what to believe." My words are noncommittal, but my mind's racing. Suppose Isabella snuck a look in my pack and figured out why I really brought everyone to Malicia?

I place the Crawly Talkie back in my pack and zip it shut. "I didn't want to freak you out. I know you're dealing with a lot of anxiety. The last thing in this world I would ever want to do is add any more stress to your life."

He brushes the back of his hand against his eyes and looks away. "That's the last thing I want to do to you, too."

I gently pull him up to his feet with me. "Let's go round up the others. Even though everyone's equipped with a flashlight, they must be freaking out about the generator."

We walk hand in hand, as if it's something we've always done, the most natural thing that can be, and I wonder why we've never done it before. In minutes, we're back at the main access hallway, and Joaquin pulls his hand away, as if just realizing he's been holding mine all this time. Isabella has joined Sofia and Carlos at the makeshift med center, under the light of one of the emergency lanterns.

They both have strange expressions on their faces and are speaking in hushed tones before stopping abruptly.

Isabella is the first to spot us, recording our approach on camera. "Where in the hell have you two been? We were about to mount a search party!"

"Sorry," I say. "I was in the generator room. Something came loose and just missed taking me out. That's why we have no power in this section. Joaquin came along and found me."

Sofia approaches me, examining me like a seasoned physician "Are you hurt, Ray?"

"I'll live, doctora." My smile morphs into concern when I notice her bandaged hand. "Forget about me. What happened to you? Are you okay? Let me see."

She snatches her hand away before I can get a better look. "Just an accident, Ray. I got clumsy when the lights went out and banged my hand against some equipment. I'm perfectly fine."

Izzy looks like she's about to say something, but Sofia shoots her a quick look that kills whatever it was.

Before I can push things, Sofia's already sorting through Joaquin's stash of medical supplies, slathering peroxide on my wound and bandaging it up.

I nudge my chin toward Carlos's prone body. "I'm more concerned about him. He looks really bad."

Joaquin pushes his hair back from his forehead. "There's nothing else we can do for him except pray, if you believe in that sort of thing."

Isabella takes a few close-ups of Carlos then glances at Joaquin. "At least if he dies, we won't have to worry about being murdered in our sleep . . . at least by *him*."

As nasty as it sounds, she's only said out loud what I'm sure all of us are thinking.

Joaquin opens his mouth to say something to her, but I give him a subtle shake of my head and the words die in his throat.

The four of us huddle around Carlos's body for the next several hours, unable to sleep, unsettled by his raspy, wheezing breaths. The entire complex creaks and vibrates as Edgar stakes his claim, accompanied by a cacophony of unholy sounds.

ISABELLA

After being cooped up in the tunnels with the others for hours, it feels exhilarating to be outside and on my own. It was suffocating down in El Nido, having to bite my tongue and pretend I have no idea who Joaquin really is, scrutinizing his every move, wondering if it's part of some secret agenda.

Yeah, I get that PTSD and anxiety can mess with people both physically and mentally, totally understandable. But even before we came on this trip, I picked up on . . . something. Algo extraño. He has this way of playing victim and leveraging that to get what he wants. Very subtle. I'm not saying he's being deliberately manipulative, but I get the sense that there's something that he's after, and it doesn't have anything to do with making a movie about this place. He came back here for a specific reason. Carajo. I can't even image how hard it must be for him to be back here after suffering that damage.

Sofia and I barely had any time to discuss my discovery of his identity before Joaquin and Ray rejoined us. We decided to not say anything for the time being until we were able to find out more. *No need to upset Ray until we have facts*, Sofia advised, always the voice of reason.

But I've been thinking about it. What if discovering the truth about Joaquin's identity is just the direction I've been looking to take my documentary in? Not some sensationalist piece about a massacre, but an intimate portrait of one young man's struggle to overcome personal tragedy and rebuild his life? Maybe to confront his inner demons? Now that's a piece Northwestern might appreciate more, focusing on the human angle rather than ghoulish rubbernecking.

I'm going to have to watch them all closely and get as much of it as I can on camera. Whatever they're all hiding, at least it will keep the focus off me and my own agenda.

This whole new direction and purpose have me really energized. I haul myself out of the floodwaters and onto the rocky perch. It's a good thing my camera's waterproof or this whole operation would be a bust. I position myself as best I can in front of the gaping hole where the lobby windows used to be, taking more pictures and video.

Coño, talk about a disaster. The dock and all the surrounding beach are submerged, along with the flight of stairs leading up to the hotel lobby. Scanning the horizon, I'm surprised to see the dome surrounding Malicia still intact, with the mountain itself still jutting straight up as if giving the heavens, and Edgar, a big Eff You with its tall, central peak.

I check my stopwatch. Shit. It's been almost ten minutes. While down in El Nido, I'd divvied most of my attention between listening to Edgar's temper tantrum, reading the files I'd borrowed from Recursos Inhumanos, exchanging knowing glances with Sofia, keeping tabs on Joaquin, and waiting for my opportunity to slip away and head topside. Once my new inspiration for the documentary hit, I was wired with pent-up energy. Of course, no one could control me if I decided to march past them and head to the surface, but I wasn't about to deal with any awkward questions that might expose my new plans for the documentary. It would be too soon. The last thing I want is for Joaquin to know that I'm privy to the truth at this point and put his guard up. That could lead to messy confrontations, which could end up with a search and discovery of my flash drive. No need to chance Joaquin's outrage or Ray throwing a hissy over me stealing confidential property or some other crap.

Sure enough, as soon as Edgar had begun quieting down, they started nodding off, first Joaquin, then Ray, and finally I convinced stubborn Sofia to take a nap by promising I'd look after that creep Carlos for a bit and would wake her if there was any change. She knew I was up to something, because she gave me a long look and mouthed *be careful*, before reluctantly agreeing. I love her to death. Joaquin and Ray, too. But c'mon, gente. I've got exciting work to do.

Then I grabbed my gear and slipped past them and up the stairs, eager to get some air and work out as many deets of my future award-winning documentary masterpiece as possible.

But I'm not an idiot. The sudden stillness didn't mean

Edgar was gone. Without access to a proper forecast, I couldn't be absolutely sure, but I'd bet the sudden stillness was the hurricane's eye passing by. Based on Joaquin's ramblings when I questioned him on camera, the calm of Edgar's eye could last as little as five or ten minutes, a tiny window to catch a breather before the hurricane unleashes round two.

I'd already pushed my luck way too far. After I grab my gear, I dip into the chilly water, wading back toward the entrance to the tunnels. I hear a soft shuffling sound coming from behind me.

El Salon de Leyendas.

Those enormous doors at the entrance have been blown away, ripped from their frames like matchsticks, leaving a jagged outline of splintered wood.

What the hell? Many of the figures are still intact, standing on their heavy pedestals. But something seems different about them.

I snap a series of photos. . . .

A ghastly show is on display in my viewfinder. The dim lighting of the hall has leeched all color from the images, giving things a ghostly black-and-white quality. The strobe effect of the flash turns the scene into one of those old-fashioned, silent Nickelodeon movies we had to suffer through in Ms. Herrera's "History of Film" class.

El Salon is a jumble of dark, contorted shapes, with flashes of stark white faces, bulging eyes, and distorted grins. But that's not the worst of it. The shadows are . . . moving, twisting, and turning grotesquely, as if controlled by some demented, God-like puppeteer. I want to back away, but I'm frozen, my muscles rusted in place.

They're just statues. Wax copies—

My heart thuds. Icy sweat seeps from my pores.

Is that La Jupia? Her face is concealed behind an enormous hood, but the outline of her sharpened claws is unmistakable. How did she get off her horse?

My finger jams on the shutter release button, snapping a rapid series of photos. . . .

The figures continue their grotesque prancing and posing, almost as if in slow motion, shadows closing in all around me. This shit's crazy. Some optical illusion caused by faulty equipment. Just look up from the viewfinder—

Eyes lie. Cameras shoot truth.

Something slithers and sloshes across the wet floor behind me. Whatever it is, it's big, judging from the deep vibration that gnaws through to the bone, as its bulk slinks closer and closer. A noxious odor nearly gags me, the stink of festering wounds and roadkill that's begun to bake in the sun. Tremors rattle my body.

Am I imagining that horrible sound and that stench, or is that shit really getting louder and closer? I need to turn around and capture it with my camera. What if I turn around and it's not a monstrosity risen from the depths of the Caribbean sea? What if instead it's something far more disturbing? Something real, and not this imagined supernatural bullshit. Like Carlos. Or . . .

I try to scream, but my jaw might as well be wired shut.

Something cold and clammy slowly wraps around one of my ankles. Tears flood my eyes, further obscuring the image on the viewfinder. The tentacle tightens around my ankle. Bile rises in my throat, while the rest of El Salon's all-stars continue their dance from hell, soundless, closing in on me.

Up. Up. Up. The tentacle slithers higher and higher up my leg. A hot, rancid stench invades my nose. I grip the wooden cross around my neck so hard I can feel it cutting into the palm of my hand. Que vaina! I don't believe in the supernatural. I won't. I'm not even sure I believe in God. The cross is just the only thing I have left of my mother and her superstitions. But in a moment like this it's hard not to pray.

Let go! I scream over and over again without ever making a sound.

RAYMUNDO

I bolt upright. I might have actually dozed off at some point. But now that I'm awake, I'm struck by the odd sensation that something is very different. It takes me a moment to figure out what it is. It's too quiet. No rumble of heavy winds. No clanging debris. Seems like Edgar has finally passed us by and moved on to menace someone else.

My eyes scan the area in the dim emergency lighting. My first thought is to make sure the contents of the backpack I've been clutching have been undisturbed during my sleep, before remembering that my idea to hold a séance is all out in the open. Now all I have to do is make sure to keep it together and get to Paranormal Place in time to perform the ritual. If we can just make it through the next two days until Halloween . . .

That must have been one of the longest nights in my life, second only to the night I lost Rudy and Mai. It's no coincidence both are connected to Malicia. For most of the night, we hunkered down without saying much. At one point, Edgar's roar was so loud, even down here, that we couldn't say anything without having to shout. Every bang, every creak, every screech threatened to pop the eardrums. It got so bad, we decided to ditch our plan to watch over Carlos in shifts for two reasons.

First, even if someone were on duty when Carlos took a turn for the worse, what were we going to do about it anyway? We had already plied him with the maximum dosage of every antibiotic and painkiller we had. An overdose would be lethal, which, considering his rapidly deteriorating condition, would be a mercy.

Second, Carlos aside, who could sleep with that constant surge of hurricane winds shaking everything around us? Maybe Isabella, but she seemed more concerned with the contents of her flash drive. Even though she'd charged her extra batteries, there's only so long those would last. She begrudgingly turned off her laptop, staring into space like the rest of us, obsessing about who knows what.

I actually started getting nervous every time anyone would walk past my pack. God forbid Isabella should be the one to discover what I had tucked away inside it, all the instruments for the ritual. I decided it would be best to get ahead of things, try and explain what I had planned in as lighthearted a way as possible.

I cleared my throat. "So, originally one of the fun activities I had planned for us on the island was to have a séance when we reached Paranormal Place, you know, the section of the park dedicated to ghosts and stuff."

Isabella had looked up from her laptop and rolled her eyes. "I don't believe in the supernatural."

I forced a laugh. "Neither do I, Izzy. But I thought what better place to have a séance and contact the beyond than Malicia on Halloween night?"

I struggled not to let them see how desperate I was, the deep need I had to go through with this, the real reason I had brought them here. According to the ritual, every single one of them was needed to open that channel, to let me connect with Rudy and find the answers I've needed for so long.

Sofia had sighed. "With everything that's happened, I guess there's no point to it now."

Her voice sounded so . . . . hollow. I'd never seen her acting this way. Sure, out of the four of us, she was the one I expected to challenge the idea. But her tone was different. It almost sounded like despair. She wasn't okay.

It was Joaquin, good old reliable Joaquin, that had salvaged my plan. "I think a séance actually makes more sense now than just as a party game," he'd said.

"What do you mean?" Isabella asked, studying him.

Joaquin turned to me. "What happened with Carlos. Him murdering the crew and trapping us here for some reason. I think a séance might be able to shed some light on what's going on here. I'm with you a hundred percent, tiguere."

I reached out and gripped his hand, not only grateful for him pushing my idea, but also the fact that he always had my back and cared about making me happy, just like I did about him.

Sofia had merely nodded her agreement after that. But Isabella cinched the deal.

She squeezed Joaquin's shoulder. "If a séance is what you want, a séance is what you'll get, despite my skepticism."

I remember it striking me as odd that she'd give in to Joaquin so easily, without her usual snark and banter, but I wasn't about to question my good fortune.

"Great," I had said. "We all have a date for a séance in Paranormal Place on Halloween night."

That's when Sofia had broken her uncharacteristic silence, looking up at us, her eyes glazed with exhaustion. "Assuming we're all still here on Halloween."

After that remark, everyone pretty much stayed silent, staring into space, listening to Edgar's tantrum.

I look over now at Joaquin, who's sleeping soundly beside me, curled against my chest. Thank God he's been able to get some rest. I brush the hair off his forehead. Then I gently untangle my body from his before moving to check on Carlos.

Damn it. He looks so much worse.

The bandages are almost all black now, as if they've been covered in soot. What's left of his skin is so pasty, it's as if someone has rolled him in dough, except for the pulsating crimson blotches of burnt flesh, oozing pus. His breathing is shallow, with occasional gurgling noises emanating from deep in his chest. Not sure what's going on with his nose. It's a swollen purplish mess, as if someone had landed a powerful right hook. I reach out a tentative hand and touch his forehead. He's burning so hot I actually flinch. Esto es imposible. If his fever is that high, he should have been dead by now. His eyes pop open and my insides turn to jelly. Probably just a reflex but creepy as fuck. Instead of healthy whites, the surface has gone from opaque to translucent, exposing optic muscles and nerves and—

Something wriggling just under the surface like maggots. I jump back as if stung. That wasn't caused by burns. What if it's some kind of contagion? The beginning of a new pandemic. What if we've all been exposed? I turn around to check on the others.

Sofia rolls onto her side, hugging her Bach like a teddy bear. She's tossing and turning, her eyes fluttering as if she's deep in dreamland. Soft groans escape her lips. Her bandaged hand is hidden from view and I fight the urge to panic. What if my jevita, my childhood bestie, has been infected with the same bug as Carlos? My heart sinks. What have I potentially exposed her to—exposed all of us to—due to my selfishness? I consider waking her until I notice that Isabella is missing. Her laptop is still by her cot, but her flashlight's gone, along with her camera, and she's nowhere to be seen.

A quick search of the designated bathroom reveals nothing. I notice the door to the stairwell access ajar, propped open with a small coffin paperweight, as if someone were afraid it would lock behind them. Isabella. Has to be.

"Izzy? You there? Where are you?" I call through the opening.

No answer. I push open the door, and start up the stairwell, up and up, each step getting wetter and wetter the higher I go. Storm surge?

Even though I'm in really good shape, my chest is heaving by the time I reach the top of the stairs. This door is also propped open. By this time, the sea is steadily flowing through the opening, soaking my sneakers and the bottoms of my pants. As prepared as I think I am, I'm not ready for the devastation that greets me when I push through the concierge area and into the lobby.

There's no glass left in the windows. It's like walking through a mine field of jagged shards. At some point, the ceiling must have caved in, and I'm forced to maneuver around a mini Malicia Mountain of rubble to make it through the gaping hole that was once the entrance.

The outside looks like a snapshot of the beaches of Normandy from one of my history classes, except, instead of bodies, what little beach is left is littered with torn trees, mangled equipment, clumps of seaweed and other unidentifiable debris. What's even more alarming is that the ocean is lapping right against the hotel, submerging the entrance in several feet of water. I'm struck by how calm the sky looks. There's some wind, but it's light and cool, the kind of conditions you'd expect on a crisp, breezy day. You'd never guess a hurricane just plowed through here if it weren't for the devastation left in its wake. Remarkably, from what I can make out, the dome covering Malicia's four terror experiences has held together. And the massive mountain itself still looms. As I gaze out at the sea, the memory hits me like a hurricane force wind.

It's like I'm four again. Shivering in the cold drizzle of rain. Except instead of the choppy seas ahead of me now, I'm staring at the reflection of the spinning blue and red lights on the water. They look like magical shooting stars, and all I can do is whisper a silent wish over and over.

I wish Rudy is okay.

IWishRudyIsOkay . . . IWishRudyIsOkay . . . Iwishrudyis okayIwishrudyisokay.

I remember the smell of blood mixing with the salty air—the stench of death—the fresh blood of all those corpses lying broken in the park. Ten body bags were lined up outside the family residence, waiting to be airlifted to the morgue. I knew it was ten because my brother, Rudy, had been teaching me to count in both English and Spanish.

Four-year-old me had snuck out of the patrol craft, watching my pai. Sobbing as he unzipped bag after bag, one through ten, uno a diez, searching for what we both didn't want him to find, me thinking *Dios Mio. Por favor. Don't let it be mi hermano, Rudy. Don't let it be Mai.* As horrifying as it all was, I remember that intense relief as he unzipped each bag, revealing each body one by one, the family chef, my father's secretary, the butler, the concierge, the nanny, the gardener, the chief security officer, the maid . . .

DiosMioDiosMioDiosMio. Gracias. I had thought. *They're okay. They're okay.* Only two more. Just get through these last two . . .

Nine out of ten. Ziiiiiiiiiiiiiiiiip.

The image of mi pai, falling to his knees, shoulders heaving, lifting mi mai's head to his shoulder is seared into my brain.

Finally the tenth bag. Ten out of ten. ZIIIIIIIIIIIIIIIIIP. A boy's arm spilled from the bag, dangling, dripping blood.

By then, mi pai had completely lost it, head back, letting loose a guttural cry. But I didn't make a sound. I couldn't. Instead, I snuck back into the transport, sucking my thumb.

My brother and my mother. Two out of ten.

A loud rumbling interrupts my memory, and I stare in horror as the winds suddenly pick up speed and a block of dark gray pushes forward. I was wrong. Edgar didn't pass us by. The temporary calm was a lie, the eye of the hurricane passing over us. The worst is yet to come.

I cup my mouth and call out, "Isabella! Are you out there?"

Still no response. What if she came out here, slipped, fell, and is badly hurt?

"Over here."

I whirl to find her standing there at the entrance of El Salon de Leyendas, pale as a ghost, camera dangling around her neck like a hangman's noose. She's clutching her wooden cross around her neck, eyes wide, trembling. "The tentacle . . . it must have heard you coming . . . let me go . . ."

I grip both her arms. "Isabella! There's no tentacle. You must have imagined it. But that hurricane's real, and it isn't done with us! We have to get back down to the tunnels ASAP!" The terror in my own voice surprises me. I risk a glance back at the horizon—

Where a wall of black clouds and crashing waves is barreling toward us. Our asses are in trouble. I scramble toward Isabella and grab her by the arm, dragging her toward El Nido. She drops her camera.

Isabella rips free of my grasp and gropes for her camera in the rising waters.

"Leave it! There's no time!" I shout.

She ignores me, tugging at the camera strap, which is caught on a piece of debris.

Edgar's winds crash through my ears, drowning out my pleas for her to give up. The pressure feels like it's about to crush my skull.

The strap finally gives. Grabbing the camera, she sprints past me, and I'm hot on her heels. As we dart toward the stairwell, the first gust of hurricane force winds slams into us, knocking the breath from me. It feels like I'm a rag doll, twisting and spinning, then—

JOAQUIN

I spring upright. How the heck could I have fallen asleep with so much to do, so much at stake? One second I'm out like a rock, having the most delicious dream of nestling in Ray's arms. Next, the adrenaline is bursting through my veins, jolting me awake as effectively as a defibrillator. The last traces of the dream, Ray and I, lying intertwined, fade away, along with the possibility of it ever becoming a reality. It's Friday already. Only two more days to make sure I get Ray up to that mountain to meet his fate and save my ass. My eyes dart about the room as I break out into a cold sweat. Where is Ray? What if he's on to me? A loud groan shakes me completely awake and I move to investigate.

It's Carlos. My god. He's hardly breathing. And what's going on with his wounds? Why are they so black underneath? He also reeks. The smell is like a pungent mix of sickening sweetness and rotting milk. My anxiety gets the best of me, as usual, and I grab the small compact mirror I scored while scavenging the tunnels.

I look like utter crap. Dark circles under my eyes, which are bloodshot, bed hair for days. But it's not the aesthetics I'm concerned about. I angle the mirror so I can check my nostrils, my ears, in any nook and cranny where something insect-like could be crawling around. I know what I saw. El Bacá has infected Carlos. Possessed him. What if the demon's not planning on stopping there? Wearing N95 masks and gloves is not CDC approved against demonic possession. Sofia and I have been the two in closest proximity to Carlos since we brought him down here. And I'm beginning to wonder if something's going on with her, too. She looks tired, out of it, which is not typical Sofia. Is El Bacá trying to warn me that Sofia, and possibly even Izzy, are in danger unless I get my shit together and do what needs to be done?

Carajo. I scratch my nose and my heart sidesteps its next beat. What if while I was sleeping, that critter crawled out of Carlos's nose and slithered into mine? What if It burrowed through my insides? Into my brain—?

Maybe It's trying to punish me for having thoughts about Ray, for dreaming about what it would be like to be with him. Maybe the demon's exploring other options—Carlos, Sofia—because It thinks I'm going soft on Ray. If It can accomplish what It wants, get Ray to the mountain on Halloween night to perform the ritual and be reborn in the flesh, in Ray's body, then El Bacá won't need me, and It won't have to honor the bargain and release my soul in exchange for delivering Ray.

Relax. Get a grip, Joaquin. Concentrate on your breathing. Inhale—Yes. My lungs. The thing's nesting in my lungs. That's why I suddenly can't breathe. That's why I'm going to choke to death. They all warned me what the punishment for failure would be. . . .

Something squeezes my left shoulder. Jesus. My heart. It's eating through my—

"Joaquin!" Sofia calls my name. She squeezes my left shoulder again. Her voice is like an anchor, holding me back from the brink. But there's something different about her. She looks pale. And her eyes are kind of glazed over, as if she were high or something. Is she under El Bacá's influence? I need to watch her carefully. As if I weren't paranoid enough.

"What's up? Where is Ray?" Her words are measured, not in their usual logical, in-control way, but more robotic. I'm probably just being paranoid about her being mind-napped by a demonic entity. It has to be the stress of our situation.

"I-I . . . d-don't . . . know where Ray or Izzy are. I was just checking on Carlos." I try and fail to swallow the lump in my throat. "I don't think he's going to make it. And I think he's already infected us, too."

I lock eyes with her, scanning for any sliver of confirmation that she knows what I really mean when I say infected, but her glazed eyes remain neutral.

Sofia breaks into a smile that's more unnerving than comforting. "Everything is going to be fine. Te lo prometo." She gives me one last squeeze before we move apart. "Let's just focus on finding out where Ray is."

I find it odd that she hasn't mentioned Izzy, but then a deep rumbling vibrates throughout the complex, getting louder and louder. Sofia and I exchange horrified glances and look above us. I can tell we're both thinking the same thing. It was only Edgar's eye passing over us. Now he's back with a vengeance.

SOFIA

I sprint past Joaquin toward the stairwell door, three words cycling through my mind.

Find. Ray. Now. If he's still out there, he'll die. And it's not time yet.

My shoulder slams into the stairwell door, pushing it open. I'm not prepared for the force of the wind and its ear-splitting howling, threatening to suck me up the stairs, as if I were in one of those zero gravity chambers. Except you don't get body-slammed by two-hundred-mile-per-hour winds in those things. I grip the nearest railing, but I'm barely holding on for dear life, my fingers slick, slipping . . .

No. I can't fail now that I have a mission. I'm the only one here capable of seeing it through. Not Joaquin. It's all so clear now.

"I got you!" Joaquin grabs my waist, trying to haul me back inside.

There's a loud clang above us. Then something dropping,

heading right for us. The metal door from the stairwell above has been torn from its hinges. And now it's a lethal projectile, careening toward us, followed by a cascade of flood waters that'll drown us if the door doesn't take us out first.

Joaquin wraps a fire hose around us. Together, we drag ourselves back inside El Nido, just as the door crashes down, inches from us. It takes both of us to slam the door against the flood waters, but we manage to, cutting off the wind, before we both collapse, soaked and breathless.

"Sofia," Joaquin finally breaks the silence. "I know what you're thinking, but we don't know for a fact they were outside. They could have been exploring one of the wings down here."

It's easier to play along than to go with my gut. "It's possible."

I spring to my feet. "We have to go look for Ray." I start to march down the corridor past Joaquin, but he grabs my arm.

"I'll go after Ray and Izzy. You should stay and look after Carlos. I mean, he shouldn't be left alone, right?"

"We don't have a choice. It might take both of us to find Ray. Besides, Carlos is sleeping. He won't notice we're gone. There's nothing else we can do for him."

I can barely stand to look at Carlos, seeing him lying there in pain. Why prolong his suffering when death is a foregone conclusion? I rub the puncture wound hidden underneath my bandaged hand. The wound caused when Carlos bit me before I could sedate him. He's already fulfilled his purpose and given me the gift. It's time for him to go. I can take it from here.

All I have to do is send Joaquin out of the room on some pretext. Then take one of those hypodermics, fill the plunger with air, find a vein . . .

It would be over so soon. Carlos would be out of his misery, relieving the rest of us from the burden of looking after him. Then we could focus on finding Ray, assuming he's not dead already. If Izzy is alive, great. If not? Oh, well. She's not the important one.

I suddenly feel off balance, dizzy, as if I don't understand my own thoughts. What is wrong with me?

I lean against a cabinet to steady myself. "Joaquin, can you grab me a water. I think I'm feeling a little dehydrated."

What am I doing? He's gone in an instant, leaving me alone with Carlos. Giving me the chance to—No. This is insane. I won't do it.

The hypodermic is already in my hand. How the hell did it get there? I am not a murderer.

I'm shaking my head, even as I'm tapping the crook of Carlos's arm. No need to, though. The veins are clearly visible, pulsing beneath his clammy skin. "I . . . will . . . not . . . do . . . this," I whisper.

I press the tip of the needle against a nice, plump, juicy vein, pricking the skin. All I need to do now is apply pressure to the plunger, inject an air bubble that will make its way to his brain, and Carlos's nightmare will be over. Then I can get on with the task at hand. . . .

This is crazy. I will not do this. I can't—I apply pressure to the plunger—

A stinger darts out from Carlos's left nostril, accompanied by a loud hiss. I yelp, dropping the needle and sending it clattering to the floor.

"What's wrong?" Joaquin's voice just beside me almost makes me scream.

"I thought I saw something . . . inside Carlos's nose. It's gone now."

My words rattle Joaquin, which has the desired effect of diverting his attention away from the hypodermic. That would have been almost impossible to explain away, especially since I can't explain to myself what I was about to do. I rub the bite wound underneath the fabric, fighting the urge to scratch and draw attention to it.

Joaquin's eyes lock with mine, reflecting fear and desperation. "I've seen it, too. There's something inside him. A parasite. It's almost like something out of a sci-fi movie. Does it mean anything to you?"

Another burst of loud clanging. Joaquin and I exchange frightened looks. This doesn't sound like Edgar. It's different, echoing down the corridor. There it is again. Something is trying to get in.

"It could be Ray and Isabella," Joaquin mutters, as if reading my thoughts.

There's no question of leaving poor Carlos behind now. The two of us scramble down the hallway, coming to a fork in the corridor.

"It's coming from the left," I say, not waiting for Joaquin to acknowledge me before I'm already sprinting in that direction.

"El elevador," he says, catching up to me.

We both stare at the closed elevator doors.

"But that's impossible," I say. "There's no power. How could—?"

Another series of clanging noises almost makes me jump out of my skin. But this time, I hear muffled voices. I bang on the doors, pressing my ear against the cold steel. "Ray! Is that you? Can you hear me?" More muffled voices. I probably sound the same to them on the other end.

"What if it's not them?" Joaquin whispers.

"It has to be them. Who else could it be?"

Our eyes dart in the direction where we left Carlos and back. We never expected to encounter him on the island either. What if there are others?

Joaquin presses his ear against the elevator doors, too, trying to pick up something over the howling winds. His eyes light up. "I think I heard my name!"

"It has to be Ray! He must have gotten trapped inside the elevator." My eyes dart left and right. "We have to find something to pry open these doors."

Joaquin jumps to his feet. "I have an idea."

He races off, rushing back a minute or two later with a fire axe. "Stand clear."

I move out of the way. He swings the blade toward the center of the door several times, surprising me with the force and accuracy of his blows. I can't help but think how his focus on getting to Ray is definitely deflecting his anxiety. Good. We have the same end goal. Ray is our priority.

"Here, let me try." I grab the axe from Joaquin and fit the blade in between the elevator doors' groove, twisting the handle, and widening the gap enough where we can also fit our hands between to help pry them apart. Another pair of hands appears above our heads from inside the elevator doors, startling me, until I recognize the fingers.

"Tiguere!" Joaquin shouts. "Are you guys okay?"

The hands disappear, replaced by Ray's face, sporting some fresh cuts and bruises.

"It looks worse than it is."

I crane my neck, trying to get a better look inside the car. "Is Izzy with you?"

"Presente," she calls from behind Ray.

"What happened to you guys? Where were you? How did you get trapped in the elevator?"

"It's a long story. The short version involves getting caught out in the eye of the hurricane, barely making it back inside before Edgar cut loose, then diving for cover inside the elevator shaft, cutting the emergency brakes, and ending up partially down here."

"Hurry, Ray. We don't have much time," Isabella calls.

I can hear her snapping pictures behind him and a rush of anger engulfs me. She has no idea how important Ray is. If it were up to me, I'd leave her out in that storm so she could take as many pictures as she wanted before getting blown away.

I reel backwards. Those aren't my thoughts. I would never want anything to happen to Isabella. What is happening to me? My fingers dig into my arm as I try to ground myself, remain in control.

There's another loud crash from above. Water seeps through the opening, splashing me and Joaquin.

Joaquin shakes himself like a wet dog. "What the hell?"

"Oh, did I mention it's flooded up there and heading our way?" Ray's eyes betray the nonchalant tone he's trying too hard to inject into his voice.

The elevator lurches violently, knocking Joaquin and me back.

"Ray, it's coming!" Isabella screeches.

Ray, Joaquin, and I pry open the elevator doors wide enough for them to fit through.

"Pa'lante!" Ray shouts, shoving Isabella through the opening and diving through the gap, shoving the elevator doors closed again before the avalanche of water and debris plunging through its ceiling can crash into El Nido.

But even now, the water is seeping through, slowly flooding our underground shelter.

Ray shakes his head. "Those doors aren't going to hold forever. We need to make our way further into El Nido and higher ground before it gets too deep." He slings his arms around Joaquin and me, ushering us down the corridor as we slosh through the deepening water.

"What about Carlos?" I ask over the bubble and hiss of the rising waters. If I can't end Carlos' suffering, I'm not going to let him die alone, especially since he's done his duty and opened my eyes.

It's that voice again. That other voice inside my head. A pang of terror seizes me. Am I having a psychotic breakdown? The idea of not being in control of my own thoughts and body is more horrifying than anything else Malicia has to throw at me.

The rest of them follow me into our improvised med center to Carlos's cot.

He's gone.

Joaquin shakes his head. "I don't get it. How could he have gotten loose?"

I shake my head, examining the straps that had held him to the bed. "These look like he ripped right through them."

Ray shoves the empty cot into the wall. "Imposible! I had him strapped down tight. And he was on death's door. No way he could have gotten free."

Isabella grabs her laptop and pack, glancing at the sea water slowly oozing into the room. "We can debate this shit later. Not all of my equipment is waterproof. Vámonos!"

"I'll carry my pack and the one with the food. Pana, you and Sofia divvy up the essential equipment, like the flashlights, in your packs." Ray is already sloshing ahead, the rest of us struggling to keep up.

He leads us through the maze-like tunnels of El Nido, pausing briefly to shut each door behind us.

"Maybe that'll slow it down," he says. But his tone doesn't sound very convincing.

By the time he leads us into a larger corridor and slams the door behind us, we all slump against the floor and walls, wet and frightened.

"What do we do now?" I ask. "This place will keep flooding."

He shoots me a look. "That's why we have to keep moving. Go deeper into the complex, into the dome, and look out for higher ground."

Joaquin's eyes blaze in the dim light. "The mountain! Malicia Mountain. That's the highest point on the island. That's where we need to go."

I try to contain my smile. Clever boy. Score one for Joaquin. At least he's focusing on our goal. Getting Ray up to that mountain by Halloween is all that matters now.

Ray nods. "The mountain makes sense. But it's going to take a while to get up there. In the meantime, that message on the cell phone in the banquet hall mentioned Serial Springs. That means there's someone else still alive on this island. Maybe they have or know where we can find one of the SAT phones located in the park, which we can use to contact the outside world."

Joaquin's pacing in circles. "While SAT phones can be used anywhere, because of the storm's interference, one would probably work best on top of the mountain anyway, so we should still plan on going up there even if we find one."

Ray reaches out and squeezes his shoulder. "Sounds like a plan."

But it's obvious as they stare into each other's eyes that Joaquin can't be relied on to carry out the master's plan.

That's why I'm here now.

As we slog through the icy water, I notice the syringe I almost used on Carlos bobbing on the surface, almost pricking me in the ankle. I pick it up now, careful not to let anyone see me, glancing at Ray as I tuck it into my pack.

I have another use for that syringe now.

This time, I barely fight that voice.

RAYMUNDO

There's always been something unsettling about these tunnels in El Nido, going back to the times Rudy and I used to sneak in to play as kids. Waves of deep cold, penetrating the air and digging into your lungs. Strange creaks and groans, as if the mountain itself were shifting in its sleep. The sometimes dank air, carrying a faint, putrid aroma, as if something dead had almost finished the bloating process but wasn't quite done. During normal park hours, with all the activity filling the crowded corridors, none of these things were ever too noticeable. But during the dark, when things had settled and most sensible people were home safe under the covers, the aftershow began. Like now.

At least the floor here isn't wet—yet.

Even in the dim emergency lighting, I can see the anxiety etched into their faces, which I'm sure mirror my own. How much longer until the generator goes?

128

I stop and they all follow suit without saying a word. "We're all exhausted. Why don't we rest up for a few until we reenergize?"

I rummage through my backpack and distribute some bottled waters, chocolate bars, and leftovers, careful not to disturb the ritual materials for the séance. Even though my plans to conduct the ceremony are now out in the open, I'm still wondering how it's going to play out when we actually arrive at Paranormal Place, the spot where Rudy died.

I catch Sofia staring at me intently. I've never seen her look at me quite like this. It's as though she's studying me like a chapter in one of her medical journals. "You really think we're going to find one of these SAT phones, Ray?"

"Each crew locking down the park is supposed to carry at least one satellite phone in case of emergencies. From what I could tell in the log back there in the security station, it looks like there were four units dispatched, one to each of the park's four quadrants. If we can get ahold of just one of those phones, we can reach the outside world, report what's happened here, and wait for the cavalry to arrive—"

"Unless Carlos gets to us first." Joaquin slumps forward, palms on his forehead.

I crouch by him, reach out, and muss his hair. "He won't." I rise and look around us. "But just as a precaution, we should keep our eyes peeled and take turns acting as lookout during rest periods."

Isabella crinkles her nose. "What's that stink? Smells like there might be something decomposing down here." She pans the camera around, taking more footage.

Joaquin is rubbing his arms as if he's freezing. "I'm not sure. Maybe it's a by-product of whatever infected Carlos . . . or something."

Sofia clears her throat. "I'm sure whatever infected Carlos is not contagious."

The look on her face is a cross between dismissive and arrogant, two qualities that I've never seen in her, even when we dated. If something's troubling her, I need to talk to her and find out what's up.

I also can't help but notice how she's rubbing her bandaged hand. "I don't know how you can be so sure about that, doctora. I think we're all going to have to get checked out when we get rescued, just in case . . ."

Her eyes lock with mine. "Are you questioning my diagnosis?"

"All I'm saying is that we still don't know what the crews may have been exposed to on the island. They could have uncovered a rare toxin, or eaten something that might have jumped from animal to human like at those wet markets. Without proper tests it's impossible to tell. I would think you would agree with that, no?"

She looks away, remaining silent.

Isabella snorts. "Or maybe the dude just went loco and murdered his co-workers. Some people are just monsters. End of story." She turns away and aims her camera at Joaquin. "What do you think about all of this?"

Joaquin's rocking back and forth now. "You think we're going to get sick like Carlos? I'm probably going to get it really bad, aren't I? I mean I've been in really close contact with him, touched him, all it would take is a paper cut—"

Isabella moves in closer to him with her camera. "Did you rub your eyes or scratch your nose after you touched him? During that last pandemic—"

"Izzy, por favor," Sofia cuts her off. "Speculation without scientific tests is pointless. It's probable none of us is infected with anything. Besides, Carlos suffered bad burns and that's why he was dying. Burns aren't contagious, people."

Joaquin's rocking intensifies. "Do burns cause parasites, Sofia?"

They exchange a knowing look that confuses the hell out of me. Just what is going on between them? What am I missing?

I move between them. "Parasites?"

"I saw something in Carlos's nose. It crawled out from a birthmark and right into his nostril. Looked like some kind of insect but not like any I've ever seen before."

My eyes flit to Sofia. "You saw it, too?"

She shrugs. Her eyes dart to Joaquin's, and I could almost swear she glares at him for a moment. "I saw something. I'm not so sure what it was."

I crumple the napkin that was holding my tostón. "I think I might have also seen something the last time I checked in on Carlos."

Joaquin jumps to his feet. "Well, I know for sure what I saw. It was a goddamn parasite. Then the blackout hit when the generator blew. All hell broke loose and I didn't get a chance to mention it until now. And now he's out there on the loose. . . ."

I move over to Joaquin, pulling him close, feeling his body trembling in the throes of another anxiety attack. "Don't get excited, pana. No one's upset with you."

Isabella thrusts her camera in our direction. "Wait a minute. You're telling me that dude's got something crawling inside him, and we weren't wearing Hazmat suits? And now he's lurking somewhere on the island, waiting to infect us if he hasn't already?"

"Weren't you the one who always wanted to go viral?" Joaquin snaps at her, breaking free of me. "Think of all your new followers, Izzy."

She gives him side eye. "Why are you so freaked, Joaquin? Is it this place? Why does it trigger you? Dime?"

Joaquin goes to grab her camera, but I step between them. "Gente, enough. I understand everyone's stressed, but we need to keep it together if we're going to get through this."

Izzy aims her camera at Joaquin once again. "You're not really mad at me, are you?"

"Yes, I'm really pissed at you!"

She lowers the camera and smiles. "And you're so angry that you aren't feeling anxious anymore, right? You're welcome."

Joaquin lets out a nervous chuckle, and I muss his hair again.

Sofia grabs her pack. "I don't know about you, but the sooner we get out of this tunnel, the better. Let's keep moving."

I lead them down the maze again. No one says a word. The only sounds are the storm winds, whining like the giant turbines of a 747, accompanied by the occasional drips and splash of rain and sea leaking into the complex.

But there's something else. Underneath it all. Sounds you can barely make out but if you listen closely between gusts you may be able to catch before they seep back into the walls.

Voices. Whispers.

I can't make out what they're saying, but I'm not sure I want to know.

I try to focus on the path ahead, half expecting something to jump out at me at every turn, like in those Halloween fright mazes. Finally, I can see it up ahead, the huge silver door with the Malicia logo. Beneath it the words:

Serial Springs.

"We have arrived," I say, half to myself. Of course, I'm leaving out the fact that finding the satellite phone isn't the only reason I've led them here. Once we make it to Serial Springs, I can lead them through to Creature Canyon, and then Paranormal Place to hold that séance.

Isabella snaps a few pictures. "Serial Springs? Isn't this the place with the psycho theme?"

I nod. "Welcome to Serial Springs, home of every single serial killer that has stalked your nightmares. Be careful. They may choose you as their next victim." I'm trying to boost morale by employing my park guy schtick, but no one is smiling.

"After you." I open the door and usher everyone inside. I could swear I hear the quiet sounds of laughter in the dark before shutting the doors behind us.

ISABELLA

Coño. Can we get any cornier?

Huge billboard-sized letters bombard us from every direction, making sure to let us know that we've arrived in SERIAL SPRINGS. They're designed to look like those magazine and newspaper cutout letters used by psycho killers in their anonymous messages to victims and authorities.

yOU'RE nEXT!

tONIGHT yOU diE!

I knOW wHAt yOU're uP tO, iZZY!

I blink the last thought away, trying to shut everything else out except what I can see through my viewfinder. I fire off another series of photos.

The whole place looks like a typical small town. There's a town square, complete with clock tower, post office, the Serial Springs housing development, featuring row upon row of suburban victim homes, and a grocery store.

But just below the surface, you can tell something's off. A broken window here and there. A boarded-up door. Crime scene tape cordoning off one of the houses. A section of lawn that appears to have been dug up in multiple places, as if someone were searching for a body. Or body parts. A gothic-looking county morgue that seems oddly out of place.

I turn to Ray. "Adonde ahora? Which way?"

He scans the façade of a horizon and points. "Over there. That's where we're heading. According to the log, the crew was stationed on the other side of Main, at El Asilo."

"The Asylum? Sounds cozy," Sofia's smile widens. "Espera. El Asilo, as in that movie series about the demented serial killer doctor that cut out his victims' internal organs and teeth and stuffed them into jars?"

I snap a photo of her. "Oye, since when have you ever liked horror flicks?"

The grin she gives me chills me to the bone. "I'm beginning to develop an appreciation for them now that I'm here."

"That demented serial killer you referred to, Sofia, is Dr. Romeo Perez," Joaquin says. "Aka El Ratoncito Perez, who killed over one hundred and fifty people throughout the course of seven movies."

I lower my camera. "El Ratoncito Perez? I remember that story from childhood. Mi mai used to tell it to me. He's the Dominican version of the tooth fairy, isn't he? Kids would leave their teeth under their pillows, and this little mouse with a red pack on his back would steal them from underneath their pillows. How the hell is that supposed to be scary?"

Ray shakes his head. "Guess you missed those flicks."

I purse my lips. "Doesn't sound like I missed much."

"In the movies," Ray continues, "the deranged doctor dressed up in a straw hat, gold glasses, and wore linen shoes so he could creep up on his victims more easily. He never spoke a word when he dismembered and disemboweled people, just squealed like a mouse, making sure to remove all their teeth and wear them like a necklace. The pack on his back was actually stained red from blood, stuffed with jars containing livers, brains, hearts—"

"That's . . . interesting. I should make it a point to watch one of those movies really soon." Sofia chuckles.

Now I'm totally confused. "Espera, niña. Aren't you the one that's always making a fuss when we have our movie horror-thons, spouting shit about some people having a warped idea of what constitutes entertainment? What happened to 'Science over séance, thank you very much?'"

Her grin disappears in a flash of anger. "So now I'm not allowed to broaden my horizons, Izzy? Here, take a photo of this." She flashes me the bird, as Ray and Joaquin stifle laughter.

What the hell has gotten into her? I know we're all stressed and shit, but she's been acting weird since she spent all that time playing doctor-patient *with that killer*, Carlos. He did something to her. Her hand. Is she infected like Joaquin was rambling about? Does she know where he disappeared to?

I snap some more photos of Sofia before focusing the camera on Joaquin's face, which is buried in one of the old tourist maps he found as we exited El Nido. He finally looks up and points. "There's a shortcut to El Asilo this way."

As we make our way down the pathway, I notice the *Have You Seen* and *Missing* posters covering the telephone poles and storefront windows, some half torn, the others yellowing, most featuring attractive young people and children. (Coño, I guess if you're ugly and old, even the serial killers swipe left.) I get the eerie sensation that I recognize some of those faces, but it's probably my brain trying to rein the freak in.

Control yourself, mija.

The whole place has been designed to maximize shadows, the streets cramped and claustrophobic, with plenty of windows, so you can never be sure who's watching you.

"I don't remember half these rides," Joaquin says, his voice filled with nervous energy. For a split second, he grows paler and his eyes widen, the scar on his ear pulsing pink.

Then he blinks it away, stuffing the brochure in his pocket.

There it is, and I got it all on camera. His stark terror of having slipped up, exposed himself. I want to reach out and tell him that it's okay, that he doesn't have to hide anymore. But a serious documentarian would never interfere with her subject that way.

"Remember?" Ray asks. "You never told me you were here before, pana."

"Once. Long time ago."

I take an extreme close-up of his face. "You must have been really young."

"What does it matter? I barely remember this place. Can you please stop recording me?"

I'm tempted to press him on when exactly it was that he was here last but decide to wait until I can get him alone. I want to tell his story, not pressure him so much that he freaks out.

Sofia points to a tavern on the next corner, Ratoncito's Labyrinth. "Ah, I could really use something besides lukewarm water. If only . . ."

I lick my lips. "I could really use una fría."

Ray shoots us his frat boy smile, which quickly turns whistful. "Reminds me of old times."

I study all of their uneasy expressions in my viewfinder as I click away, bouncing between Sofia's strange, detached face, and Joaquin's anxiety ridden one.

Just what is going on with you two?

We finally reach El Asilo. If buildings could brood, this would be a perfect example. I give mad props to whoever designed the façade. What a monstrosity. Towering spires, ivy strangling the façade, set back on a hill and surrounded by barbed wire. The look, coupled with Edgar's tantrum taking place just outside the dome, punctuates the foreboding atmosphere. If you weren't crazy before you arrived, you would be after you left.

Ray steps forward to scan the area, finally pointing off to the side. "There. One of the work crew's forklifts next to the trailer. If there's a SAT phone to be found, that's where it's going to be." He starts off alone.

"Ray," Sofia stops him in his tracks. "I think all of us should come with you. Just in case."

He nods.

As we follow him through an opening in the barbed wire, I grab ahold of Sofia's arm and hold her back for a second while Ray and Joaquin continue.

"Qué te pasa, Sofia? Are you okay? You're really weirding me out. And that hand looks worse—"

She wrenches free of my grip. "Maybe I'm just tired of your whole gossip mongering disguised as a human interest story about Joaquin!"

I pause like I've been struck. She's never looked at me like this before, such anger in her eyes. No, not anger. Hatred. "You know it's not like that. I don't give a shit about Malicia. It's Joaquin I'm interested in. His story is very compelling and—"

"Bullshit," she hisses. "It's still all about Izzy and her quest for fame. You'll never change." She gets up in my face. "Drop the snooping into Joaquin's past before it bites you in the ass."

"Hey! You guys coming or what?" Ray calls from the distance.

I catch Sofia's cold stare in my viewfinder. She's framed by one of those tacky serial killer billboards that says:

YOU'LL nEVER lIVE TO sEE aNOTHER dAY!

JOAQUIN

We pass through the barbed wire fence. My heart and lungs race to catch up to my mind. It's hard enough dealing with the trauma of being back here and the betrayal I'm about to carry out, and now, because of a slip of the tongue, they're going to be suspicious of me, especially Izzy, who caught it all on camera. All my planning and scheming will have been for nothing, and my own very soul is toast.

"This way." Ray doesn't slow down or glance back as he leads us toward the work site.

Is he purposely avoiding looking at me? Even if he has figured out who I really am, he can't possibly know what it is that I have in store for him. No way. Even I can't believe it now that it's about to happen at last. It was one thing having it drilled into me in that attic room for years, through the haze of incense and chanting. But actually meeting Ray in the flesh, befriending him for years, gaining his trust, developing feelings—

I can't swallow. Throat dry. Have to get out of here. Going to break down in front of them. Start crying. They'll think I'm crazy. . . .

I almost laugh then. Loco. A lunatic. And here we are at El Asilo. We'll just drop you off here, Joaquin. No need to worry. Such a nice cell! Later, looney. If I'm not crazy now, I will be after I do what I came here to do to Ray, sacrifice him so that El Bacá can use Ray's body as a vessel to manifest in the flesh and unleash Its dark reign on all of humanity.

What good will my soul be then? I'll lose either way. But the coward in me doesn't want to think about any of that. I just need to concentrate on my short term goals to avoid the crippling anxiety trying its best to overwhelm me. Bring Ray to the island while making him think it was his idea. Check. Set things up so that I have an excuse to take him to the top of the mountain under the guise of a better SAT phone signal. Check. I just need to time things so that we're there on Halloween night. Just two days from now. In the meantime, I have to make sure it's me that finds the SAT phone. We don't need any rescue teams showing up and destroying well laid plans before then.

I also have to watch out for some wild cards, like Carlos and Sofia. If El Bacá has possessed them, it can only mean one thing. The demon doesn't trust me and is taking out an insurance policy to ensure the plan doesn't fail. That would mean El Bacá has lost faith in me. Does It think that I'm weak? That I've gotten too close to Ray? And if that's the case, and either Carlos or Sofia accomplishes what I fail to, then the deal the demon made with my coven will be broken, and El Bacá will be free to destroy me as well. So either Ray dies, or I do. There's no Hallmark ending on our horizon.

My eyes flit to Isabella, who's snapping away with her camera. Great. She'll capture my full meltdown for the world to see, just like all those reporters did so many years ago.

Enough. Breathe. Relax. That's it. You're in control.

I have to find a way to neutralize her curiosity. One way or another.

We stop when we reach the work crew station. Not much to see here. Abandoned equipment, no trace of the actual crew.

I turn to Ray. "I don't get it, tiguere. If this place is supposed to be demolished, why does it look like there's some excavation going on?"

Sofia inspects the scene as if she's looking under a microscope. "I was thinking the same thing."

Ray's eyes narrow as he surveys the site. "From what I understand, while some of the teams are responsible for planting charges to bring these structures down, others are working on salvage and assessing the existing infrastructure and structural integrity for the new owners, which explains all the digging."

Isabella yawns and records the scene like a crime scene investigator. "Definitely B roll footage."

Ray ignores her. "Everyone spread out and see if you can find the SAT phone or anything else that'll be useful, but make sure you stay within line of sight of everyone else."

Oh, I definitely don't plan on taking my eyes off you, Ray. So much depends on it.

But after about ten minutes of ransacking the trailer and

surrounding equipment, the only thing we come up with are a couple of warm bottled waters, which Ray stuffs in his pack along with the rest of the rations.

We all glance at each other's haggard faces. The implication is clear. He has no idea how long we're going to be stuck here. If only I could tell him that it's not going to be for much longer, just not in the way he's hoping.

"Let's take a break. But just a five minute water break." He opens one of the bottles and passes it around so we can each take a swig.

When the bottle gets to me, I have to make a real effort not to gulp it down to drown out the latest wave of anxiety.

My tremors cause some of the water to dribble down the corners of my mouth. Ray gently takes the bottle from me and dabs my lips with the corner of a spare T-shirt he had in his pack. "Just imagine you were taking a sip of some ice-cold Presidente beer."

At that moment, I hate him for being so naïve, so trusting, making the monumental task I'm facing so much harder. I want to shout *Open your goddamn eyes, Ray. I'm getting ready to royally fuck you over.* But all he does is smile warmly, and I have to suppress my rage, my despair, and pretend to be comforted like a good little pana. God I hate him. God I hate me. And then I remember that god has nothing to do with any of this.

After resting a few minutes, Sofia finally breaks the silence. "If they were working inside El Asilo, we need to check it out just in case." She seems a little too eager as she pulls out four flashlights, handing one to each of us, before slinging her pack over her shoulder. "It'll be dark in there, so everyone stay close."

I maneuver myself in between Sofia and Ray as we walk up to the entrance, making sure he's closer to me than to her. There's a part of me that's always resented Sofia's bond with Ray, even after they finally broke up. I used to think those feelings had to do with how much harder she made my task of influencing and manipulating Ray by having to constantly compete with her effect on him. But sometimes it feels there's a deeper reason for my resentment, one that creeps out in my dreams. And now, there's the added threat that she's actually in league with El Bacá, conspiring against me, trying to fulfill the demon's will before I can.

We pause before stepping inside. "People died in there. I remember . . . reading about it on the Internet."

Except for the clenching of his jaw muscles, Ray's face might as well be made of stone.

Sofia's eyes bounce from mine to his. There's a sparkle in them, an excitement, that feels . . . off. "Nothing can touch the Quisqueya Club when we all stick together." She leads the way inside.

If the outside of El Asilo screams gloomy, the inside is even worse. The front desk area reminds me of a medieval torture chamber, elevated on a dark wooden dais, crammed with patient files so stuffed with sheaves of yellowed paper that they resemble ancient, arcane scriptures. On either side, rows of padded patient cells extend into the darkness. There are tracks on the floor to accommodate the passenger cars for the ride portion, which have been ingeniously designed to resemble hospital gurneys with room for up to six guests on board. An icy draft knifes through the lobby, bathing me in a cold sweat. My flashlight almost slips through my fingers.

"How quaint." Isabella is busy recording the area with her infrared lenses. But unlike when we first got to the island, she seems to just be going through the motions, almost bored of it all.

Sofia pans the room with her light. "Yes, it is quaint, isn't it, Izzy?"

Ray cocks his head. "I wouldn't think *quaint* would be a word you'd use to describe this place, doctora. We should definitely get in and out as quickly as we can." He looks in my direction and purses his lips.

Here it is. He's finally taken off those sickening blinders of his. He's going to call me out now. I can feel it. I just know—

Instead, he grips my ice-cold hand and whispers in my ear, "I'm going to need you in here, Joaquin. I'm un pendejo when it comes to scary rides."

Anxiety gives way to another wave of rage and bitterness. Sí. You definitely are un pendejo, Ray. "I would never let anything happen to you." I squeeze his hand even tighter as he leads me deeper into the gloom.

SOFIA

I can't imagine this place being any creepier when it was operational. The unsettling storm sounds ripping and roaring all around us are not the product of sound effects but a real live upper category hurricane. The dark tunnels we're carefully maneuvering through are full of real danger—one false step and we can plunge down a steep drop intended for a rollercoaster surprise. And yet—I'm not afraid. Somehow, I know that it's here, in the icy draft of these dark tunnels, that I'll find the SAT phone. It wants me to find the SAT phone before the others do, including Joaquin. We can't leave the island—not yet. Not until after Halloween night when the ritual has been performed and It walks in Ray's flesh. Once again, it's like another voice, one that doesn't belong to me, is infecting my thoughts. But the more I hear it, the less afraid of it I become. I've been so used to always taking charge, always stressing out over the most minute detail, that there's a comfort knowing that something else is in the driver's seat and I can just kick back and see where It leads me. And I owe it all to Carlos for pointing me in the right direction. The others think he was diseased and crazy, but now I understand that he was enlightened. Everything is much more clear now. Is this what Eve felt like when she took a bite of the forbidden fruit? If so, no wonder she shared it with Adam. Just like I intend to share it with Joaquin, Isabella, and Ray. Especially Ray.

I step carefully over one of the metal tracks, uneasy at the thought of all the voltage capable of passing through them. "It was smart of you to turn off the breakers, Ray." I've been trying to keep my tone more measured, but it's hard with all the excitement of this newfound awareness and purpose coursing through my veins.

"It wouldn't do any of us any good to get zapped if the power should decide to return without notice, not that it's very likely," Ray says.

Isabella snaps a few more photos with her infrared lens, then tucks the camera away. "I need to recharge soon."

I lead the way with the bobbing beam of my flashlight another fifty feet or so through sheer instinct, until we reach a fork in the tracks, going off in three different directions.

Isabella snorts. "Coño."

"Now what?" Joaquin's voice quavers as it echoes down the corridors.

He's nervous. He knows El Bacá's disappointed in him. That he's been deemed not up to the challenge. But I'm here now. And I always get things done.

We're here. This is where It wanted me to lead them. I'm not quite sure what It looks like yet, but with each passing moment,

Its features are becoming clearer, just like my thoughts, emerging from a cloak of darkness that is my own ignorance. I used to think I had all the answers, that science was everything. That becoming a doctor was going to be how I would help people. But now I realize sometimes you have to force people to take their medicine when they don't realize what truly ails them.

Ray aims his flashlight in each direction, left, forward, right, bouncing it back between them. "Guess we're going to have to search these one by one."

Isabella shakes her head. "That'll take a lot of time."

I lower my flashlight. I need to stall them before they leave this spot. The voice in my head is overwhelming now, making it hard to hear what's left of the old me, the unenlightened me, trying to stretch the seconds until *It* gives me a sign. "The only safe option is to stay together. We can't split up, especially with Carlos on the loose, although I still can't understand how he can be ambulatory in such a weakened condition." But I really can understand now, and they will soon, too.

Ray trains his light on me. "We're in agreement, doctora."

Joaquin shines his own light up at his face. "I definitely agree as well. And if someone should get separated and lost, we meet back at the front desk."

Izzy frowns as she checks her camera's gauges. "Sounds like a solid plan. I would have preferred taking time to recharge my battery first, but it looks like I'm outvoted."

I grin at her, making her so uncomfortable that she looks away. Then I aim my light at the first tunnel. "Fine. Let's—"

There's an ear-splitting crack, and then the ceiling collapses.

The sign that I've been waiting for.

JOAQUIN

I barely have time to register the shouts and the screams before I feel Ray shoving me out of the way.

"Watch it!"

Then I'm slammed to the floor, covering my ears against the deafening roar as the tunnel collapses in a storm of debris and dust.

It takes me a few minutes to get my bearings. I take a deep breath, then go into a coughing fit, hacking up my lungs.

Jesus. What if I've breathed in asbestos? Or some deadly chemical the crews were using? My lungs could be dissolving as I lie here. What if I've broken some bones? Punctured my liver? Ruptured my spleen? What if—?

STOP IT.

The wave passes and only one thought propels me.

"Ray!" I shout into the darkness. If something's happened to him prematurely . . .

No response.

Luckily, my flashlight's still on and within reach. I grab it and flail it about, catching flashes of destruction all around me.

"Raymundo!" I shout again. "Tiguere! Are you okay?"

Still no answer.

My heart's pounding against my ribs. I'm not sure if it's hard to breathe because of my panic attack, the swirling dust, or a possible collapsed lung.

My stomach twists into knots. It's bad enough that Sofia and Izzy might be severely wounded, or dead even. But if anything's happened to Ray prematurely, then all these years of planning for this moment, my entire lifetime, will have been a colossal waste, not to mention the unspeakable price for failure.

"Pana!"

It's Ray's voice. It's muffled, but he's still alive! The irony that I'm thrilled he's still breathing, knowing that I'll be responsible for him taking his last breath, is not lost on me.

"Where are you, Ray?" I shout over and over, until I'm led to a small crack in the debris, a thin sliver really.

I rush over to it, shining my light inside, as a pair of fingers slips through the crack.

"I'm here, Joaquin!" Ray calls. "Are you hurt?"

I reach out and press my fingers to his. "I'm okay. Y tú?"

"Just a few scrapes and bruises. I'll survive. Sofia is okay, too. Can't get through to her though. The opening on my side is bigger than this one but still too small to crawl through." He pauses for a minute, and I can hear him taking a deep breath. "Not sure about Izzy. Sofia hasn't heard from her either. I'm so worried about her."

"What if something's happened to her? What if—?"

"I know. We have to regroup and search for her. Together. We're all cut off from each other. I've already talked with Sofia and we've agreed to continue down our tunnels until we find a way out. You're closest to the lobby where we came in. I want you to go there and wait for us. And try and stay out of sight."

No. That is not going to work. I have to stay close to Ray until I can get him exactly where I need him to be, especially with Sofia and Carlos lurking about trying to beat me to the punch. Is this cave-in a test of my resolve and loyalty?

I shake my head, even though Ray can't see it. "I don't think I can hack being alone, Raymundo. I'm . . . I . . ."

"I'm scared, too." His fingers disappear and are replaced by his eyes.

I hunch closer until just inches apart, staring right back at him.

"Don't worry, Joaquin. I'm going to come for you as soon as I can, even if I have to barrel through these tunnels with my bare hands. I promise you."

I let out a nervous laugh. If he were smart, he'd barrel through in the opposite direction from me. "Don't make promises you can't keep." Tears sting my eyes, but I wipe them away furiously before he can notice. I can't afford to pity him . . . feel anything for that matter. That's why El Bacá recruited Carlos and now Sofia. My feelings for Ray are a liability that are going to condemn my very soul.

"The sooner I start making my way down the tunnel, the sooner I'll see you back at the lobby. Now go. Por favor, pana."

"Be careful, tiguere."

He gives me a wink. "You, too. See you on the other side."

The last thing I see are his eyes, and I can tell he's smiling at me.

Then he's gone, his footsteps echoing through the crack until they fade away completely, leaving me alone in the darkness.

The only sounds now are Edgar's winds, beating against the dome, alternately wailing, then howling to get in. I feel like I'm having withdrawal symptoms, as if thousands of tiny bugs are crawling their way through my skin.

Holding the flashlight out like a weapon, I force myself forward, step by step, moving faster and faster, propelled by fear and adrenaline, until I push through the doors and find myself back in the lobby. But I can't just sit around and wait calmly. I have to be the one to find the SAT phone before any of the others do. Ray and the others will be here soon. In the meantime, I can hunt for it myself while I strategize how I'm going to get Ray alone and incapacitate him before conducting the necessary rites on the mountain. I check my pocket where the vial of powder is still hidden. A tranquilizer I can slip into Ray's water bottle before we hike up the mountain so he'll be nice and tired by the time we get there. Then after he passes out, I can tie him to the altar. Once he's totally incapacitated, I can begin the ritual—

A soft, distinct sound like the tinkle of a little bell startles me. There it is again. Where's it coming from?

Slowly, I make my way to the reception area. That's not possible. There's no power. How can it be?

One of the room numbers on the control panel is flashing. The patient in 13B is requesting the nurse's assistance.

B as in Bacá.

SOFIA

About fifty feet in, I'm already having pangs of regret at leaving Ray to fend for himself. He's the important one in all of this. Joaquin and Isabella are afterthoughts, although their blood might prove useful. That other part of me, the old, primitive one, feels a pang of revulsion at that thought, until the more evolved version I'm becoming snuffs the spark before it can become a flame. It, the one cloaked in shadow, wanted this to happen. It wanted to separate us, so that I can be the one to find the SAT phone. My heart races with exultation at the thought of carrying out Its will.

The dark is oppressive, my beam cutting into it like a butcher knife. For a split second, that other me that's growing dimmer and dimmer considers turning back and trying to find Izzy and the others instead. But Sofia 2.0 quashes that thought.

I stumble over one of the tracks, losing my grip on the

flashlight, which goes rolling off to my left. Damn it. Please don't let it go out. Please don't let it go out. It goes out.

Don't panic. That's the old me talking. The one with the need to be in control. You don't need the flashlight. It's guiding you now. All you have to do is crawl about ten feet in an angle and you'll be where you're supposed to be.

I smile as I feel my way across the cold metal tracks, fanning my hands out on the ground, going slowly. I used to think I knew what confidence was. But this, this is true confidence: feeling my way through the dark, knowing I'll find what I'm looking for.

I stifle a bout of nervous laughter before rising and continuing my way down the tunnel. And then I'm rewarded with a sign cloaked in bloodred emergency lighting, just like I knew I would be:

Maximum Security Ward. Only Authorized Personnel Beyond This Point.

From the way the brochures teased the visitors, this is supposedly where the most vile, violent serial killers were housed, the ones that gave you nightmares during the daylight hours. This is where the gurney cart would stop, and either animatronic or costumed psychopaths would jump out and scare the crap out of unsuspecting park visitors.

Except it's only me now. And I have to go inside and do my new master's bidding.

ISABELLA

Que jodienda.

If I hadn't lost my flashlight when the tunnel collapsed, I wouldn't have to rely on the infrared of my camera viewfinder to guide me. The battery indicator is already blinking, which means if I don't find my way out of this place soon, I'm going to be stuck in pitch black, waiting for the monsters to come out and play. And by monsters, I mean human monsters, like that creep Carlos or one of his buddies. Still don't buy the supernatural bullshit. Anything I thought I saw back at the Hall of Legends was just stress related. That's what I'm going with.

Not sure if the others made it out, but if there's one thing about the Quisqueya Club, it's that we are persistent and a force to be reckoned with. I'm betting if anyone else is lost in the tunnels, they're doing what I am now, following the tracks back to the ride's exit.

That would be the logical thing to do, as Sofia would say. At least what she would have said before she started taking shots of the Malicia Kool-Aid.

My battery blinks again. If I'm going to get stuck here in the dark, I need to find somewhere to hunker down and wait where the others will hopefully find me. I maneuver down the tracks for a respectable distance before I spot the ideal location.

One of the old gurney passenger cars is still resting on the tracks. Guess no one ever bothered to shove it back into storage when the park shut down. For a few seconds in the dark, I imagine what it must have been like that day, the screams, the loud report of semi-automatic weapons fire, the ear-splitting crash of explosive devices being detonated around the park, as terrified visitors scrambled to escape without getting trampled.

I approach the car and inspect it under the greenish glow of my infrared. Can't take any chances that rats might have decided to bunk here. The last thing I need right now are rodents and rabies. Aside from some old candy wrappers and a couple of Malicia park maps, there's nothing else inside. Using the retracted safety bar as leverage, I haul myself into the car and spread out. The car's built to accommodate approximately six, three in the front row, and three in the back. I take out my laptop, place my pack in the back seat, then, with the front row all to myself, stretch out horizontally, and power up the computer, resting it on my thighs. Luckily this battery still has some life.

While it boots up, my thoughts drift back to what Sofia said about me not having changed, always chasing gossip rather than substance.

Am I really just full of shit and kidding myself? Is being

a legitimate journalist what I really want out of life, instead of becoming some click-chasing influencer feeding on the carcasses of other people's tragedies and dreams?

I'll show her. I'll show Northwestern. I'll show them all.

My computer completes its start-up routine, and the first thing I do is check how much juice I have left. The little battery icon taunts me with a fifteen percent reading. Que mierda. I'll have to find a power source soon, or the rest of this docudrama will be D.O.A.

I search for all the personnel files I borrowed from Recursos Inhumanos, detailing the park's sordid history, the cover-ups, the payoffs, the tragedies. Here they all are, a treasure trove of dirt, right at my fingertips. The info in just one of these files would make me go viral in a heartbeat.

I hesitate, thinking about my original plan of being catapulted to stardom. I imagined myself giving interviews about how I hunkered down during Edgar, more concerned with exposing the hidden truths of the notorious Malicia Massacre than my own personal survival.

As I slowly drag each file to the trash bin, I imagine getting rejected by every college I applied for, and not being able to afford them even if I were to be accepted. These files could all but guarantee that none of that happens. But going that route wouldn't be true to myself. If Northwestern is going to admit Isabella Fuentes, it has to be the real Isabella Fuentes. Hot tears burst down my cheeks, snot running down my nose. I'm trembling all over, my finger hovering over the *Empty the recycle bin* option. I tense every muscle and jam my finger down, watching as every file vanishes in the blink of an eye—

A creaking sound causes me to whip my neck to the right, then left.

"What was that? Who's there?" I call into the dark. No response. Just the continual wail of the wind and the constant drip of the rain seeping into the cracks and crevices of Malicia's wounds.

I sit upright in the gurney, using the camera's waning infrared to scan my surroundings. Through the greenish haze, I can make out the outlines and shapes of El Asilo, the tracks that disappear into the darkness, the façades of patient rooms flanking my position. I'm just about to call out again, then I stop myself. If someone had heard me, they would have responded by now. I was not about to be the horror movie redshirt that continually called out in the dark and didn't get a clue when no one answered her back.

Another long creaking sound, off to the right. Much closer this time.

Que carajo. I'm tempted to slam the lid of my laptop closed, but there's a comfort in the light of the screen.

There it is again. That creaking noise. So much closer. It's goading me. It wants me to leave the safety of the gurney car and try to find it. A chilling thought creeps through me. What if it's Carlos?

Not a dumbass here. Going to stay put, not wander into the dark. All I have to do is scan the area with my viewfinder to make sure it's clear. Nothing can get to me if I maintain my position.

The gurney's safety bar slams down all by itself, locking me in place.

RAYMUNDO

It's funny how you never forget some things from your childhood, like riding a bike, your favorite video games, comics—

The layout of El Asilo at the scene of a mass murder. Yup. My childhood was definitely fucked up.

I barely need my flashlight as I work my way down the tunnel. I anticipate the next stops before I even get to them: the patient rec room with its decrepit card tables and wheelchairs, now a haven for scurrying rats eager to escape my beam of light, the stark showers that look like something out of an internment camp with their broken pipes, rusty showerheads and faucets. In some ways, this was more of a home than the one I shared with my parents. At least this place didn't pretend to be real.

As I pick my way across a broken track littered with debris, I can barely keep my worries at bay. I'm worried sick about

Isabella. No one has had any contact with her since the collapse. What if she's badly hurt? And even though Sofia is strong, she's been acting so strangely lately that I can't help but obsess about her safety as well. What about Joaquin? It killed me to leave him back there all alone, knowing how terrified he is and the toll the anxiety and panic attacks take on him. I was an ass for getting them all into this mess. Sure, they all made the decision to come here this weekend of their own free will. But if I hadn't been so insistent—so desperate—they probably wouldn't have come. Joaquin was always a given. He's been my rock. But Isabella and especially Sofia? And all because I need them to perform a séance. Just thinking about what I'm putting all my friends through makes me sick, no matter the why.

It's freezing in here. Que vaina. Even with Edgar doing his thing, it shouldn't be that cold in here. It never was before.

My head's throbbing. Must be a tension headache from all the stress. Or maybe I hit my head harder than I thought when that tunnel collapsed. I pause to rub my temples as the pain knifes into my brain, making my eyes water. Then the wave subsides to a dull throbbing.

Rounding the next corner, my heart triathalons at the sight ahead of me. An entire section has been cordoned off with orange cones and tape by the construction crew. There's equipment everywhere—forklifts, drills, a massive tractor, all scattered about haphazardly, as if whatever team was here had to leave in a hurry.

Something scared the shit out of them. But what could have scared them enough to leave the place like this? This doesn't make any sense. Sure, the teams were doing some excavating to survey infrastructure or plant demolition charges, but this looks more involved.

I scramble throughout the site, searching all the compartments in the vehicles, inside and under toolboxes. Nothing. Except for a half-burned work log. I scan what's left of the final pages. It's almost unintelligible. Something about coming across a series of tunnels not in the original plans. But it's the last six words that make my mouth go dry.

It's down there. Waiting. GOD HELP -

That biting cold reaches out and nips me again. I flinch when a ghostly silhouette invades my peripheral vision. It's a tarp, fluttering in the artic draft blasting through the tunnel. What's it covering? What did they discover in the deep dark? I hop off the forklift I've been inspecting, clamber over more gear, and grab one of the tarp's edges, pulling as hard as I can until it rips away from its anchor.

It's even colder now, my breath creating frosty plumes as I gaze down into the crevasse. Whatever crew was working this sector has set up some sort of pulley system stretching down to the depths of the chasm. There are various outcroppings surrounding the rim of the crevasse, varying in depth. There's one about five feet down. Another about ten and so forth. I can't be sure how far down it goes, but if that's an emergency flare down at the bottom, I'd say maybe fifty feet? Seventy-five? What the hell were they looking for down there? My eyes flit to the heavy tracks on the floor and the empty, oblong block of earth. And just what the hell did they dig up?

A sudden loud ringing pierces the silence and scares the crap out of me. I teeter on the edge, life flashing in front of my eyes for a few seconds, head pounding, before I regain my balance. That sounds like—the SAT phone! I hunch down and peer over the fissure's edge again.

More ringing. Even from my vantage point, I can make out the red blips of the SAT phone, dangling precariously on a perch about twenty feet below, tantalizingly out of reach.

I scan my surroundings, searching for anything I might be able to use to ensnare the phone and fish it out. I finally find a roll of electrical wire in the cab of the forklift. As I unspool it, I can tell it's definitely long enough. But wrapping it around the phone tightly enough so that it won't slip is going to be really tricky.

The first thing I do is secure the flashlight with a wire at an angle to the surrounding outcroppings, so I'll have sufficient illumination. One miscalculation and the phone will be lost, along with our chances for a rescue.

There it is! In the flickering light, I spot my prize, approximating the width of the handset, adjusting the loop on my wire accordingly.

I take several deep breaths and lower the wire, unspooling it inch by inch, watching it pass one outcropping, then the other, closer and closer until it's dangling just above the phone. I need to adjust the angle, so I lie on my stomach, inching my torso over the precipice as much as I dare, dripping with sweat from my efforts, despite the polar vortex engulfing my body. With my arms outstretched trying to catch hold of the phone. I finally manage to pass the loop over the phone, tightening it excruciatingly slowly, before I begin hauling it up. Twenty-five feet. Then twenty. Fifteen.

The wire snags. The phone slips out of the loop and into the chasm. Motherfucker. But instead of crashing at the bottom of the pit, the phone lands with a gentle thud on another outcropping a few feet below and rolls to the edge before coming to a stop. I let out the breath I've been holding. I've got no choice. I have to go down and get it.

After testing the pulley with my weight, I lower myself down, foot by foot, trying not to look down, farther and farther, until I'm within arm's reach of the SAT phone. I pause to catch my breath, then reach for the phone, my fingers brushing against it, momentarily sending it closer to the edge, before I grip it firmly.

Another sharp pang stabs through my head like an ice pick, much worse than the last one. My vision blurs. An intense surge of nausea hits me. Everything starts to go dark. It seems like it takes forever for the wave to pass.

Again, the piercing ringing cuts through my senses. The hell . . .? Someone's calling.

I hit the activation switch on the SAT phone and press it to my ear. "Hello?"

JOAQUIN

The light on the control panel above 13B flashes again. This is not possible. The power is down. That buzzer shouldn't be working. This isn't even a real asylum.

With El Bacá's malevolent presence, anything is possible. I try my best to ignore the buzzing, but my thoughts aren't much of a calming distraction.

What's taking the others so long? Surely, they should be back by now.

What if they got injured? What if they're dead? If Ray is already dead, my fate will be much worse.

Relax. Breathe. Slow. Just like that. Easy . . . The light on that control panel flashes again. 13B. The buzzing is louder and more insistent, as if someone's finger is repeatedly jabbing the button and growing more impatient and angry. This isn't just some Quisqueya Club prank. It's Its doing. And if It's getting more involved, that means my time is running short.

I glance behind me. None of the others are coming. I squeeze my eyes closed. My breathing's still shallow. I can't hear a thing except that annoying and terrifying buzzing.

I cover my ears but can't block out the incessant buzzing, an angry insect waiting to sting—Damn it. STOP.

I open my eyes again, grip my flashlight tightly, and take a tentative step forward, then another, slowly making my way down the corridor, draped in a shroud of shadows. My footsteps echo in the cold stillness. I pass Room 8B. Room 12B . . . Then finally I'm staring up at it. 13B.

And in that moment, I know It's waiting for me in there, if not in the flesh, then in the temporary body of one of Its minions, a helpless vessel like Carlos and Sofia, all part of the one. As terrified as I am, I know that if I refuse, it will be much worse for me.

I take a deep breath, reach out a hesitant hand, and grip the cold, steel handle.

This isn't a real asylum. It's probably a fake door, with nothing behind it. I twist the handle and a loud click cuts through the stillness. It actually works. The Malicia players probably came in and out of here dressed in costumes during the tour to scare the shit out of the guests. . . .

I nudge the door open wider with the toe of my shoe, the long creaking conjuring images of withered bones. Scanning the room with my flashlight, I take in the grimy walls. They were once white but have been soiled by yellowed splotches of who knows what. There's a curtain dividing the room, one of those privacy deals patients use when they're sharing a room and need their own space. There's some kind of cart filled with pill bottles, syringes, and electrodes. Props. Eso es todo lo que son. Just little details to create the illusion you're trapped in a creepy sanitarium—

The piercing alarm makes me jump, and I bang into the cart, spilling its contents all over the broken-tiled floor. It came from right over there. From just behind the curtain. My instincts tell me to run. To get the hell out of here while I still can. But I'm drawn to the curtain like Pandora to that blasted box, drawn to It, despite my terror.

My heart's fully primed, pistoning blood through my arteries. I can feel it thrumming in my ears, drowning out Edgar's moans in a disturbing duet, in time with that insane buzzing. I take another step closer and stop dead in my tracks. I can see the outline of . . . something . . . on the other side of the curtain. Something long, gangly, skeletal, undulating as if it's strapped down on a bed. There's a gurgling noise now. The kind someone might make if they had a long feeding tube lodged down their throat.

I try to shake off the building panic. You're just imagining things. Hallucinating. Whatever is behind that curtain, it can't get to you. It's strapped down. But what if it's It? And what if It's already decided that I've failed my mission?

"I'm . . . doing everything that . . . you've asked . . . ." I don't even recognize the sound of my own voice. My mouth's so dry every syllable is an effort.

There's a slow ripping sound that solidifies the blood that's been churning through my veins into frozen gel. This. Is. Not. Happening. Those are not the straps giving way to whatever's trying to slither out of the bed. Whatever's been calling for the nurse, waiting for someone to show up to sink its teeth and claws into. Waiting for me . . .

"Ray means nothing to me! I swear it. My only allegiance is to you. I promise I'll get him to the mountain. Just tell me you'll still spare me if I do. Please . . . I need to know that we still have an understanding. I beg you . . . !"

More ripping. One limb's loose, accompanied by more thrashing and gurgling. That infernal buzzing is almost constant now. Despite my terror, I'm angry at myself. Don't be a wuss. Grab the curtain. Pull it open. Take a good look at what's inside the box and face your fear. Face It.

But I can't move. When I try to look away, I catch sight of the patient file, its contents strewn across the floor, exposing glimpses of a skeletal face, black eyes, notations of dismemberment and . . . cannibalism. The sound of another strap torn loose. That horrible shadow slinks off the bed with a loud thump. One foot hits the ground. Followed by another thump. Then another. My legs are numb, jellylike. I can only stare in terror as the shadow moves toward the edge of the curtain. Are those fingers gripping the edge? Talons? Its talons? At that instant, I know if I see what's on the other side of that curtain my mind will snap, plunging me irrevocably into madness. The claws pull on the curtain—

With a burst of adrenaline, I whirl, scrambling for the door, slamming it shut behind me, even as I hear those feet shuffling across the tiles toward me.

I'm out of breath by the time I get back to the lobby, shaking all over, bathed in a cold sweat. Except there's something different, something on the front desk that wasn't there before. I reach out a trembling hand, snatch the note, and shine my light on it. It's comprised of cutout letters from newspapers and magazines. The type of message a serial killer would send his victims:

SEE YOU AT THE MOUNTAIN. TICK. TOCK.

Sofia

eart racing, I take a deep breath and push through the doors of this mock maximum security ward, expecting to see all the behind-the-scenes ordinariness beyond the elaborate set dressings.

To my shock, it looks like a real ward at an asylum, either side lined with steel and glass cell doors. At the far end of the corridor is a guard station with no one on duty. This doesn't make any sense. The tracks don't lead inside the building, so why bother to be so elaborate if none of the guests are supposed to see this?

That's the old me talking, the dying me that was always interested in finding a logical explanation for everything. Now I can see how limiting that all was. It's easier to just accept things, no matter how strange or terrifying they may seem. And once the Quisqueya Club—once the world—has accepted It,

169

they'll finally be able to see clearly for the first time.

Most of the cells I pass are dark inside. But there's a light on the far end, a sickly shade of yellow oozing out of the last cell, which is conspicuously set apart from the rest.

As I pass the security station, I catch sight of the patient roster lying haphazardly on the rectangular stand. Sure, it's only a prop, but according to the list, there's only one patient currently being interned in this wing. Notorious cinematic serial killer Romeo "El Ratoncito" Perez.

That mixture of exhilaration and fear grows stronger. It suddenly feels chillier in here. From what I remember, good ole Ratoncito Perez would start by slicing off victims' tongues, then removing their teeth, which he used as a necklace, making the victims stare in soundless horror while he devoured their organs, like a mouse nibbling on cheese. And according to this chart, El Ratoncito Perez is waiting just up ahead in that last cell.

I let out a nervous laugh. It might call Itself El Ratoncito at the moment, but that's just one of the many masks It wears at Malicia. Its true form is much more glorious.

I creep past the last remaining cells until only one remains, taking up the whole end of the corridor.

The light is coming from a crack in the cell doors. They're unlocked.

The dying embers of the old Sofia rear their ugly little head and genuine fear grips me. This is all part of the Malicia experience, Sofia. How many times had Ratoncito Perez escaped El Asilo in the movies, each time going on a culinary killing spree that would end with his demise . . . at least until the next sequel?

During the park's heyday, this was probably the part in the tour when unsuspecting visitors would step through these doors, only to be greeted by a cheesy actor playing El Ratoncito Perez, popping out of the dark amid screams and laughter in the jump scare performance of the year.

Only this time, there aren't any actors. And it doesn't explain where the light is coming from. My muscles tense. I push open the doors and slip inside.

The source of the light is the dying glow of a flashlight. It's lying on the floor, aimed toward the far wall, illuminating it in shades of orange embers.

The scream freezes in my throat, my vocal cords paralyzed as my mind struggles to make sense of what my eyes can't look away from. Hanging from the wall is a man, another member of the ill-fated work crew assigned by Ray's father, judging by what's left of his uniform. The name, Miguel, is stenciled on the left breast pocket. In the shadows, I can't be sure what's holding him up, but he's spread-eagle, his torso cut open with all the precision of a surgeon. Stacked in a series of small glass jars in front of him are what appear to be his internal organs, laid out like the contents of a picnic basket.

So much cutting. So much violence. And another thought hits me, this time from the new Sofia, who's back in the driver's seat. Where's all the blood?

I stare at the body, fascinated. There was a time when I would have been terrified, might have even screamed. But now I'm more curious than anything.

The worker's eyes pop open, fixing on me. He opens his mouth . . . but only gurgling noises come out. There are no words.

He has no tongue. He gestures feebly, pantomiming his pleas for help. But I can only stare at those haunted eyes, begging for release. Do it, Sofia. Finish him off. Kill him.

I move forward, studying this Miguel as if he's an exhibit in a museum, trying to figure out how he's attached to the wall, nodding when I realize he's been strung up by his own torn muscles, his ligaments keeping him pinned in place.

Miguel's eyes begin to bulge. At first, I think it's because he's in excruciating pain, until I realize he sees something behind me. There's someone else in the cell with us. Another wave of excitement washes over me as I whip my head around.

Standing there, framed in the doorway, is Romeo "El Ratoncito" Perez, wearing nothing but Its straw hat, gold glasses, and linen shoes. It's sporting an ear-to-ear grin, Its mouth twitching erratically as It emits piercing squeals—like a rodent.

I drop to one knee, bowing my head, feeling unworthy of this honor.

"Dígame," I say. "Tell me what you need me to do to him."

I listen intently as the rodent squeals. Then he hands me one of the SAT phones we've been looking for. A new understanding dawns on me and I nod. Taking the phone, I dial it and listen to it ring, until I'm rewarded with the sound of a familiar voice saying hello.

I pause, look up at El Ratoncito, and smile.

"Is anyone there?" Ray asks on the other end.

ISABELLA

"No me jodas!"

As hard as I try to push the safety bar up, it's not budging.

"Are you friggin' serious?" I think the time for Malicia to be worrying about safety precautions and lawsuit prevention is way over.

I'm trying to squeeze my body past the bar and out of the gurney when it lurches forward, almost ripping my mother's cross from around my neck. Looks like I'm going on a ride after all.

Ray must have started one of the generators while searching for the SAT phone. That's the only explanation. Rides don't start by themselves. At least, that's what I'm going with, because the alternatives are just not cutting it. Besides, this will save me the trouble of trudging back through the dark by depositing me at the main entrance.

While the car creaks along, I gather my equipment so I'm ready to roll the first chance I get.

There's a sharp crackle behind me. It looks like the gurney's speaker system is shot and there won't be any ride narration accompanying my impromptu journey. That's okay. The last thing I need are more theme park bullshit scares piped into my ears.

Up ahead, an ominous sign in gothic lettering heralds *Experimental Wing,* hovering above a pair of wrought iron gates, which creak open just before my gurney can collide with them. As soon as I'm through, they slam shut, with a loud, echoing clang.

My jaw drops at the chilling scene before me. The most lifelike animatronics loom on either side of me. Doctors and nurses hovering above patients who are strapped in all sorts of painful looking gadgets, including electrodes, while their bodies writhe from the current. One doctor, a gaunt, balding man with wire-rimmed spectacles is hunched over a haggard female patient with long, stringy gray hair. He's pressing the impossibly long needle clutched in his hand to her temple. As my gurney slows to a stop, he pauses what he's doing and turns my way.

Oh, God. He's looking right at me. No. That can't be. No es possible. He can't possibly see me. He's a machine, just like the one I'm riding in.

His wide, thin-lipped grin makes my stomach crawl. He continues to stare at me with those cold, insectile eyes, even as he presses the plunger into his unwilling patient's head. Why does he look so familiar? I've seen that face before. Where?

Then it hits me. Antonio Jimenez. The Malicia CEO. The guy who blew his brains out on live TV during a press conference right after the massacre. His file was in the flash drive I found in Recursos Inhumanos.

And the woman. She lifts her head and smiles at me, too, foam pooling at her lips and oozing down her soiled hospital gown, even as the enormous hypodermic protrudes from her temple.

Cara Vargas. The Malicia Director of Public Relations, who died of an aneurism, probably stress induced, shortly after the murders. The smile in her company profile photo looks the same, minus the drool, the unkempt hair, and the needle, of course. I can't bear to look Cara in the eyes any longer and turn away.

Qué carajo? These two died after the massacre. After Malicia was closed down. There's no way the park designers could have molded their likenesses into animatronics after the fact. Yet all around me, it's the same deal, faces I recognize from the personnel files, Malicia employees cast as demented doctors and patients, ogling me, winking, licking their lips.

Maybe the park designers just based all their animatronic designs on employees while they were still alive, and it was just a coincidence that most of this lot were victims of the massacre. Yes. That's it. Logical. Sofia would be proud of me. Because we don't want to get into the alternative. That would be some crazy shit.

I'm getting really antsy, ignoring the sudden drops and twists and turns the gurney takes, anxious to get off this thing and rejoin the rest of Quisqueya Club. Several times I have to hug my equipment tightly against me so it won't go flying. It's almost as if the ride is trying to destroy it, if I believed in such nonsense. The gurney heads toward a metal door with a little view slot cut out of one corner. The sign above it reads:

CONFINAMIENTO SOLITARIO.

Solitary confinement?

The door opens slowly, swallowing up my gurney and slamming shut once I'm clear. Gone are the padded walls, the surgical equipment, and the staff. Instead, I'm in the middle of a gothic graveyard, surrounded by a rusted spiked fence and cracked and crumbling gravestones surrounding a mausoleum. As my gurney rolls closer, I can read the names engraved on the headstones. Joaquin. Sofia. And me.

What the fuck? How is this possible? While I applaud whoever set this up for their ingenuity and recognize that it's a stunt I would have pulled in a heartbeat to juice up my doc back when I was into such things, it doesn't explain how anyone would have had time to set this up, unless they had special access.

Almost as if on cue, a figure steps out of the mausoleum. It's Ray. Of course. I knew it. He set this up before we got to the island. But there's something different about him. When he opens his eyes, they're glowing red. His grin is impossibly wide, just like the creepy way Sofia smiled at me before entering El Asilo. I can feel the cold radiating from Ray's body. Not just temperaturewise, but a feeling, despair, torment, sucking the very hope through my pores. Whatever this thing is, it's not Ray.

As soon as I realize this, the figure dissolves into a cloud of black smoke, morphing into something else, becoming more distinct in its new form as it hovers toward me.

Fuck. This is supposed to be SOLITARY confinement. As in ALONE. No one else. No supernatural shadow slinking toward me. My blood turns to lava. I hate this ride. I want to get off.

I batter the safety bar with my fists, rearing back, slamming it with my knees despite the pain. The casing is bent and battered from my frenzied assault. Then the gurney's doing its rollercoaster thing, tumbling down a steep incline, zooming back up, spinning, careening backwards—all over the place, just like my emotions. I'm screaming at the top of my lungs, giving voice to all my fear. All my rage. The gurney jolts to a complete stop.

Seconds later, the safety bar disengages, and I thrust it up as hard as I can and grab my gear, stumbling out as a low, menacing laughter chases after me.

RAYMUNDO

"Delvalle Base One," the female voice on the other end announces.

There's something familiar about that voice, but I can't quite place it.

"This is Ray Delvalle!" I answer. "We need your help ASAP—"

"Looks like you guys are getting hammered by Edgar. We won't be able to get to you for a while. Hang tight for the next two days. We will land a chopper on the helipad on the mountaintop on Sunday. Make sure you are ready and waiting for evac, copy—"

Before I can answer, the phone lets out a series of beeps and then dies. I stare in silence at the darkened screen. The phone may as well be a brick for all the good it's going to do us now.

Que vaina. I should have led with Carlos murdering the other crew members. But they did say they'd be here after the storm, on Sunday. The same day I need to conduct that séance and contact Rudy. If I tell everyone about the call now, they might be tempted to just go directly to the top of the mountain before I'm ready. What harm could it do to delay the news just a bit . . .?

The sound of a loud snap dices through my thoughts. The cable I'm dangling from lurches, dropping me a foot or two, my feet losing their purchase on the ledge and flailing wildly. Damn it all to hell.

I try to pendulum my body back to solid ground. It's too late. The pipe I tethered the spool of cable to must have dislodged. In seconds, I'm hurtling toward the bottom of the chasm, the cable sizzling and slicing my palms. I stop with a jerk, dizzy from the sudden drop, only having time to register that I'm about ten feet from the bottom, before I lose my grip and plummet the rest of the way.

My body slams into cold earth, rattling my jaw and causing me to bite my tongue from the impact. All I can do is lie there on my stomach, dazed, spitting out a gob of blood, trying to regain my senses. When I crane my neck to look upwards, my muscles ache from the strain.

Up above, in the opening of the chasm, I can see the metal pipe I tied the cable to has fallen across the opening. Luckily, it's wider than the hole, and the cable is still tied to the other end, albeit dangling ten feet above my head. How the hell am I going to get out of here?

I sit up and inspect myself. Lots of cuts and bruises. At least I can move all my limbs. I crawl to the cavern's wall, press my hands against the cold stone, and use it to push myself upwards to a standing position.

I notice a passage off to the left that I missed originally, which would be easy to do considering it's a crude, circular opening, barely wide enough to fit through. I shine my light on it and can make out a larger opening on the other side, maybe ten feet, give or take. Normally, I wouldn't bother with it, but I'm kind of desperate to get back to the others. If the work crew was digging around down here, they may have left something I can use on that end. In any event, it won't really take that long to crawl in and have a look-see before I tackle the larger problem of how I'm going to get back up to the surface.

I crawl into the opening, gripping the flashlight in one hand and propelling myself forward with the other. It's extremely cold in here, and as I make my way farther inside, I quickly regret my decision when a noxious wave of something rotten hits me hard, stinging my eyes.

Holy fuck. It smells like shit. What the hell is that all about? It reminds me of that odor oozing off Carlos. I'm halfway through, I could just turn around now—

Nope. I must keep going. What if there's someone injured on the other side, unable to move or speak? Besides, I have to get out of here, make sure Sofia and Isabella made it out safely, and get back to Joaquin. He's all alone and vulnerable. And no, it has nothing to do with the fact that I need the three of them to perform the ritual before any rescue team shows up.

I push forward again and a mound of earth collapses from the tunnel wall, locking my right ankle in place. I break out into a cold sweat as I struggle. Quickly, I realize the more I panic and thrash about, the more dirt I'm causing to be dislodged, making my situation worse. It's a good thing I'm not claustrophobic.

I slow my breathing and try my best to make all my muscles relax, while at the same time pushing forward. It's impossible to shake the feeling that something's behind me, watching me, getting closer, reaching out . . .

There's a squishing sound, and I don't stick around to find out what just made it. I thrust forward, the adrenaline surge propelling me ahead, spitting out dirt, ignoring the sharp edges tearing at my skin, until I plop out the other side.

At least the ceiling here is high enough for me to stand, but just barely. My body is throbbing almost as badly as my head, but I'm just grateful to be out of the tunnel.

My relief dies a quick death. The stench is much stronger now, and I fight the urge to gag. A constant buzzing sound assaults my ears, and it takes a minute to place it through my dazed state. Insects. Flies.

I slowly revolve, scanning the earthen walls with my flashlight.

Why would there be flies down here? It's coming from the wall opposite me. At first, I think it's an optical illusion. The wall seems alive with movement. I must have hit my head real hard. Then it registers. Son of a bitch. The movement and the buzzing are flies, hundreds, maybe thousands all clumped in patterns on the wall, patterns that are actually letters.

The whole thing is ripped straight out of a serial killer crime scene in a movie. I'm so numb that I can't even feel my body's aches and pains anymore. I step closer, wondering how it's possible that flies can form letters—

I choke on a gust of rot. These aren't just letters. They're body parts. Hands, feet, fingers, ears forming every letter.

As the flies crawl about these rotting body parts, I catch

glimpses of torn uniforms, enough to realize it's the remains of the work crew stationed here. I can't resist the wave of nausea and heave, splattering my guts in the corner.

It takes my shell-shocked brain a few seconds to decode the obscene message:

JACK AND JILL WENT UP THE HILL. TO BETTER VIEW SOFIA'S KILL.

Sofia's kill. Could Carlos be responsible for this? Oh, my God. Sofia's in danger. She needs me. What if it's already too late? The "hill" must be Ratoncito Hall at the top of Serenity Hill. I dive back into the tunnel, not caring about the pain, burrowing through the mound of dirt that trapped me before.

Bracing myself, I manage to find foothold in the jagged cavern wall and scale a few feet. Then I leap from the cavern wall and grab the cable, praying it will hold all two hundred pounds of me.

Shit. There's a sickening moment when it looks like the cable isn't going to hold. For a split second, I picture myself crashing to the cave floor, my body twisted and bloody like a gruesome mosaic. But the cable is still intact. I grip it as tightly as I can and use my aching legs to walk up the tunnel walls.

Above, the pipe lurches to one side, throwing off my balance. I struggle to maintain my grip, then I'm climbing back up again, just five feet away from the surface. Then three. Then one. . . . The cable snaps loose, and I just manage to hook a hand on the end of the cavern. I struggle from the strain, before finally pulling myself up and out.

I run as fast as I can, hoping I'm not too late. Terrified I already am.

JOAQUIN

I don't know how long I've been obsessing over the note.

Who could have put it together? Who could have left it at the front desk in the relatively short time I'd been gone exploring Room 13B? Could Sofia have somehow doubled back and done it? Or is another member of the Quisqueya Club in league with It, spying on me to make sure I carry out the plan?

The sound of running feet congeals my blood. Reflexively, I crumple the note in my fist, just as a figure bounds into view.

Isabella, camera in hand. She looks frazzled and out of breath. "Qué pasa? Is anyone else back yet?"

I shake my head and measure my words carefully as I explain about Ray and Sofia having escaped serious injury and the plan we made to meet back here, studying her reactions carefully to see how much she actually knows.

"I've been alone ever since," I continue. Of course, I leave out the part about my experience back in 13B.

"You obviously didn't find the SAT phone either."

I shrug and lock eyes with her. "I haven't found a thing. But I strongly get the impression that you have, Izzy."

Isabella chuckles. A front. I can tell she's nervous. "Now what could I have possibly found that could be of any use to us?"

"Maybe not of any use to us, the Quisqueya Club. But just you and your documentary."

She sighs. I can tell she's trying to appear nonchalant but I'm not buying it. "Seriously, with the mind games right now, Joaquin? We have more serious problems."

Since we're alone, I decide to go for broke. "You heard when I said about remembering being at Malicia before as a kid."

She shakes her head too energetically. "Sí! Claro. And you already explained that to Ray, to his satisfaction."

Now it's my turn to chuckle. "But not to yours."

I move a few steps closer and she backs away, until she's pressed against the front desk without anywhere to go. We stare into each others' eyes.

More running feet. I pull away from Isabella, just as Ray appears a few seconds later, looking paler than I've ever seen him.

"Tiguere!" I rush forward to throw my arms around him, but he bolts past me toward the entrance, calling back, "Sofia's in trouble!" before disappearing into the park.

SOFIA

*E*verything is going smoothly. The master will be pleased, especially since It won't have to rely on Joaquin's ineptitude any longer.

Of course, I couldn't have done it without Carlos's help. After all, he planted the SAT phone for Ray to find it. And I did my part, assuring Ray he must be at the top of the mountain on All Hallows' Eve. Carlos scrawling that note at the dig site to get Ray to come here now was a work of pure genius, nothing Joaquin could have ever dreamed up.

But now comes the more delicate part of the plan. It's time to give Ray his medicine. And who better to administer an injection than Ray's trusted *doctora*?

I grin and pull the hypodermic from my pocket, the same one I had originally planned on using on Carlos, except instead of air, it's now filled with a dark blend of special herbs necessary to prepare his body for its new inhabitant before the ceremony.

Joaquin was probably going to wait until he had him on the altar and try to clumsily get him to drink it instead. It's safe to say the poor boy has outlived his usefulness, and the master can break any contract he had made to spare his pitiful soul.

I peer through the curtains of the old house. Just on cue, Ray is running up the hill toward the entrance, and I make my way down the cracked marble stairs and down into the basement, where I lie down on the cold steel table to play my part, making sure to slip the needle into my pocket.

RAYMUNDO

I burst through the double doors of Ratoncito Hall, home of the infamous serial killer, located at the top of Serial Springs' tallest point, Serenity Hill.

"Sofia! Are you in here? Sofia!"

I'm breathless as I dash through the old house, searching every room, sprinting upstairs to the attic, until the only place left to search is the basement. When I reach it, the door is open a crack and I peer through it.

The room's lit by candles, maybe hundreds of them, flickering in the icy draft. Cobwebs dangle from rotted paneling, while flurries of dust dance in the air. There's a figure hunched over a steel table, wearing a straw hat, busy toiling with something that's blocked from my view, shoulders working in a circular motion but otherwise silent.

The walls are covered with photos. Most of them are a blur,

but I can make out a few things. Faces. Mouths open wide, eyes gaping in fear.

The figure stops what it's doing and turns to me, making my blood run cold.

It's a ghost. A very pale ghost with an extremely wide grin. It's not a ghost. Not really. It's a doctor.

Dr. Romeo Perez. Aka El Ratoncito Perez.

Something flashes in the candlelight, temporarily blinding me. It's a long, shiny surgical knife. The one he's been sharpening.

Dios, ayúdame. But God probably doesn't want to have anything to do with this place.

El Ratoncito stretches out a white gloved hand and reaches under the table, cranking it, rotating it from horizontal to a vertical position.

And that's when I see her, Sofia, strapped to the table, eyes staring vacantly ahead in my direction.

My instinct is to charge in and help her, but then I remember El Ratoncito's big, sharp knife. I need to plan my move more carefully, or I could end up getting us both killed.

He nods at Sofia, pantomiming a clapping gesture, before rolling out a steel tray in front of her. The only things on it are ten small empty jars, their lids resting underneath each one. Hot, angry tears burn my cheeks.

My hands ball into fists as El Ratoncito approaches her and places a finger over his twitching lips, all the while grinning. And occasionally squealing.

Tears are dripping down Sofia's cheeks. El Ratoncito rests the knife on the table, using both hands to mimic an exaggerated crying gesture. He moves toward her again, extending his gloved hand to push her mouth open, producing a silver clamp with the other to hold it securely in place, then pulling out her tongue. Before he can reach for the knife again, I spring, tackling him to the ground, using all of my strength to pummel him with my fists until those white gloves of his are saturated in his own blood. But despite my beating, he somehow manages to scurry out of the basement like the rodent he is, that terrible squealing ringing in my eardrums.

I turn to Sofia, ripping her free from the straps confining her to the operating table, cradling her against me as we slide to the floor. Her skin is cold and clammy.

My hot tears stream onto her cheeks. "It's okay, doctora. I got you. I'm never going to let anyone ever hurt you. I love you so much. . . ."

She looks up at me then and her expression goes from vacant to lecherous. She grabs me by the neck and pulls me to her, pressing her lips against mine. But it's not a passionate kiss, it's more like a violent act, and I push away from her, even as she laughs, a laugh so unlike her.

She looks at me in mock sorrow. "Awww, poor Ray. You never had a problem kissing me before. . . ."

I back away, trying to make sense of all of this. "Sofia. I know you've been through a lot, and that monster did something to you. But you're like my sister now. One of my best friends. You don't know what you're saying."

She lets out a long sigh. "Let me guess. You don't want to kiss me anymore because you have feelings for someone else. But let me tell you something, Ray. He's not everything you think he is."

I shake my head and pull her to her feet. "C'mon, let's get

you out of here. Can you walk? Do you need me to carry you?"

Her response is to reach into her pocket and whip out something long and shiny. I barely have time to make out the hypodermic plunging toward my neck when I grip her hand just before it skewers me. But she's strong. Way too strong for it to be natural. Before I know it, I've crashed to the floor on my back, struggling to keep the needle from my neck. She's relentless, pushing forward, forcing me to use both hands to hold her off. Her face is contorted into that of a wild animal. She growls, snarls, and snaps at me, hot flecks of drool spraying my cheeks.

"Sofia, what the hell's wrong with you?"

"You know you like it when I'm rough," she hisses.

The needle moves closer to the throbbing vein in my neck.

"Don't . . . make . . . me . . . hurt . . . you," I squeeze through clenched lips.

"Like you actually could," she whispers back.

This time, when she opens her mouth, something crawls partially outside and perches on her lips, a parasite of some sort, just like she and Joaquin were discussing what seems like ages ago.

The sight gives me a last surge of adrenaline and I push her off me. She goes crashing into a corner. But in seconds, she recovers and whips around like a reptile, her mouth opened in an even wider grin. She's gripping the hypodermic as if it's a dagger.

"C'mon, Ray. Give me another kiss, for old times' sake."

She lets out a loud roar and leaps. Without thinking, I grab the nearest thing, Ratoncito's surgical knife, and plunge it into her leg.

Someone screams. I turn around and see Joaquin and Isabella framed in the doorway, their eyes opened wide and mouths agape.

I rush to Sofia, just as the parasite slithers all the way out of her mouth, scurrying toward the doorway. Joaquin's waiting for it, crushing it with a chair.

But I don't care about any of that now. "There's too much blood! I need something to wrap her leg! Fuck. What have I done? I was just trying to keep her away from me."

I'm not sure if it's Joaquin or Isabella through my blurry tears, but someone hands me a torn piece of fabric and I'm wrapping it around her leg like a tourniquet. But it's soaked in seconds.

I turn to the others. "Why isn't it working? Why the fuck isn't it working? Oh, God. Please. Dios mio."

I cradle Sofia in my arms, whispering over and over into her ear. "Hang on, doctora."

But she only stares at me, the life draining from her eyes and onto the basement floor.

SOFIA

What . . .? Adonde . . .? Where am . . .?

It's a struggle to focus my vision. It feels like lead blocks have been attached to my lids. And even after I open them, I can't quite figure out what's going on. Everything has this hazy quality about it, like someone's coated my eyes with . . . vaselina? Am I dreaming? No. Not a dream. A nightmare. Not sure why I should be feeling giddy. I should be terrified.

Ray is looking down on me. Dios mio. I led him here . . . to this place. I was waiting for him. Waiting to . . . inject him? It's all so hazy. My poor Ray's crying. He thinks it's his fault. I want to reach up, stroke his cheek, ask him to forgive me, but I can't. I'm so weak.

I can't feel the wound in my upper thigh any more, the one that nicked my femoral artery . . . the one that's bleeding me out. I don't have much time. If only I could have explained everything to Ray, made him understand . . . but that look in his eyes, the shock, the sadness . . . I don't want him to remember me like that. I don't want any of them to remember me like that.

Hang on, Sofia, Ray's saying. *Please don't leave me.*

Izzy and Joaquin are at his side, all clinging to each other, all crying as they stare down at me, stroke my hair. I want to tell them that the Quisqueya Club are badasses, that even without me to take care of them they'll be fine.

I do wish I could go home. See my parents one more time. They'll be worried about me. I have to get ready for college in the fall. Need to keep studying if I want to be a good doctor. And bedside manner is important.

Ray's expression is full of compassion as he strokes my cheeks, whispering that everything's going to be okay. He might have made a good doctor himself. But all I want is for him to be happy. I can see the way Joaquin looks at him. Whatever he's going through, I know that he loves Ray, too. That the two of them could be good together. If they could just talk . . .

It's a chore to move my head to look around, but I need to see Izzy. I want to tell her so badly that I'm proud of her sticking to her guns and deciding to be a journalist with integrity. I want to take back what I said—what the other one in my body said—but I can't. I can only trust that she knows that I love her and would never hurt her. She bows her head and kisses me on the forehead, collapsing into the crook of my neck. How lucky I am to have them at my side at the end. The Quisqueya Club. My best friends in the entire universe.

Ray's forehead is pressed to mine, and he's telling me a story. Mai and Pai used to tell me stories, too, whenever I was sick or couldn't sleep because of bad nightmares, like the one we're living now. I'm never going to see Mai and Pai again, am I?

Somehow, I reach up and touch Ray's face, and when my hands drop down to my side, I can see that his cheeks are the color of bright red roses—and then every single color fades away. . . .

RAYMUNDO

I stare at the blood dripping from my hands, in time with the tears trickling from my burning eyes.

The sense of horror and loss topples over me like a boulder, now that I'm back outside on the top steps of Ratoncito Hall, crushing my ribcage, piercing my heart and lungs, making it impossible to breathe. I collapse to my knees, the floodgates in my eyes now opened. Pain in my head. Excruciating.

What the fuck did I do to her? Oh, God. Sofia . . . I'm a murderer. All I can do is stare at her blood on my hands.

I'm barely aware of Joaquin and Isabella joining me on the manor's steps. I'm clutching Sofia's Bach, which I found in her pack, like a pillow. It still smells like her.

I bury my face against Joaquin's neck and cheek, bawling like a baby, not caring what anyone thinks of me. Sofia is gone. And I'm responsible.

"I loved her, too," he whispers, and we cling to each other.

It feels like every single emotion is draining away with each tear, leaving me a hollow shell of my former self. Suddenly, I'm reliving the aftermath of the massacre all those years ago, the sight of those body bags that were once my mother and dear Rudy.

It's Isabella who remains stoic. She's clutching the wooden cross around her neck and staring up at the manor's windows, as if she's expecting to see something.

My grief erupts into anger and rage. I drop the book on the steps.

"She was going to medical school! She was going to be una doctora!"

I storm back into the house, pushing Joaquin and Isabella away as they try to stop me from tearing it up with my bare hands.

Isabella blocks me with her body. "If you want to honor Sofia, there's a better use of your energy."

I stare at her, confused. "What do you mean?"

"Something did this to her, possessed her. Something evil. This place. That Ratoncito Perez. The only way to cleanse it is with fire."

Her words surprise me. "You want to burn it down?"

She nods.

Joaquin shakes his head. "I thought you didn't believe in the supernatural?"

She gives him a pointed stare. "I've evolved."

Without saying a word, she digs into her pack and pulls out a bottle of Brugal, as well as a lighter. Dousing the heavy drapes in the foyer with the alcohol, she flicks the lighter and turns to us. "For Sofia. And to burning that rat ass motherfucker down in whatever stinking hole he's hiding in."

She tosses the lighter onto the drapes, and they immediately ignite in a blaze.

The three of us exit down the steps and pause one last time in front of the manor.

"Tranquilo y tropical," Isabella whispers.

"Tranquilo y tropical," Joaquin and I respond in unison.

In seconds, Ratoncito Hall's engulfed in a cloud of billowing dark smoke and becomes a bright orange pyre, the topmost flames licking the underside of the portion of Malicia's dome that covers Serial Springs, as the three of us watch in silence, clinging to one another like children.

I stuff Sofia's Bach into my pack, resting at my feet. Not only is it a symbol of Sofia, it's all I have left to represent her in the séance, which now, more than ever, is crucial to contacting Rudy and finding out how to stop this evil once and for all.

JOAQUIN

I'm still numb from Sofia's death. But I'm the only one that knows the truth: Sofia is dead because It was trying to use her to bypass me and get to Ray. She came after him with a hypodermic filled with the sacred herbs necessary to prep his body to receive El Bacá's consciousness. If I wasn't one hundred percent sure before, I am now. El Bacá's planning on double-crossing me and using someone else to perform the ritual. That way, not only does It get Ray's body, It gets to claim my soul as well. At least It can't use poor Sofia any longer, but Carlos is still out there, and I have to be on my guard. The only way I make it through this with my soul intact is if I eliminate any competition and perform the ritual on Ray myself.

I sigh as I check to make sure the hypodermic Sofia had prepared is still safely hidden away with my things, after I slipped it in my pack back at Ratoncito Hall. I give El Bacá credit for thinking of a more effective way of delivering the necessary dosage than I would have. It's less subject to chance than offering Ray a drink he might refuse or not finish.

Poor Ray thinks he's responsible for Sofia's death, but it's me. I may as well have plunged that blade into her femoral artery myself. I've been playing them the whole time and now the game has become real, and I've gotten my first taste of the very real consequences this will have on my friends. We've only been here for little more than a day and one of us is already dead.

As the three of us continue to trudge through Malicia, the difference between Creature Canyon and Serial Springs is still jarring to my dulled senses. Gone are the cookie-cutter houses, the quaint little barrios with their myriad shops and homely atmosphere. Instead, as we emerge from the tunnel between lands, we're confronted with a sprawling landscape consisting of ancient ruins to the west, a foreboding medieval castle to the north, and menacing swampland to the east, shrouded in giant, twisted trees. To the south, there's a post-apocalyptic wasteland, complete with the dilapidated husks of enormous skyscrapers, the perfect cover for whatever creatures are lurking in the shadows, all of Its minions, ready to pounce at Its will.

"Follow me." Ray leads us down a street named Burial Way, stopping at a shop named "DeathSpresso," which purports to *put the coff-in coffee.* The booths are set up to look just like coffins, the open lids acting as tables. Ray enters the back room, flipping some switches. A small generator sputters into life, causing the electric candelabras throughout to glow.

If I haven't really processed what happened to Sofia yet,

I can't even imagine what he must be feeling. She is—was—his best friend since childhood. I've cared for Sofia as much as I could under the circumstances, always trying to keep that barrier around my emotions ever since I became a part of the Quisqueya Club. I always knew that the day would come when I would betray their trust, but it's been so difficult, especially the last year or so, keeping my guard up. So many parts of our friendship have become real, seeping through the cracks of the concrete prison I've built for myself. I always envied the fact that Sofia got to have Ray in her life—really in her life— for so long. But I can't afford to think about what my life might have been like if I would have truly let in someone like Sofia did with Ray. Sofia is dead now. Gone. Just like my chances of living a normal life, even if I actually make it off this island. And who knows who's going to be next? I choke back a spontaneous wave of tears. No wonder El Bacá has his doubts about me.

Ray's cheeks and hands are still faintly pink with traces of Sofia's blood. At least he was able to find a stray Malicia T-shirt to replace his bloodied one, though having to see that decal of Master Crawly's face leering at me every time I look at Ray is unnerving, to say the least. He might be known as Master Crawly to the rest of the world, but I know who He really is.

"I guess I should charge my camera," Isabella's pale face looks like a ghost in the dim light as she steps around Ray and plugs in her equipment.

He fixes her in a death stare. "Sí. Why don't you do that?"

"Meaning what, exactly?"

"Meaning maybe you should try giving a shit about something other than your documentary for once."

She jabs the plug in the outlet, turning toward him. "I know you've been through hell. We all have. Sofia is—*was*—my best friend."

Izzy's shoulders begin to heave and a fresh wave of silent tears streams down her face, though she makes no sound.

Ray goes to her and wraps her in his arms. "Sorry, Iz. I'm not sure what I'm saying. I just . . . I . . . " His eyes mist over and he squeezes them shut.

"I know. I can't believe she's . . . gone."

Isabella catches me staring, and for a second, her eyes freeze over in a stone-like glare. Unnerved, I turn away, choosing to look out the window instead.

"What's that pit thing at the crossroads?" I point toward a dark crevice in the middle of an eerie, gothic cathedral.

"It's the entrance to a ride: It's a Small Underworld. For park dwellers who are dead tired and want to experience some of the other attractions in an aquatic hearse transport, rather than on foot. From there, you can experience the dangers of Creature Canyon, including a face-off with the Queen of the Chupacabras, in a fraction of the time it would take to hoof it."

He's trying to sound like his old tour guide self, but it's obvious the enthusiasm just isn't there anymore.

While Isabella busies herself with charging and checking her equipment, Ray and I search the premises for anything useful, but turn up nothing noteworthy. Sofia's death, and the fact that we've all been running on pure adrenaline, is finally taking its toll, based on everyone's haggard faces.

Isabella looks up from checking some gauges for the umpteenth time. "Why don't you and Ray take a power nap.

I'll keep watch and let you know if anything comes calling, then you can relieve me in an hour or two."

I'm too tired to say anything, so I follow Ray into the outer part of the restaurant, selecting one of the coffin lounges, kicking off my shoes, and trying to settle on the cushions. But I can't get comfortable. My teeth are chattering, my body trembling. How the hell am I going to pull this off? Sofia's death was a wake-up call. It's one thing to plan something out over such a long period of time that it almost becomes abstract. Seeing a good friend bleed out right before your eyes is sobering, as is knowing what comes next.

"You look like you're freezing." Ray peels his T-shirt over his head and holds it out to me. "Here, put this on. It'll keep you cozy."

"But what about—?"

"I'm cool."

When I slip Ray's T-shirt over me, I can't help but inhale his scent, a soothing combination of earthiness and warmth. As my head pokes through the v-neck, I try not to stare at Ray as he takes off his shoes and socks, gazing at his torso, the smooth skin pulled taught over his muscular chest, tree-trunk arms, and chiseled stomach, framed by the waves of his loose, cascading hair. Very soon I'll be driving the sacred dagger into his heart, destroying that perfection forever.

Ray catches me staring and manages to crack a little smile, the first one since Sofia died. "Better?"

"S—sí."

I curl up in the coffin lounge next to his, still shivering, my body unable to retain any warmth as I twist and turn.

Eventually, I feel him shift positions and settle in right beside me, spooning me, his chest pressed firmly against my back. "It's all my fault. I'm so sorry for all of this, Joaquin. I'll keep you and Izzy safe. Promise."

As his arms fold tight around me, I can feel him sobbing, feel his hot tears on my neck. In that moment, I hate myself. He's the one feeling guilty. He's the one vowing to protect me. While I'm the one that's been plotting his death since before we ever met. I grip his arms, pulling him as close as I can against me, giving in to exhaustion, drifting off—

The next thing I know, Isabella is shaking my shoulder. Instantly, I'm alert and anxious. "Qué pasa?"

"Do you hear that?" she asks, her eyes scanning the view right outside the glass. Ray already has his face pressed against it.

I shake my head. "I don't hear any—"

There is something. I hear it then. I can't quite place it at first. But there it is again. Música. Not just any music. More like something you'd hear at a funeral procession from long ago. And there's something else. Cheering? It's all coming from outside. I push out of the booth and join Ray at the window.

"You hear it, too?" he asks me, without even glancing in my direction.

"Where's the music coming from? What does it mean?"

Izzy and I follow him outside, the three of us sticking close. Other sounds now, faint, but distinct. Screaming. Not the terrified variety. More like the *you scared me that was so awesome and funny* kind.

Something flutters by in the chilly breeze and Ray snatches it out of the air. It's a Malicia brochure, containing a map and attraction guide. He scans the page it's open to and nods. "That explains it. Medianoche."

"What happens at midnight?" Isabella struggles to find a direction to aim her camera.

Ray holds out the brochure to both of us, tapping a finger on the schedule of events.

Don't miss Scaretacular, the number one horror parade at midnight!

It's to die for . . .

ISABELLA

I spend most of the night unable to sleep, seeing Sofia's face in the dark, my heart breaking over and over again as I dread every creak, every moan of the wind. Forget the monsters outside. I'm worried about the potential monsters in here, especially Joaquin.

I should tell Ray the truth about him, even if Sofia advised me not to. But that was before many horrible things happened. I saw that parasite in her mouth, heard her at the end before she attacked Ray. That wasn't her. She was definitely possessed, and I'm convinced Joaquin knows all about it. If there's anything I'm sure of now, it's that the supernatural does exist. I clutch the wooden cross around my neck. My mother's superstitions have turned out to be true after all. I have more than enough for my documentary. But no one will see it if I don't make it out of here alive. I just want to leave this hellhole and never look back.

After what we heard at midnight, and what Ray pointed out in the brochure, we all decided on a comfortable lie by osmosis, attributing the sounds to some kind of group audio hallucinatory experience shit, caused by Edgar's strong winds playing tricks on our senses . . . yada yada yada. Uh . . . yeah . . . that's it . . . that's all it was . . . because if we accept the truth of the matter, we may as well pack it all in and head back to El Asilo for a nice, long vacation. Well, Ray and Joaquin can choose to stick their heads up their culos. I'm done denying the evidence. Malicia is haunted as fuck.

I shift in my coffin booth for the thousandth time, searching the dark for the others. There's a kind of desperation in the way Ray and Joaquin are spooning. It's like they're clinging to each other, rather than sleeping. I actually feel sorry for them. They've had a thing for each other for the longest time but have both been too pendejo to act on it. And now Malicia is calling them out, forcing their hand, turning something beautiful into something driven out of fear and desperation.

I toss and turn, unable to get comfortable. I still expect to see Sofia spring up from the darkness and poke me in the ribs, like it was all some sort of big joke, a Halloween prank we'll laugh about for years to come. I'll call her *cabrona*. And she'll come back with *sucia*, and we'll laugh and figure out a way to scare the shit out of the boys.

But seeing Ray and Joaquin curled up like that, looking so frail and vulnerable, the finality of it hits me. Sofia's never coming back. Nunca.

It's easier to cope by shifting focus. I'm all about getting off this godforsaken island now. But while I'm still here, maybe

I owe it to Sofia to find out why Joaquin has returned here after the tragedy and what he knows about what ultimately killed her.

I reach for my camera, make sure the infrared's activated, and take some photos and video of Ray and Joaquin lying there. Is it betraying a trust? Maybe. But so is leading your friends into a death trap for the weekend.

I target Joaquin in my viewfinder. Why has he hidden the fact that he is the sole survivor of the Malicia Massacre? We're his best friends. His only friends. The Quisqueya Club has always had his back. Why not trust us? What's so bad about surviving a tragedy?

I set the camera aside and stare at him in the dark, making a silent vow to Sofia. If I find out that Joaquin is the reason Sofia is dead, he won't have to worry about getting off this island.

I'll kill him myself.

RAYMUNDO

I feel like a robot, emotionless, trying hard to keep myself busy. There's no time for slackers. Pai was always calling me un haragán, a lazy oaf, no matter what I accomplished, making honor roll, leading my sports teams to victory. Acing all my classes. None of it mattered. I was never good enough according to him, never putting forth my best effort. Just coasting through life on my good looks. But laziness is not what I'm feeling now.

I fill my backpack with the few items I found that might be useful: a hunting knife and a torch. Along with the master control unit to control the rides I picked up at the security station and a fire axe, it should give us an advantage, if we're lucky. Even though at this point I'm not sure if I'm more afraid of unseen forces than myself.

After not finding any other SAT phones at the Creature

Canyon crew station, we finally decide to head in the direction of the park that I've been anxious to get to since we first arrived, Paranormal Place.

I glance over at Joaquin and Izzy and curse myself for bringing them here, but at the same time, I don't know what I'd do with myself if I didn't have them at my side. Then thoughts of Sofia flood my brain. Not only do I feel gutted for killing her, I'm not even sure I can go through with the séance with her book as a proxy, even though it was the sole reason for bringing the three of them here to Malicia. Whether we go through with the séance or not, I have to tell them soon. Considering it's already Saturday morning, I only have one day left to decide before Halloween.

I swipe a fresh wave of stinging tears away. After everything I've done, I'm not good enough to be with Joaquin when, or if, we manage to get off this cursed island tomorrow when the rescue chopper arrives on the mountaintop. As I check the master control unit for the It's a Small Underworld ride, making sure the generator's hooked up and the system's online and functioning, my heart feels heavy.

Sofia can't be dead. She just can't be. But it's true. No getting around her ice-cold skin, the lifeless eyes . . . her blood all over the basement floor. A wave of anger tenses all my muscles. I slam the panel I'm working on shut. What the fuck did I do by bringing her here?

I punch in the initiation sequence on the circuit board, the deep low hum vibrating through my body. The lights flicker and the ride comes to life, resurrected after all these long years. The animatronic demons guarding the entrance growl and hiss, as they play tug-of-war over a globe of the earth, their long talons embedded on either side. The infamous It's a Small Underworld theme song belts out through the ride's speakers, an irritating mantra on an infernal loop, repeating constantly:

There is just one Hades and Beelzebub
You belong to us and your soul is grub
Kiss your family goodbye
And get ready to die
Let it burn, burn, burn . . .
It's a small underworld burn in hell,
It's a small underworld burn in hell,
It's a small underworld burn in hell,
Let it burn, burn, burn . . .

"Gente, we're ready," I call to Joaquin and Isabella.

Joaquin accepts my offered hand and allows me to escort him into the ride. He lets out a nervous chuckle as he lets go. "Why did it have to be another boat?"

Isabella bustles past Joaquin and into the ride without saying a word or glancing in his direction. There's been something odd going on between the two of them, especially since this morning. I've caught her staring at him several times, a strange expression on her face, as if she's sizing him up, but I'm not sure for what, and I don't have the energy to figure it out.

I shrug. Maybe it's just me. With everything that's going on, I've been hyper-scrutinizing everything, anything to fill that gnawing in the pit of my stomach.

The three of us grab the supplies and load them in with us. Unlike the gurneys at El Asilo, these ride cars are shaped like a fiery sled, being led by the snarling, three-headed Cerberus.

Ours is missing one of his six eyes, probably caused by a stray gun shot.

Izzy takes the back seat, while Joaquin climbs into the front beside me. She pulls out her camera and starts recording. "Ready."

I check the ride's palm-sized remote unit. All lit up and ready to go. "Hang on everyone. We're off." I jam my thumb against the start button and the car lurches forward.

It's a small underworld burn in hell,
Let it burn, burn, burn . . .

Next thing you know, we're zooming through a dark void, the car careening and spinning toward our first unholy destination. I glance behind us, making sure no one's following us, like Carlos or El Ratoncito Perez. Nada. I let out a breath as we continue our journey into this underworld. Up ahead, the passage opens up, revealing a vaulted ceiling and a series of nichos, which remind me of graves.

"We're passing through the Valley of Las Ciguapas, the home of the seductive and deadly mythical sirens of the DR."

A mournful, eerie song petrifies every hair on my body. It sounds almost like the song of crying children, punctuated with a soft, woeful whining.

"Qué es eso?" a wide-eyed Joaquin asks.

"'El Canto de la Sirena,' 'The Mermaid's Song,' is what Mai used to call it when she would tell Rudy and me the story."

Isabella points to a group of moving figures hiding in the caverns. They appear to be female, some with brown skin, the others with dark blue. Each of the figures has a mane of smooth, glossy hair that covers their bodies. And when they walk, their backward facing feet give the impression they are going in the opposite direction. "What the hell are those?"

I shake my head. "Relax, Izzy. Those aren't real. They're animatronic Ciguapas. They can't harm us."

Maybe coming this way was really a good idea. A boring ride after all the horrors we've faced.

I toggle the switch on the control unit, and our floating hearse picks up speed. Suddenly, we pull a rollercoaster move and drop. Isabella struggles to hold onto her camera, while Joaquin's fingers dig into my shoulder.

"Sorry about that, guys," I say. "I just want to get to Paranormal Place before it gets dark."

After a few more twists and turns, we glide into a cave illuminated by flickering torches. Ancient hieroglyphics line the walls, a series of crude drawings depicting small, childlike creatures dressed in red.

"La Cueva de Los Duendes," I mutter.

Joaquin shakes his head. "I've seen the movies. Those goblin mutants are nasty bitches."

I nod. "Except these are just more animatronics dishing out cheap scares."

As if in response, one of the goblins rushes toward the boat, waving a machete, but at the last minute its mechanism yanks it back into the dark to wait until it can pop out again and scare the occupants of the next boat.

Isabella stifles a yawn. "This is really lame. And I'm here for it."

In the center of the cave is a large, dark opening, like a well. A horde of dark, animatronic figures is crawling out, some of them missing body parts, others with exposed mechanisms.

Joaquin lets out a nervous laugh. "I don't think this ride is going to pass its next inspection."

I gun the controls again, swerving as we zoom out of the cave in a rapid series of dips and turns. When we finally level off and start slowing down, we find ourselves in a cavern designed to look like it's underwater, complete with lighting effects simulating the shimmering ocean.

"The Chupacra Lair," I announce.

It takes a minute for everyone to get their bearings. Joaquin has been gripping my hand so tightly it's numb, which I actually find comforting.

I let out a long sigh. "This ride brings back a lot of special memories. Rudy and I used to scurry through these eerie caverns, hiding from the legendary Reina de los Chupacabras, the Queen creature herself, who supposedly lived in the deepest trenches of the oceans."

Joaquin rubs my arm. "Sounds like you two had a lot of fun."

I smile at the memory. "See, there was an enormous tank, filled with dark and murky water, which housed the Chupacabra queen. Every night at sunset, the big event was watching the pool fill with thousands of bubbles, as the queen rose from the depths in the presence of the crowds, literally hundreds of gaping onlookers, spitting up their soda and popcorn as their seats buckled and the tank overflowed. Everyone in the splash zone, which often included Rudy and me, were drenched to the bone. Finally, the attraction operator would use a sacred scepter to banish the queen back into her watery prison, before her cache of hundreds of eggs could hatch and attack the audience, much to the cheers of everyone."

Joaquin pauses to consider all this. "According to the movie series spawned by the legend, the Chupacabras would cause madness and death to anyone unfortunate enough to make eye contact, before getting all their organs sucked out and blood drained."

That last thought makes me think of Sofia, and I can tell Joaquin instantly regrets mentioning any of it.

"Sorry," he says.

I'm grateful when he squeezes my hand again, as Isabella continues to stare ahead in silence. Tank after tank is filled with the grotesque bodies of animatronic Chupacabras comprised of a row of razor-sharp spikes jutting down the middle of their backs, short arms ending in nasty claws, long legs like kangaroos, and grayish skin erupting in fur and feathers. The creatures' eyes are black and soulless like a great white shark's, their mouths open and revealing horrifying sets of fangs.

My heart races and my breathing picks up as we round the last corner and enter the lair belonging to La Reina de los Chupacabras herself. The tank's dark. No murky water. Nothing to see inside except pitch black darkness. One of the tank's glass panels has been completely shattered. Even in the dim light you can see the grotesque footprints, if you can call them that, leading directly out of the tank and into one of the channels leading into the actual ocean. They're dinosaur-like, enormous talon shapes that look like they could rip anything to shreds—or puncture the thick safety glass keeping its owner prisoner for so long. Whatever made these must be huge, given the size of these prints. And what's even more unsettling is the fact that the prints are wet. Fresh.

Isabella notices that detail, too. "That's not part of the ride, is it?"

I shake my head. Chupacabras have been unleashed at Malicia.

Just as we exit the Chupacabra Lair, a terrifying groan cuts through the air, a wretched wail of primal anger. Something heavy lands in the back of our boat and I stare at it in disbelief.

It's Carlos.

JOAQUIN

"Stop the boat!" I yell.

As the ride comes to an abrupt halt, Isabella slips under the safety bar, scrambling to the front of the boat to join Ray and me.

"Holy shit," I mutter.

Carlos looked bad before, but now he's almost unrecognizable, except for the tattered name tag still hanging ridiculously from the last bit of his shredded poloché. His body has shriveled up, the burnt skin creating a maze of thick scar tissue strangling his limbs, making him grotesquely deformed and shorter. His ears are larger and pointy, his hair is practically gone, with only a few remaining scraggly strands. But it's the eyes that really freak me out. Both are bulging, almost pulsating, glowing with iridescent light. El Bacá's light. In my gut I know he's here for Ray, trying to pick up where the possessed Sofia left off. Trying to shut me down and cheat me out of the chance to keep my soul.

Carlos leaps into the backseat of the boat with the ease of a monkey, never taking his eyes off us. His mouth opens, letting loose a stream of drool through rotting teeth.

Ray shoves me and Izzy behind him. He's holding the fire axe, making threatening motions at Carlos. "Cuidado. Keep your distance. I'll use this if I have to."

In response, Carlos let's out an inhuman groan that echoes through the tunnel. His pulsating eyes remain fixed on us, his cracked lips twisting into a gnarled grin.

My adrenaline is in overdrive. I can't stand idly by and let El Bacá's puppet control my destiny.

"Coño! What do we do?" Isabella shouts.

Ray takes a step closer to Carlos. "You and Joaquin climb down into the water and head for shore—"

"We're not going to leave you!" He has no idea why I'm so desparate.

"Listen up, " he snaps. "It's the only way. I have to hold Carlos here."

Before I can protest, Carlos lets out another primal shriek and leaps toward us. But Ray's just as quick. He slams the axe handle into Carlos's head, causing him to collapse against the boat's console. Carlos is foaming at the mouth, body violently convulsing.

"What's happening to him?" Isabella shouts. Her hands are held out in front of her as if she can't decide whether she can stand touching him to help us.

Ray shakes his head, confused. "I didn't think I hit him hard enough to be causing this."

Neither of them get it. El Bacá's inside of Carlos. Those demonic parasitic drones, controlling Carlos's will.

"It's just like with Sofia," I say under my breath.

Carlos continues to convulse. Ray throws himself on top of him, trying to restrain him with some cord from his pack.

"Help me!" he shouts.

Isabella scrambles to his side, trying to get ahold of one of Carlos's flailing limbs.

Ray snaps his head toward me. "What are you doing? We need your help!"

But I can't help. I'm frozen in place, watching everything unfold like a movie in my mind. I shake my head. Mute.

"Damn it, pana. Now's not the time to panic. You got this! C'mon!" Ray's losing it. He's not angry, he's scared.

Between the two of them, they manage to bind Carlos's hands enough to push him off the boat, jump into the water, and drag him to shore.

"Shit," I mutter. I break through my paralysis and slink into the water. Luckily, the water level here isn't too deep, and I manage to scramble to shore after them. Thinking of that escaped Chupacabra possibly lurking in the dark waters is the only fuel I need to move as fast as I can.

Ray and Isabella are still struggling with Carlos on the simulated sandy perimeter of the lake, practically collapsing from the effort. But the crisis isn't over yet. Carlos is growling, breaking loose of his restraints as he must have before. Ray and Isabella are no match for his demonic strength.

I can only watch, horrified, as Carlos dislocates his own joints, bending bones in ways they were never meant to be bent, as he squirms his way free.

"Can't you shoot him up with something? A sedative?" Isabella shouts at Ray.

He shakes his head as his eyes grow wide. "We used them all up. . . ."

Isabella lets out a yelp. "Oh, God. I can feel them. In his arm. Moving . . ." she mutters, bursting into heaving sobs, even as Carlos lets out another agonized roar.

I get close enough to pick up the strange movement in Carlos's arms. Something definitely wants out. I need to do something fast.

Ray's eyes bug. "What is that?!"

I still can't believe what I'm seeing. Carlos's skin is pulsating like his eyes, twisting, the topmost layers tearing open as if multiple somethings are trying to gnaw their way through his flesh and out. I kneel down as close as I dare, keeping a safe distance.

Ray belts out some choice Spanish curse words under his breath as Carlos tosses both him and Isabella like rag dolls. There's a loud ripping sound as the taut skin around Carlos's stomach rips open. The stink hits us like a wave, a noxious blend of rotting sweetness that makes my eyes burn, gagging me.

That's not the worst of it. Carlos's entire body is now purple and bloated, every inch of skin and scar tissue covered with strange symbols, carved into his flesh, similar to the ones engraved in those trees at Boneyard Bayou. Each of the symbols is pulsating with life, twisting tentacles tearing through the markings and Carlos's flesh, popping pustules oozing out more dark rot.

While some are trying to burst through the gash in his stomach, there are hundreds of wriggling tentacles visible under his skin, popping free throughout his entire body.

One tentacle finally bursts through Carlos's forehead. It's gray and insect-like, its body coated in Carlos's blood and its own slime.

Raymundo tries to hit it with the axe, but the tentacle rips it from his hand and flings it aside. It hisses and sprays out a mist into the air that burns our eyes and has us all coughing.

The insects slithering out of the gaping wounds in Carlos's body screech and snap as they skitter toward us—toward Ray.

I pick up a nearby stone with both hands and slam it down on the closest parasite. That should have crushed it, but the still-moving tentacle poking out from underneath says otherwise.

Carlos convulses again as more of the critters spring from every orifice, one heading right toward Ray with a glistening pincer, which I'm sure is coated with the same substance Sofia was going to inject him with.

No. I can't let that happen. Carlos is not going to rob me of the opportunity to save my soul from hell.

Grabbing the axe, I shove Ray out of the way, just as Carlos makes a final lunge for him.

With an animal cry, I swing the axe as hard as I can, lopping his head off in a spray of blood and gore that spatters the glistening blade, as well as Ray and Izzy.

I've finally done it. I've finally gotten blood on my very own hands. I drop to my knees, puking my guts out until I'm only dry heaving. I can now officially add murder to my growing list of sins.

Ray squeezes my shoulder. "You didn't have a choice. He was going after me. There was no other way to stop him."

I look up, tears glistening down my cheeks. The confusing part is I'm not exactly sure why I did it. Was it to save my own soul? Or was it because I couldn't bear the thought of Carlos touching Ray, hurting him?

Ray pulls me up and we hug fiercely. In that moment, I don't want to think about anything else.

I suppose I should be in shock, or scared shitless, or both. I've only bought myself a temporary reprieve. With Carlos gone, it's now up to me to perform the ritual on that mountaintop tomorrow night. That's what I need to focus on, not feelings or emotions. The last thing I need to do is lose it when I'm on the brink of saving my eternal soul.

Ray and I finally separate. But when I turn to Carlos's decapitated body, it's still moving. What the fuck?

"It's not dead!" Isabella yells.

We can only stare in horror as Carlos's headless body continues to writhe.

I shake my head violently. "Eso es imposible! He has to be dead!"

Isabella points. "Claro que sí. He *is* dead. It's those things squirming inside him."

Ray springs into action, grabbing the gas can and dousing the body. "We have to burn it!"

The body continues to flail as he lights it on fire, the air filled with the high-pitched squealing of the parasites trying to escape their fiery prison.

I can't help but stare at the squirming parasites in fear and awe. El Bacá's determined to get what It wants. And so am I.

The stench of rotting, burning flesh is overpowering. I can't stop gagging. Ray and Isabella cover their mouths and noses.

An inhuman howling pierces the silence.

This new horrific sound might be what's going to push me over the edge. I'm sure if I could see myself in a mirror, I'd be as pale as a white boy.

"Sounds like it came from . . . everywhere . . ." My voice trails off.

The hum of the generator decreases. The lights flicker, threatening to die out.

While Ray and I whip out our flashlights, waving them about, Isabella uses her camera.

"Going into infrared mode," she calls.

As scared as I am, I refuse to let the fear get the best of me and plunge me into panic mode. It's all too much. Instead, my body shifts into autopilot. "The park's coming to life," I whisper.

Isabella's still holding her camera. "So now what?"

Ray stops suddenly, wrapping one massive arm around Isabella and I and pulling us close. "Oh, God," he whispers.

A half a dozen workers, looking much like Carlos—soulless black eyes, disease-pocked skin—are closing in on us. Each of them is carrying an axe or other sharp object, still dripping dark blood.

"I take it they aren't going to let us pass?" Isabella asks.

In response, there's more horrific howling and screeching that fills the air, seemingly coming from every park speaker. The armed workers advance toward us. But I do a double take to make sure what I'm seeing is really happening. Some of them are dropping to all fours, their bodies contorting, the sound of snapping bones and tearing flesh cutting through the air. They're changing. Unlike Carlos, who was filled with those toxic parasites, these workers are transforming into something else . . .

I shoot Ray and Isabella a look. "Are those werewolves?"

Ray nods. "The Dominican version. Lugarus. The dog form of the legendary El Galipote. Back to the boat, now!"

"Wait a minute," I whisper. "If we take the boat back and they follow us, we won't be able to outrun them."

Ray sighs. "That's true. What do you have in mind, pana?"

I point to the nearest ride, something called Runaway Hearse. A high-speed rollercoaster. "I saw in the park brochure that this rollercoaster also leads into Paranormal Place. Is that true?"

A light goes off in his eyes as he begins to see where I'm going. "Yes."

"And the coaster would be much faster than the boat we came in on, right?"

He gives me a wink. "Absolutely."

Isabella's eyes flick between the ride and the distant Lugarus. "Ray, can your remote activate the coaster?"

He shakes his head. "But I can activate the manual release in the control box, which will propel the cars to run one full cycle. That should get us to the other side and into Paranormal Place!"

Ray starts walking toward the entrance to the coaster, Isabella and me at his heels. The Lugarus are still staring at us, slowly padding in our direction.

"No sudden movements," I say. "We got this."

Once through the entrance, Ray instructs Isabella and me to get into one of the cars as he tinkers with the control box. There's a loud hum as the coaster powers up. Anxiously, we glance at the Lugarus, whose curiosity has definitely been aroused.

"We're off," Ray whispers as our car rolls in its track, gaining speed as the first of the Lugarus reaches the entrance, heads tilted as they watch us climb.

When we reach the top, there's that sickening pause just before we plunge downward again. Then we're swerving and spinning at breakneck speed, looping and twisting as we accelerate and decelerate. For a brief moment, it's almost like we're the Quisqueya Club on a typical amusement park vacation again. Except there's no Sofia, and none of us are making a sound, which is eerie in and of itself, in addition to the howling filling the air.

As we start to slow down and finally stop at the entrance to Paranormal Place, I take a deep breath. It's just past midnight on Sunday morning. Halloween. I need to get Ray up to that mountain today.

RAYMUNDO

I glance toward Joaquin and Isabella, huddled together in a corner of the Psychic Inn, where we've sought refuge. After arriving here right after midnight, we were all too exhausted to do anything else but crash. Joaquin's curled up in a fetal position. Isabella's clutching her camera like a security blanket. I don't know what I'd do if anything happened to them, too.

The sooner I get Joaquin and Isabella away from here the better. There's just one thing left for me to do today. Hold the séance before the rescue chopper arrives.

I stare at the backpack again, in such close proximity to Joaquin and Isabella. At one point, I even thought of "accidentally" ditching the backpack during our escape. But that would have been a pendejo move, being that we depend on some of the other supplies inside it to make it through this. Who am I kidding? I didn't get rid of it because there's still a part of me that wants to go through with the ritual, especially now that we've actually arrived at Paranormal Place, the place where it happened.

While so many met their deaths in other parts of the park, thirteen years ago to the day, Rudy was murdered right here in Paranormal Place. According to the ritual in the book, this is where we have to conduct the séance.

With Joaquin and Izzy sleeping, now would be the perfect opportunity to scout the exact location where he died and start setting things up.

I grab the pack and slowly make my way outside the inn. There it is. Just as I remember. A small cemetery that supposedly contains many of the bodies of Paranormal Place's ghostly denizens. The pack feels heavy on my back.

Maneuvering through the rows of gravestones and crosses, I head toward a plot of land set off on a tiny hill. This is where they found his body.

Before continuing, I kneel and unbuckle the pack, reach in without looking, and rummage through its contents, my hands trembling as I check to make sure all of the ritual materials are there, including Sofia's book.

"What are you up to?"

The voice makes me jump, and I whirl. It's Joaquin. My muscles relax and I stretch my arms wide. "I couldn't wait. I had to see this place."

"This is where he died, isn't it?" he asks.

I nod. "Just over there in that little mausoleum on that small hill. I think he was hiding when . . . when the massacre started. I wanted to have a moment alone with him before the séance."

"I'm sorry. I should leave—"

"No. Stay with me. Please. Now that I'm here, I'm not sure I can handle it alone."

He sits on the grass beside me. "I'm always here for you. Siempre."

I nod. "Gracias."

After the adrenaline rush of our escape from Creature Canyon, I've really missed my quiet alone time with Joaquin, whether it was just shooting the shit about a new movie or discussing our hopes and dreams after graduating high school and venturing into college. The truth is, I don't really have much to look forward to right now. I want to hug him, but I couldn't deal with it if he were to reject me right now and shatter the last sliver of hope I have left.

"You haven't been looking too good since . . . since Sofia. It's really starting to hit you, too," he says.

"I guess the shock is wearing off, and the fact that I'm never going to see her again is really kicking in." I squeeze my eyes shut, rubbing them.

"It's okay to have anxiety," Joaquin says.

"I don't have anxiety," I say, instantly regretting my defensive tone.

"It's perfectly understandable under the circumstances. I could give you something for the stress, an anti-anxiety—"

"I'm fine, really. I guess hunger pangs are starting to set in. That's all. Not that I feel like eating anything. Shocking, I know." I laugh for his benefit.

He shakes his head. "It's more than that. Trust me. I recognize the signs."

"I can cope. I don't need any pills to get through this."

"You mean like I do," he says quietly.

"I wasn't trying to put you down. It's understandable you might need to take something, considering everything you've been through."

His eyes narrow. "What exactly do you mean?"

"Losing your parents at a young age in that accident and having to be raised by your grandparents."

The muscles in his face relax. "Sí. It's been tough. What about what you've been through? I know you lost your brother and mother during the massacre here. And now Sofia. It's okay to lean on someone else, Ray. You don't always have to be the protector. No one will judge you."

No one except me.

A small twinkling light appears above Joaquin's head. Then another one off to his right. Yet another one to his left. The air above us is soon filled with the twinkling lightning bugs, giving the impression of a starry night sky shining just for us.

I point. "Where did those come from?"

Joaquin turns to look at me and smiles. "Las Nimitas! I remember running through the fields behind my abuela's house in Santo Domingo, chasing them, trying to catch one and make a wish."

It's so great to see him smiling after so much tragedy. As he reaches out to try and catch one of the fireflies now, I can't help but grin myself. One of them lights on his hand, its glow reflected in his eyes.

I move closer to him. "Why do they twinkle?"

He's still staring at the glow, mesmerized. "It's a mating ritual.

The males flash their bright tail light, hoping to get a return flash from an interested party."

Very gently, he cups the firefly in his palm and offers it to me, carefully depositing it in my own, our hands touching, sparking a fire of a different kind inside me.

Joaquin chuckles, nodding at the firefly nestled in my palm. "He likes you."

I look Joaquin right in the eyes. "I like him, too."

We stand in silence, just staring at each other, basking in the glow all around us, one magical light show after all the sorrow, tears, and pain.

Las Nimitas swirl faster around us. One of them lands on my nose, then moves off hovering, as if wanting me to follow.

I shake my head. "Why's it doing that?"

"I don't know. It looks like it's waiting for something. According to the legend of Las Nimitas, these fireflies represent the souls of the dead, our loved ones, always watching over us, shining their light through the darkness."

My heart starts to race. "Souls of our loved ones? Then that Nimita leading us could be my brother, Rudy."

"Now wait a sec, Ray. You shouldn't jump to conclusions based off a legend."

I hold out my hand and he takes it. "C'mon. Let's see what it wants!"

As if in response, the head Nimita circles me again, lands on my nose, and then moves off again.

The other Nimitas crowd us from behind. If I didn't know any better, I'd say they were pushing us to follow their leader.

We make our way deeper into the cemetery. I squeeze

Joaquin's hand tighter, pulling him along as the firefly disappears inside the mausoleum up ahead. It's no coincidence it's led me to the exact place where Rudy died. Pushing open the rusty gate, I make my way down the stone steps, two at a time, Joaquin racing to keep up.

The stairs dead-end at a solitary crypt, with one name engraved on the cracked stone plaque.

DELVALLE.

My heart's thudding against my chest, my breathing on fire. La Nimita is hovering just above, illuminating a strange series of symbols and glyphs carved into the wall, which trigger half-memories, things I hadn't thought about since I was a kid.

"Brujeria," I finally say.

"Witchcraft? Are you sure?" Joaquin's gone a shade paler, and I'm convinced he's about to have another panic attack.

"I'm pretty sure. I remember things from when I was a kid growing up here. Some of the workers whispering things. At the time, I didn't understand. But it does make sense, doesn't it?"

"What do you mean?"

"Everything that's happening now. All this supernatural shit. Once you accept the existence of brujas and their spells and curses, it would make sense they're responsible for what's going on here. The thing is, why? What do they want? And why did Las Nimitas lead us here? Was it just because Rudy died here? Or was his death actually caused by whatever these symbols represent?"

Joaquin studies every minute detail of the strange glyphs, avoiding my eyes. "So brujas are all evil, right?"

"Yes. I mean . . . some. Brujas have nothing to do with

Wicca or anything like that. Most brujas are evil, part of covens, casting dark spells, unlike Wiccan witches who believe in doing no harm."

Joaquin turns to me. "So if you encountered one of these brujas, you'd try to destroy them, just like I did with Carlos, right? I mean, in theory."

I chuckle, relishing this moment of comfortable normalcy, like when we would lie on my bed back home coming up with all sorts of "what-if" scenarios.

"Yes, brujas are evil and should be destroyed on sight, but like everything else, there are exceptions."

He leans in close, his face glowing in the fireflies' light. "Such as . . .?"

"Have you heard of the legend of El Tumbador y La Bruja?"

He shakes his head. "The Witch Hunter and the Witch? I don't think so."

"My mom used to tell my brother Rudy and me the story sometimes before bed. It's pretty romantic. The way it goes, on the eve of his marriage to his betrothed, the Witch Hunter, aka El Tumbador, hunted his mortal enemy, a mysterious witch that could change into a bird, eluding his pursuit."

He scoffs. "That doesn't sound very romantic to me."

I give him a playful shove in the arm. "Hold up. I haven't gotten to that part yet. One fateful day, after reciting the magical incantations to ensnare the witch in his trap, El Tumbador felled the enchanted bird with one of his arrows, knocking it to shore, just as the sun was rising over the horizon on his wedding day."

He shakes his head and smiles at me. "Why would anyone go hunting on their wedding day?"

"Jesus, stop being so impatient and let me finish. Only in the light of a new day was the Bruja's true identity revealed, as the bird transformed back into its human shape, that of El Tumbador's beloved."

All the lighthearted playfulness disappears from Joaquin's eyes. "So he misjudged the one person he loved most in this world, who then died in his arms. Very romantic, but so tragic."

"Some of the most powerful romances are the most tragic. That's why we should appreciate true love when we find it."

His eyes light up. "If I were to do script rewrites on that legend, I'd give it a happy ending. There aren't enough of those in the world. I'd make it so that on the anniversary of the Bruja's death, El Tumbador returned to the same spot just before sunset, breaking the curse, so that the two were finally reunited and able to live a long, happy life."

His enthusiasm is infectious and I give him a big smile. "I like it. Why don't we make your version official?"

"What do you mean?"

I dig into my pocket and pull out a small charm bracelet. "This belonged to my mother. One of the only things I've kept. There are two charms on it, this little arrow representing El Tumbador, and the bird representing La Bruja. I was planning on burying it here on the island as a sort of memorial to her and Rudy, but I think they'd like this better."

I unclasp the bracelet and hand him the charm with the bird symbol on it.

He examines it in the shimmering light and looks up at me. "Ray. I can't keep this, it was your mother's—"

I wave him off when he tries to give it back. "I want you

to have it. You . . . you mean so much to me. I've lost . . . my brother. My mother. Sofia . . . Just promise me, if anything ever separates us, we'll find our way back to each other. Just like in your version. Please."

I look away as the tears well in my eyes. I feel his hand on my cheek, gently turning me to face him.

"I promise." He takes the two charms and holds them up toward the unseen sky. "You hear that universe? I hereby cast this spell."

I'm not sure if it's a coincidence, but the swarm of fireflies chooses this exact moment to coalesce around us into a bright halo, before dispersing and leaving us in the waning light.

I wipe away the tears as we both laugh. When he hands me back the arrow charm, his hand feels so warm in mine.

Rising, I hold out my hand and pull him up. "We should see what Izzy's been up to and hold that séance."

JOAQUIN

We trek back to the inn, where Isabella's already up and waiting.

"You finally showed up," she says. "I was beginning to think something happened to you."

She smiles, but I can see the fear and worry in her bloodshot eyes.

"We found something," I say, quickly filling Izzy in on our exploits at the graveyard, except for the part about the legend and exchanging of charms.

After listening to our account, she leans back in her chair. "So you want to have this séance now to see if Ray's dead brother can shed some light on what's going on here?"

Ray nods. "That's the plan. I think we can learn a lot."

I fake a big smile. "Ray's right. We should do it."

In truth, I have no desire to bring the spirit of Ray's brother into the mix. Who knows what it could tell him? I planted the seeds in Ray for him to come back to this island. I even made sure he came across that book with the specific ritual to perform to make it happen. As far as actually contacting a ghost though, an unwelcome visit from Rudy is one contingency I haven't planned for that could really screw me over.

I try not to think about that. If Rudy doesn't show up, Ray will be crushed to the core. But if his dead brother's ghost does make an appearance and rats me out, Ray will crush me.

Isabella clears her throat. "So I've listened to you guys, but now I'd like for you to listen to me. I've been thinking about everything, going through some of the park diagrams I downloaded onto my computer, and there's something I want to try."

I try to make light of her statement. "Uh-oh, I guess we should be worried."

She shoots me a look and I glare back at her. The reality is, I'm so close to achieving my goal, I don't need her upsetting my plans at this late stage in the game.

Even Ray doesn't seem to be too thrilled, but he nods politely. "Let's hear it."

The three of us settle into the highbacked lobby chairs to hear her out, facing each other.

Isabella leans forward. "We all agree something's going on here. Something out of the ordinary. Supernatural. The bottom line is the attractions are developing a life of their own."

Ray nods. "De acuerdo."

"No arguments here," I say.

"And whatever is causing this to happen," Isabella continues, "it seems intent on driving us from one end of the park to another."

"What can we do?" I ask, failing to see her point. "Unless we're able to contact the outside world, we're screwed."

"Joaquin's got a point." Ray leans forward. "We don't really even know what we're up against at this point. Spirits?"

Isabella shrugs. "Does it really matter what it is? Ghost, parasite, whatever. My point is, it's time to stop playing this thing's game."

I prop my legs on the antique coffee table, not liking where this is going. "What exactly are you proposing?"

"Let's change things up. Instead of following our predicted path around the park, we'll go outside and explore another way off this island."

My eyes narrow at her. "Outside? What about Edgar? It may be more dangerous out there than it is in here."

"Not necessarily. It sounds like the worst of the storm is over. We may be able to find another way off the island, some transport that we missed, or maybe set up a signal to contact outsiders. According to the park plans, there's a WaveRunner rental shed off the beach—"

"That might have been blown away by the storm," Ray finishes, looking at me to back him up.

She ignores him. "In any case, I think it beats the hell out of staying in here and waiting. . . ."

I clear my throat. "You do have a point. But don't you think our chances would be better if we hiked up to the highest point on the island to try and signal a boat or plane?"

Her eyes grow wide at my proposal.

"You mean climb to the peak of Montaña Malicia itself?" she asks, incredulous.

I'm trying to play it off, sounding as nonchalant as I can in order to maneuver her to do what I want, like I've done to Ray for years. Time is running out. I need to get Ray to the top of that mountain to perform the ritual tonight. Thinking about what will happen to me if I don't, it's all I can do not to spiral into a panic attack.

Ray nods. "It sounds like a logical plan to me."

Isabella is studying me closely and it's a struggle to retain my composure. "I'm surprised you, of all people, wouldn't be afraid of heights, Joaquin. No offense."

I look at her and force a smile. "None taken. Desperate times call for desperate measures, Iz."

Her eyes bounce between Ray's and mine. "I'll make a deal with you. We try my beach idea, and if it doesn't pan out, then I'll agree to go along with the séance or climb any mountain you want. Does that work for you both?"

Well played, Isabella.

We're both silent, pondering the idea.

"Anything's better than spending another night as prey inside this park." Ray looks at me. "Let's just do it her way, pana. Okay?"

I'm trying to hold it together. But I can't afford to push it. She's backed me into a corner by making it an anxiety issue. If I push for the mountain too strongly, she and Ray will be suspicious. A wave of anxiety hits me as I think about the repercussions of failure. "I'm pretty freaked out about the mountain thing, but I still think it's the more logical choice of the two, and I feel if Sofia were here she would agree."

There. I did it. I used Sofia into guilting Ray to do what I want him to do. What I need him to do.

Ray seems torn, just like I knew he would be. As bad as I feel for him, for trying to manipulate him, my terror is just too strong to ignore. I'm a coward. I always will be. I feel the charm he gave me burning in my pocket as if it's trying to brand me as a hypocrite. But it's darkly poetic that he gave me the charm representing Las Brujas.

Ray lets out a long sigh. "As much as I agree with you, I don't see the harm in trying the beach first. We can always try the mountain later, after the séance. We don't even know how safe it is out there, so we just have to make sure not to take any unnecessary risks . . . without a doctor in the house." His voice cracks at that last part.

Isabella nods. "Bueno. Then it's settled."

Ray stands. "Let's do this thing."

We take a few minutes to get our gear together. Then Ray leads the way back into the access tunnels below the park. It's dank in here, smelling of decay where the ocean has seeped through the pressure doors.

"Be careful." Ray waves his flashlight. "It looks like this section sustained a lot of damage from the storm and partially collapsed."

He doesn't have to tell me twice. He takes my hand as we maneuver across exposed pipes and electrical cables, over mounds of rubble, deeper and deeper into the tunnel.

The light from Ray's flashlight grows noticeably dimmer, and he shakes it. The beam flickers and, for a frightening moment,

I think it's going to snuff out completely, leaving us in total darkness. But it steadies, though not as bright as before.

All I can think about is the time that we're wasting, the time we could be using to climb up that mountain. Hopefully, we can speed through this debacle and get on with the plan before time runs out.

"We should probably pick up the pace," I say, and Ray does exactly that.

We finally reach a door at the end of the corridor. Ray tries it, but it won't budge.

"I'll have to try and bypass the security system." He searches inside the backpack, pulling out some tools and one of the schematics he lifted from the security station.

With Isabella holding the flashlight on the door's control panel, Ray uses one of the tools from the kit and cuts wires, splicing them together. At one point, there's a spark, and then a deep vibration, followed by a loud click as the door unlocks.

"Wait," I say, before Ray can open the door. "Can you hear anything on the other side?"

He presses an ear against the door, before turning and shaking his head. He pushes the door open—a loud alarm goes off, filling the corridor with a blaring siren, accompanied by a robotic voice.

"¡Advertencia! Brecha de seguridad en el sector doce! Warning¡ Security breach in sector twelve. Repeat, security breach in sector twelve . . ."

As the alarm drones on and on, Ray again consults the schematic and tinkers with the door panel. "It's good. I got this."

He cuts one of the wires, silencing the alarm. At last, he

pushes the door open. The first thing I sense is a blast of oppressive heat, the opposite of the bone-chilling cold permeating the access tunnel. Nothing like good old tropical humidity after a storm. It takes a few minutes for my eyes to adjust to the outdoors. The three of us slowly emerge from the darkness, taking in the effects of Edgar's destruction.

RAYMUNDO

amn. The island is practically unrecognizable. I can barely take it all in. It's a barren landscape. A post-apocalyptic battlefield.

Most of the hotel is underwater, trees and landscaping are virtually nonexistent. The demolition equipment has been reduced to parts scattered and bobbing in the sea. The park's dome is still mostly intact, with the exception of black smoke billowing over Serial Springs. Increíble.

In the center of it all, Malicia's peak overlooks everything, defiant, as if it's won the battle with Edgar and is daring anything else to try and cross its path unscathed.

"It barely touched the park," Joaquin says, gawking at the landscape.

"I don't mean to geek out, but the park was built to much higher safety specifications required by code," I say. "But even so, something's off here. Most of it should have flooded."

Isabella shoots me a look. "Uh, shouldn't we be grateful about that? I mean, if the park was razed, we'd be pretty much dead."

"I guess Malicia isn't ready to close down yet." I stare at the skies, shaking my head.

"You dragged us out here. What's your plan now, Isabella?" Joaquin asks.

She scans the horizon, searching, until she finds what she's looking for.

"Over there." She points to the remnants of a dock area, where some sort of storage shed is half submerged. "According to the docs I downloaded, it says they kept WaveRunners in there for the tourists." She turns to me. "Does that sound right to you, Ray?"

I sigh. "At one time they did. But that was a long time ago."

"If we're lucky, there may still be one inside with enough gas to reach the mainland."

Joaquin sighs. "That's a lot of ifs and assumptions."

She locks eyes with me. "I'm actually surprised that there's a possible way off this island and you didn't tell us before. Why's that?"

"We weren't desperate enough to swim out there before," I explain as calmly as I can. "I think I might be able to make it all the way, hop on a WaveRunner, and swing by to pick you guys up. Then we can hightail it out of this shithole."

"Don't those wave running thingies only fit two people?" Her eyes pan the horizon.

Ray grins. "We'll make it work, I promise."

Joaquin's fidgeting, struggling to breathe, and I rub his shoulders. "If you get there, and there's no WaveRunner or gas, you'll have to swim back here, too."

"What's the problem with that?" Isabella asks, looking as if she's getting annoyed.

"Tiburones!" Joaquin says. "These waters are infested with sharks. Even if Ray makes it to the shed, there's no way he's going to cheat death a second time and get back here. He'll be stuck out there."

I give him a hug. "I'm willing to take the risk."

"You mean you're willing to die by suicide." Joaquin looks like he's on the verge of tears.

"I can make it to the shed and come back for you guys," I continue. "Besides, do you see those dark clouds on the horizon? There's another storm front moving in. We'll be forced to go back inside the park. I don't see how that's going to be any safer. Me swimming out there is worth the risk."

"Imagine if we would have gotten caught on that mountain during a storm?" Isabella says to Joaquin pointedly.

Joaquin's not ready to give in. "Let's find something and create a signal fire. A recon plane might see it and send help. We have to try—"

I shake my head. "Everything's pretty wet out here. Besides, any fire we start will get snuffed out the moment that incoming storm hits us."

"Then we'll burn down another section of the dome if we have to." Joaquin hugs me fiercely. "I won't let you go on some suicide run because you blame yourself for what happened to Sofia."

"This is not about Sofia—"

"You're right. It goes deeper than that. Your brother. You still feel guilty about what happened to him on this island. But it's not your fault. *None* of it is."

I gently break the hug and stare into Joaquin's eyes. "Just remember. I never meant to hurt any of you. No matter what it looks like. I'm going to prove it. I'm getting you both safely off this island."

Isabella laughs. "Actually, you're not. See you around."

What the hell does she mean by that?

Before I can stop her, Isabella takes a deep breath and dives into the ocean, swimming toward the distant shed.

"Izzy! Come back! Damn it! I should be the one doing this!" I shout after her.

ISABELLA

I'm exhausted. Every muscle aches as the shed grows closer. The others must think that I'm bat shit crazy for doing this, but I have no choice. After losing Sofia, none of it matters anymore. Not the documentary. Not Northwestern. Not even Joaquin and his secret. Her death has left a hole in my heart that nothing will ever be able to fill. I just need to get as far away from this terrible place as I can, even if that means swimming all the way back to Miami. I think part of me doesn't think I could actually make it and was at peace with that. But spending one more day on that island is not an option.

I struggle to scramble out of the water and onto the storage shed. I've come this far and can't give up.

Maybe Ray and Joaquin deserve a shot. Even though I

haven't trusted Joaquin since I found out the truth, Sofia thought there was another side to the story. If I die right now without at least trying for the WaveRunner, it could mean their only chance off this death trap dies with me. I need to do this. If only to make up for all that time and energy I wasted into capitalizing on other people's lives online just to get clicks.

I finally pull myself out of the water, reaching for a metal railing—coño! It breaks free, plunging me downward toward the dark seas.

Something bursts free from the ocean between us, a mass of teeth and claws.

My heart's racing. I choke on a mouthful of sea water. What the hell is that? Beneath the surface, a giant shadow appears. Whatever's down there is huge.

I've wasted too much time already. I finally pull myself out of the water and race for the shed, throwing the rotting wood door open. My heart leaps. There's a WaveRunner inside. I rush to it and check the gas tank. Half full. That should be enough to pick up Joaquin and Ray and haul ass to the mainland. It had better be. But what about that thing lurking in the water? No. Can't think about that now.

I waste no time untying the WaveRunner from its moorings and pushing it out to sea, quickly climbing aboard. I turn the key. Nothing happens. Hijo de la gran puta! As I curse, the engine finally sputters to life.

I can barely contain my whoops and hollers as I squeeze the lever on the handlebar and gun the engines toward shore to pick up Joaquin and Ray, bouncing on the rough waves of the approaching storm, doing my best not to tip over, despite my speed.

For the first time since this whole ordeal, I feel a rush of excitement, the wind whipping through my hair, cleansing me from the stench of Malicia, my obsession with documenting. The sense of freedom is short-lived. Giant claws shoot out from the ocean toward me. I swerve, losing my balance and toppling into the sea. For a few seconds, I'm disoriented in the murky water. Then I break the surface, gasping for breath.

Above me, the behemoth looms, a ghastly maw that's enormous, elongated. The creature's crimson eyes pulsate as they leer at me. I can only stare in stunned silence as the WaveRunner is ensnared by the grotesque claws and glistening fangs, quickly torn apart, the pieces mangled together and tossed like sheets of crumpled paper.

It all finally makes sense in the twisted way of this new bizarre world we're living in. That behemoth. It's La Reina de los Chupacabras, escaped from its tank back at the Malicia exhibit. It's grown some, and given birth, based on the gooey remnants of the egg sac dangling from its abdomen.

Defeated, I start swimming back to shore, debating if I should just end it right now and let La Reina take hold of me, rather than play this cat and mouse game. I expect to feel those powerful claws wrapping around my body any second now, squeezing tight until I'm pulp, like the WaveRunner.

But nothing happens. It's as if La Reina has lost interest. Or maybe I'm not worthy. It doesn't matter why.

Somehow all the legends we grew up with are all real enough to touch us with their claws, their fangs.

Adrenaline propels each stroke, my arms slashing the water like knives cutting through the surface. Ray was right. The séance seems to be our best shot at gaining answers.

I pause a moment to catch my breath and see shapes waiting on the shoreline up ahead. Ray and Joaquin. Ray dives in and swims toward me, carrying me to shore, back to the prison I'm so desperate to escape.

There's growling all around us. The three of us look up. Approaching from either side of the shoreline are creatures, short and hunched, with a row of spikes down their back, and red, pulsating eyes.

"Chupacabras," I mutter through labored breath.

As they approach, the lead raises its head, revealing a missing eye. Just like that one stone Chupacabra statue hanging from the castle like a gargoyle, that greeted us when we first arrived. Somehow, after everything that's happened, I know it's the same one.

The three of us lock hands and start walking, slowly at first, until we're running back toward the entrance to the underground tunnels. I glance behind us and pull the others to a stop. The Chupacabras aren't chasing us. Instead, they're positioning themselves around the perimeter of the island like hideous sentries.

The three of us plop on the beach, breathless, trembling from the cold sea. I'm not sure how long we stay that way, but as soon as the first flash of lighting and rumble of thunder hit, the spell is broken.

"This island isn't going to let us leave, verdad?" I ask no one in particular.

Ray shakes his head. "I don't think so. This island—whatever

IT is—has a plan. It could have killed you, the same way It destroyed the WaveRunner. But It let you live."

Joaquin sits up. "It needs you alive . . ."

There's another lightning strike, which illuminates the silent Chupacabras, followed by a powerful burst of thunder that rattles the entire island. The rain begins to fall. First, cold pellets, quickly turning into an onslaught.

"Let's get inside." Ray moves through the doors into the tunnel.

I tug his arm. "We can't go back in there. That's what la isla wants us to do." Joaquin nods. "We should try and get to the mountain like I wanted."

"We can't do that in the middle of a storm. If you stay out here, you'll either catch pneumonia or end up a Chupacabra snack," Ray shouts over the peals of thunder and pelting rain. "We'll figure this out, Joaquin. Together."

Ray grabs both of our hands as the three of us stumble through the door, descending into the dark access tunnel.

"It's too dank in these tunnels," he says. "We have to go back into the park and get out of these wet clothes."

Neither Joaquin nor I say a word, but our expressions do all the talking. We're terrified of going back inside, but too tired and cold to argue.

We trudge the rest of the way in silence, finally reemerging into Paranormal Place. All around us are snatches of sounds, as if someone is scanning through stations on the radio. The hustle and bustle of crowds on a busy park day. Peals of laughter, music, fireworks, echo all around us. Is that the smell of buttered cocalecas in the air? Candy? Fresh burgers?

Don't forget tonight's Specters Soiree at midnight, a voice echoes from the speakers. *It promises to be the attraction of the century, a real heart-stopper!*

I cover my ears and weep.

RAYMUNDO

By the time Joaquin and Isabella manage to join me in the mausoleum, I've already set things up for the séance. Using chalk, I've drawn a large circle containing a pentagram. The top of the five-pointed star is pointed directly at the spot where Rudy was shot and killed.

"Are you sure you know what you're doing?" Isabella asks. "I mean, do we really want to open up more channels into the world beyond in such a paranormally charged place?"

I nod. "I've never been more sure of anything in my entire life. That's why we have to do this now."

"What's the point of all this?" Joaquin surveys the scene with anxious eyes.

I take a deep breath. The time has come to finally come clean with them. "There's something I've been keeping from you all. I don't know why. Maybe I was ashamed. Maybe it was fear."

Isabella locks eyes with me. "I'm not sure I like the sound of that."

"You can tell us whatever it is, Ray. No judgments."

Isabella shoots him a look. "I should hope not."

I knew at least Joaquin would be open. "You both know that this is where my brother was murdered. Right where the pentagram is pointing." I nudge my chin in that direction, barely able to look at it.

Isabella nods. "Ay, Ray. Lo siento mucho. So sorry. But why should you be ashamed of that?"

Joaquin gives me a hug. "It wasn't your fault."

"I thought if I could just speak to him one last time . . ."

Isabella shakes her head. "I'm not trying to be cruel, but you really think these types of ceremonies work?"

I pull out an old scroll from my backpack. "I found this old invocation in my family albums. It's supposed to be really potent. But it has to be performed at the place of death, with four participants who fit certain criteria."

Joaquin is shaking his head. "I said it before. I'm not sure we should be messing with this stuff."

I grip his arms, staring intently into his eyes. "With everything that's going on, maybe Rudy can shed some light on what's happening here. Please, pana. I really need to try. I'll beg if I have to."

He hesitates, then nods.

I turn to Isabella. "And you, Izzy?"

She chuckles. "After what I've seen, I'm definitely a believer—and no, I won't be recording it for my channel."

I place Rudy's cap in the center of the pentagram. Then I

position everyone sitting cross-legged inside the circle, one of us at three of the remaining points of the star, reserving the one to my left for my backpack and Sofia's Bach book. Joaquin is at the point to my right, and Isabella's sitting at his right.

"Whatever you do," I warn, "make sure not to break the protective circle around us."

I place black candles in holders, one for each point in the star, and one for its center, lighting only the central one. Then I look up at them through the flickering flame. "Since Sofia . . . since she isn't with us . . . you'll notice I've included her favorite book in her position. Hopefully, it will channel her energy."

They both nod.

"Spirits of those who have passed," I begin. "Please listen to our call through the veil. Only those beings of love and light are welcome in this circle." Using my candle, I light the point facing the spot where Rudy died. "For the love that was taken." Then I light the candle in front of me. "For the love that was left behind." I proceed to light the candle in front of Sofia's position. "For the past love." Isabella's candle is next. "For the chaste love." Then I hesitate a moment before lighting Joaquin's candle. "For the new love."

At my instruction, we all repeat these words three times. At first, nothing happens. I'm crestfallen. All that planning, all that subterfuge for nothing. My emotions start to boil over; I brought everyone here needlessly, and now Sofia is dead, and I'm the only one to blame.

An icy wind picks up out of nowhere. The candles start to flicker and the temperature drops. Not just a few degrees either. In seconds, our breaths are visible as frosty plumes.

Then a feeling of warmth and light. I look up.

It's Rudy. My brother. He looks exactly like I remembered him. Fresh-faced and innocent, the cowlick in his hair, big brown eyes.

Joaquin and Isabella are stunned, but I'm in the fevered throes of a dream.

I literally slump from the weight of all the emotions I'm feeling, reliving the agony and heartbreak of his death, and experiencing the utter joy of having him with me again.

"Rudy? Is it really you?" I ask, terrified it's just my addled mind playing tricks on me after the stress of everything that's happened, and he'll be gone the moment I blink.

"Hola, carajito!" he says.

Then we're hugging each other fiercely, me lifting him in my arms, twirling him around while making sure to stay in the circle, tears streaming down my eyes, followed by laughter. He's not a ghost. He feels real, if a bit on the cold side.

Reluctantly, I set him back down again, staring deep into his eyes. "Is this really happening? Or am I going crazy?"

His chuckle sparks my heart.

"I'm really real, carajito." He pulls away looking me up and down. "You got so big. Bigger than me!"

The tears are coming faster than I can wipe them away. "I've been waiting so long for you to come home again. I missed you." He gives me a peck on the cheek and buries his face in my chest.

"I'm here now," I whisper in his ear. "And I promise I won't ever leave you again."

"Never ever?"

"Never ever. I'm so sorry I wasn't there when . . . when you got hurt, Rudy. Por favor, forgive me."

"It's good that you weren't here. It would have been bad for you if you'd stayed. Very bad."

I don't care if this is some sort of delusion or breakdown. It feels so real. Rudy feels real, the smell of the sweet shampoo in his hair filling my nostrils, his candy-coated fingers, every detail just as I remember.

We stay huddled together like that for a while, until I finally, reluctantly, pull away. "What have you been doing all this time, Rudy?"

"I was lost. It was so dark and fuzzy. And I was really, really afraid I wasn't going to ever see you again. But he told me if I concentrated real hard, you'd hear me and come back to me again. And I did think, harder than I ever have, over and over, and then things weren't as fuzzy anymore, and I saw the lights, like on my birthday cake, and you came home." He looks at me, eyes glistening with tears. "Por favor don't leave again, carajito. It's scary here without you."

I grip him gently by the shoulders, our roles reversed for the first time. It breaks my heart to see my big brother as he really was. A frightened child himself. "I'm not going to leave you again, Rudy. I promise you. But you said someone told you to call me back here so I can find you. Who is that?"

He looks away, sheepishly. "I'm not supposed to say."

"Aw, c'mon. Dímelo. Don't we tell each other everything?"

Rudy shakes his head. "If I tell you, he might get mad and make you go away again." He throws his arms around my neck. "Please don't go away again. Por favor."

"I already promised you I wouldn't. There's nothing to be afraid of."

He nods. "I get scared sometimes. There are others here who aren't so nice to me."

Anger warms my blood. "Has someone been scaring you?"

He shakes his head. "Sometimes I hurt though, like the first time when I was hiding in here away from all those loud noises and I got hurt. Bad. A long time ago, I think. There was a lot of blood, but it's mostly gone now. Sometimes, it comes back, especially if he's angry with me."

Rudy's clutching his jacket closed, and I gently pull it away—revealing a series of bullet holes in his Tykes of Terror T-shirt. The same ones as in his autopsy photos.

I rock back on my heels, in shock and despair. I carefully cover the wounds with his jacket again.

"Nothing's going to hurt you again," I say. "From now on, I'll be the one protecting you."

"But who's gonna protect you?" The expression on Rudy's face is one of stark terror.

"You said there were others here. Who were you talking about? The work crews closing up the place?"

"The other people. People who got hurt here and can't ever go back home again. Some of them don't know they've been hurt. But some of them are very angry and want to punish anyone they can. Those are the ones I hide from. And those are the ones that have been getting stronger ever since you and your friends got here."

"It was you that guided Joaquin and me here. You wanted us to see those symbols, didn't you?"

He nods.

"Rudy, there's something really important I need to ask you. Something I've been carrying with me for a very long time."

Now that the time is finally here, I can barely muster the courage to ask the question. What if my suspicions have been right all along?

"When we used to play down in El Nido together, I found a book once. There were all sorts of strange writings in it, bad spells, how to make bargains with bad things. I even tried to cast one of those spells myself, one day, when I was really angry with Mai and Pai. Do you remember that?"

"Yes, I know what book you mean," he says.

Fresh tears are streaming down my face. "Was it me, Rudy? Did I summon . . . summon the demon El Bacá? Am I the reason you and all those other people died here that day?"

I can't tell if it's Joaquin or Isabella that gasps, but I don't dare take my eyes off Rudy.

He hugs me again and whispers in my ear. "It wasn't you, carajito. It was him."

I feel like a crushing weight has been lifted. All these years of blaming myself for the massacre, thinking I had caused it, to finally find out all of that guilt was for nothing. A lump forms in my throat. I look deep into his eyes. "Quién, Rudy? You have to tell me. You're my brother. Who made the deal with El Bacá? Who's responsible for what happened here? I need to know. Rudy, please. You've got to tell me. Dímelo!"

"Ray, calm down!" Joaquin cries. "We have to stop this!"

Joaquin gets up to leave the circle and I push him back down.

"You can't break the circle, pana! I need to know."

"It was Pai," Rudy says. Then he turns to Joaquin and points. "And he's a part of it. He was here when it happened."

Joaquin springs to his feet and crosses over the circle.

There's a gust of wind and Rudy vanishes.

It feels like my heart's been ripped to shreds, like Rudy's died all over again. "No Rudy, wait. Please don't go. I love you so much. I . . . love . . ." I tumble out of my chair, knocking over the candles and smearing the circle.

Joaquin hunches down beside me. But everything Rudy said has confused me. When he reaches out, I recoil. "What did Rudy mean, Joaquin? And why did you try and stop him from telling me? Dímelo!"

I've never directed so much anger at Joaquin. But I need to know what the hell just happened. Instead of answering me, he turns to Izzy, but she's just shaking her head.

"Why are you keeping up the charade, Joaquin?" she asks. "Just tell him. Come clean."

"Stop it!" He shouts, his face a mask of fear and desperation.

I turn to Izzy. "Tell me what? Something's been going on between the two of you for a while now. Might as well put it all on the table."

Isabella looks at Joaquin again. "You should be the one to tell him. Not me. Ray deserves to hear the truth from your mouth."

"What truth?" I ask, trying my best to control my anger at Joaquin. "It's okay, pana. Really. I'm not going to judge you. I just need to understand."

He glares at Isabella, then clears his throat. "I've been to Malicia before."

I sigh. "So what? It's no big deal. So have millions of other people. That couldn't have been all that Rudy meant."

He looks like he's on the verge of tears. "I didn't just visit the park with my parents on any random day. I was here. The day that it happened. The day of the massacre."

My jaw drops. When I look at him again, it's like I'm staring at a stranger, a stranger I don't quite trust anymore. "You're him? You're . . . the sole survivor?"

He can only mouth a yes.

I shake my head. "I don't understand. We've been close for years now. How is this even possible? Why didn't you tell me before?"

So many emotions seem to flash across his face. Guilt. Betrayal. Despair. I desperately want to understand how he could have done this to me.

"I've wanted to tell you for a long time now. But I was afraid to." He looks away, unable to meet my gaze.

"Scared of what?" I shout. "We hit it off right away when we met. It was just a coincidence we're both connected to this place—" My thoughts grow dark. A coldness wraps around my heart. "It wasn't a coincidence that we met, was it?"

He swipes at the free-falling tears. "No. It wasn't a coincidence. I specifically sought you out. I planned it."

"But I would have recognized your name—"

"After the massacre, my grandparents adopted me and changed my last name so I could escape all the notoriety and try and have a normal life. But I couldn't escape the emptiness. I figured if there was one person who could help give me closure . . ."

He takes a deep breath and continues. "I tracked you down

online. Finding out what private school you attended. My abuelos agreed to let me transfer there under the pretense they had a good film program I was really into. Arranging an 'accidental' meeting in the hallway, where we were both 'surprised' to discover we enjoyed many of the same horror movies you'd posted about online."

All I feel for him is contempt right now. "You stalked me. Spied on the guy whose family is responsible for destroying yours."

"That's not true. I mean. At first, yeah. I was curious to see what you were like, what made you tick. If you could relate to what I was going through. I mean, you had lost your family, too. But the more I got to know you, the more we grew closer—"

"Except everything we've shared has been a lie, hasn't it, Joaquin?"

He can't say a word. Can't even look me in the eyes.

My heart's breaking. My blood's boiling. How could he? I thought we . . .

Joaquin reaches out for me.

"Don't touch me! I hate you!"

I push him away in a blind fury and he goes sprawling. "Get out of here, now!" He dashes out of the mausoleum, ignoring Isabella's pleas, while I pound my fists against the marble floor, leaving bloodied prints.

JOAQUIN

Ray and Izzy have been holed up by the fireplace in the inn, so engrossed in the files from Izzy's laptop that they never heard me sneak back in. I'm hidden just out of view on the second floor landing, hanging onto every word, wishing I could look at Ray face to face. But I'm afraid of what he'll do to me. Maybe now even more so than I'm afraid of what El Bacá will do, now that it's more than likely that I'll fail my mission. Izzy looks up from her computer screen. "So your family was going through some deep financial shit, then all of a sudden things turn around and everything your dad touched turns to gold, until the massacre here at Malicia."

Ray's eyes meet hers over the top of the book he's been buried in. It's a history of the island that he lifted from a souvenir shop called Creepsakes before we had our big blowout. "Yep. And after the massacre, my father lost everything. Completely broke. Not a pot to piss in."

"Talk about a reversal of fortune." Izzy sighs. "So you aren't in the least bit worried about Joaquin? He could be out there facing God knows what—"

Ray slams the book closed and sets it on the table. "I don't trust him, Izzy. Who knows what else he's lying about?"

My heart sinks. He's never going to give me the chance to explain. And if I'm really honest with myself, I can't say that I blame him.

"Hey! I think I found something!" Isabella announces, pulling up a new full screen window large enough for me to see it. She glances in my direction and I can't help but think she knows I'm here and is trying to help. "According to these security footage logs, the head of security, one Orlando Ortega, purged the system of this footage but kept a copy in his own private files."

She taps on the play button and a clip shows grainy footage of a half dozen hooded figures lowering a chained, oblong box into an excavated tunnel. There's a very familiar symbol visible on the lid of the box, that horned figure with the letter 'B' emblazoned on it. Its mark. My heart's racing. Once the box is lowered into the ground, the hooded figures begin the process of covering it in cement before the video abruptly cuts off.

Isabella looks up. "According to the notes, this Orlando guy died in the massacre less than a week later. He was beheaded."

Ray leans forward. "Wait a sec. Let me play that again."

He taps the play button and allows the clip to replay, and all I can do is watch, helpless to stop them from peeling away at the truth.

As soon as the clip is over, Ray slams his palm against the table. "I knew I recognized that box and that tunnel! When I was alone in El Asilo, I came across that excavation site, except that chained box or coffin or whatever the hell it was had been removed by the work crew. They must have dug it up after all these years. But what's inside it?"

I feel like I'm about to throw up. They're learning too much.

"I'm one step ahead of you, Ray." She fast forwards through the footage and freeze frames on the symbol on the coffin-shaped box.

Ray nods. "I remember seeing that symbol when we first came through the gates at Boneyard Bayou. But I don't remember it from when I was a kid. I suppose we can't look it up without any Wi-Fi, huh?"

Isabella smiles. "No need to. I ran a cross-check in the system and found this." She taps a few keys and the symbol appears full screen, accompanied by text that makes my mouth go dry.

Ray studies the screen. "El Bacá. It says here he was rumored to be the inspiration for the park mascot, Master Crawly himself."

She nods. "You can give yourself a ten out of ten for that one, Ray. Yes. El Bacá is a demon, some believe the devil himself. It's also a shape-shifter and can be conjured by those seeking to make a deal for wealth, power, or whatever else one desires in exchange for some grand sacrifice."

Ray shakes his head. "It's all beginning to make sense now. My father, son of a bitch that he is, made a deal with this demon, but something went wrong. Probably my father got greedy, and he double-crossed El Bacá, trapping It somehow and burying It in that tunnel. That ended the deal, and then the massacre happened as a result. This Orlando person, one of the only people who knew what went down, was one of those killed, so there was no one left to reveal it."

Isabella nods. "Until the work crew came through, uncovered El Bacá's prison, and accidentally released It."

"Or deliberately released It. The only thing we don't know is what Joaquin has to do with any of this."

Isabella closes the laptop. "All this time we've been thinking this is a haunting, that all the park monsters were coming to life, but it's only El Bacá. We've just been encountering different parts of It, pieces of the whole."

"We need to find out what it is El Bacá wants and how to stop it. The rescue team will be here before tomorrow, and by then we'll be out of time."

Isabella gives him a hug. "I'm still exhausted from that swim. Let's get at least an hour's rest before Malicia throws something else at us."

But I can't rest. I should, but the anxiety welling inside me is like a live wire.

Ray and Isabella are so close to finding out everything. By tomorrow morning I could be dead, or worse. El Bacá doesn't forgive failure.

I watch them a little longer from my hiding place. Unbelievably, Ray's dozed off. I can hear his light snoring and wish I could crawl in next to him, and pretend we still have a future to be excited about. But my time of being able to share anything with him has probably dwindled down to mere hours at this point.

Even Isabella finally nods off, after spending an eternity fidgeting with her camera and laptop.

I sneak back out of the inn, desperate, not knowing where else to go. I can hear noises all around me. Some subtle. Footsteps. The beeping of a cash register as a server calls out an order number. The sound of murmuring.

El Bacá won't relent until I do what It wants me to do. Sacrifice Ray Delvalle. I have to get him up to that mountaintop somehow.

In addition to feeling like I have to throw up again, I have to take a piss. It would only take a few seconds to reach the bathroom just across the way, another minute or so to do my business, and a few more seconds to sneak back into the inn and find a way of reasoning with Ray. Piece of cake. Easy.

Something creaks. The sound of a turnstile. Someone unseen trying to board a ride. Cold sweat saturates my forehead, and I swipe it away with my forearm. The sensation in my bladder intensifies. I dart across the pathway and duck into the bathroom.

The place looks like a funeral home, all paneled in dark wood, with each stall door resembling the lid of an old-fashioned wooden coffin. A light blinks to my left, and I almost shit myself.

It's a Nimita, flitting above el zafacón, which is overflowing with trash. But unlike the fireflies that Ray and I saw before, this one's glow is dark and murky. It finally perches on the trash can, like it's staring at me, until I finally look away.

I opt for the first stall, but it's locked, which makes my heart skip a beat. Is there someone else in here? Cautiously, I squat and peer under the stall door. No feet visible along the entire row.

I go to the second stall. Same thing. Locked. In rapid succession, I try the next door and the next, locked as well. Why are all these stalls locked if there's no one inside them? The only door that's wide open belongs to the stall on the very end.

I hesitate. I could just slide underneath to the closest stall. But that would mean making contact with the floor. Germs. Bacteria. Serious staph infection. I almost chuckle at myself worrying about something like disease or illness when I have a demon on my tail that's demanding I do its bidding or it will devour my soul.

The pressure in my abdomen is too great. And again, that deep sense of decorum prevails. I hurry inside the last stall and take care of what I need to. I just finish zipping up my pants when the restroom door creaks open and freezes me in place.

"Raymundo?" I call out, before I can stop myself, like one of those stupid movie characters that's about to get slaughtered.

The lack of response chills me to the bone. It must have gotten twenty degrees colder in here. As I breathe in through my nose and out my mouth, puffs of icy breaths come forth. There's no sense calling out again. Ray would have answered. So would Isabella if she had for some reason decided to visit the men's room.

The familiar treadmill sprint of my heart begins. Can't breathe. Another sound. Slow footsteps, tapping against the tile floor, echoing down the row of stalls.

What are you waiting for, Joaquin? Get on the floor and peek under the stalls, get a good look at what's coming for you. Can't move. I can hear something tinkering with the lock on one of the stalls on the other end. Then whatever it is starts singing and it chills my blood. The voice is raspy, androgynous, mocking the voice of a child as it sings an old nursery rhyme, the Dominican equivalent of Patty Cake:

Doctor Jano, cirujano.

Hoy tenemos que operar.

Doctor Jano is a surgeon, and today we have to operate.

Images of Sofia's fate at the hands of El Ratoncito Perez come to mind, and I start to shake. Click. The lock gives way and whatever it is pushes the stall door open with a loud creak, before moving on to the next stall.

En la sala de emergencias

Un paciente lo espera.

In the emergency room, a patient waits for you . . .

Another click, and that stall door creaks open. Then the next stall door lock is picked open, then the fourth, and the fifth. Click. Click. Click.

And all the while that blood-curdling parody of an innocent children's song, getting louder and closer.

Pero recuerde que es un loco cirujano

Con tijeras en las manos y cuchillos en los pies.

But remember he's a crazy surgeon with scissors in his hands and knives on his feet.

El Bacá has come to punish me for my failure.

So sweet. I can taste it. Un esquimalito?

"Izzy?"

My eyes spring open.

I was having a dream. But it felt so real. I can still taste the sugar on my tongue, smell the tantalizing sweets wafting in the air—

"Izzy?"

That voice. Calling my name. That's not part of the dream. I sit up, looking all around me. Joaquin's still gone. Ray's sound asleep. I grip the tripod at my side. I need to be on my guard.

"Izzy?"

I look down at my lap. It's coming from the earbud connected to my camera. I pick up the camera and glance through the viewfinder. According to the indicators, there's a recently recorded video. Imposible. I just woke up. There's no way I could have shot anything. I don't sleepwalk.

I lift the earbud and hesitate a second before nestling it in my ear. Then I press play. Images of Paranormal Place come to life. Whoever shot this started at the entrance to this region, at the display of giant ghosts twirling in mid-air, seemingly not connected to anything visible. The movement of the camera is very fluid, as if whoever shot this used some sort of steady-cam accessory. The camera pans across the façades of numerous rides—wait. What's that?

Materializing out of thin air are hundreds of glowing lights fluttering about. Las Nimitas. But the fireflies transform into orbs of varying shapes, sizes, and intensity, many coalescing into more substantive forms, strolling through the park.

"Izzy?" There's that voice again coming from the video.

Ray's still sleeping. Where the hell is Joaquin? I suppose I should wake Ray so we can both go look for—

"Izzy?"

The recorded image shifts, as if the user has switched the camera to selfie mode. I squint against the glowy screen. I can't make out who it is. The camera's too tightly focused. An eye encased in cataracts fills the screen.

"Izzy?" The voice half croaks, half whispers, sending icy shivers crawling up my spine.

Before it can speak again, I rip the earbud from its nesting place. But I can't stop watching. The video turns away from that grotesque eye, panning left to right as whatever's recording this wanders through Paranormal Place. I recognize most of the surroundings from our own trek through the park. Ahead, it's the Psychic Inn, the same one we're hiding in now.

My heart's pounding against my chest to be let out as the video reveals the interior of the inn and both our sleeping forms: Ray and me. Something grotesque was right here, beside us, watching us while we slept, and we never had a clue.

RAYMUNDO

"Ray, wake up!"

The voice comes from far away. I don't want to pay it any mind. Kind of like how I would roll away from my mother's voice as a kid, burrow myself under the sheets, not wanting to go to school. It's the same feeling now. I want to stay in a deep sleep. Sí. No worries when you sleep like the dead.

Hands shake me. For one blissful moment, a feeling of relief washes over me. This whole ordeal has been nothing but a nightmare. I'll wake up and laugh about it with Joaquin, relishing his smile as I tell Sofia I dreamt she was murdered, that I, in fact, was the one that murdered her. She'd probably make some crack about fitting one of my particular organs in one of El Ratoncito's very little jars unless I stopped being lazy and woke up.

271

"Raymundo! Wake the fuck up!"

It's not Sofia's voice. It's Isabella. The delusion is shattered. My eyes pop open and I spring up. "Qué pasa?"

She's hunched over me, eyes wide, camera around her neck at the ready. "Something visited while we were both asleep, took my camera, and shot this."

"Joaquin?"

She shakes her head and hands me the camera. I look through the viewfinder as she fast-forwards the footage. But all I can think about is Joaquin.

"Do you know who that was in the footage?" I ask distractedly.

"No clue." She snatches the camera away. "The bigger question is *what* was in the footage? Ghosts? This place is crawling with them."

I nod. "Maybe we should try and find Joaquin first. Whatever he may have done, I don't want him getting hurt." I turn to leave.

"What are you doing?"

"We have to go look for him now."

Before she can argue, I grab my pack and I'm off, leaving her to scramble after me. Cupping my hands around my mouth, I call out Joaquin's name. "Joaquin, can you hear me? Yo, Joaquin!" Nothing. My heart's sick. If anything's happened to him, too—

Something on the floor catches my eye and I stoop to pick it up. It's a pill. Looks like one of Joaquin's. I hand it over to Isabella for confirmation. "You recognize this?"

She turns it over in her fingers. "Looks like one of Joaquin's anti-anxiety meds."

"That's what I thought." Then there's another. And another. A trail of pills. Joaquin would never be without these unless . . .

"Joaquin!" I call again, unable to hide the panic in my voice this time.

Isabella tugs my arm. "We can't keep following these breadcrumbs."

I pull my arm away roughly. "What are you talking about? Joaquin's obviously in trouble."

"Don't you get it? El Bacá wants us to follow the pills. It's leading us into some sort of trap, using Joaquin as bait."

"You can stay here if you'd like. I won't stand by and lose another member of the Quisqueya Club, even if I currently hate him."

JOAQUIN

lick. Another bathroom stall door down. Just two more to go. Easy, Joaquin. You survived worse than this. Watching your parents get blown away right before your eyes. You're tougher than some poltergeist. But not tougher than El Bacá himself.

Click. This is it. One more door. I'm about to come face to face with the demon that's plagued my life as far as I can remember. Maybe if I beg for mercy . . .

The dreadful singing has stopped. I wait for the inevitable click. And wait. And wait. It doesn't come. Instead, there's a gentle rattling of the lock on my stall door. Insistent but not violent.

El Bacá wants in but is being polite about it.

"Excuse me, anyone in there?" the unfamiliar, androgynous voice says. "This is Malicia Maintenance. The park is closed.

All visitors must leave. If you require any guidance, I'll be happy to assist . . ."

There's a gravelly cackling that makes me break out into gooseflesh. The door rattles more aggressively. Now's my chance.

Ignoring my germaphobe tendencies, I dive under the opening to the next stall, crawling as fast I can, especially when I hear the door of the stall I previously occupied clicking and then creaking open, like all the others.

I could just run out the now-open door of this stall. But the idea of being fully exposed with El Bacá lurking just next door in whatever shape It's assumed is just too fucking terrifying. I need to stay hidden as long as possible until I make my move in the open.

"What's the rush?" That strange voice hisses again. "I'll take you on a private after-hours tour with so many special rides . . ."

I snake under the last stall, slipping as I scramble for the exit door. A loud click from the door. Someone—or something—has locked the restroom door from the outside. I tug it, but it won't budge. There's a loud crash. I glance behind me. El Bacá's in that last stall, the one I was hiding in, and It's really pissed now, smashing it to bits, ripping through the wood, pulling out the pipes from the wall.

Why aren't Ray and Isabella here? They can't be sleeping through all this. All this commotion would have woken them up. With all my strength, I kick the exit door repeatedly, determined to get out.

Behind me, El Bacá's plowing through the interior stall doors, one at a time, sending wood and metal shrapnel raining through the restroom.

"You should have delivered him to me by now, boy," It says. "Now, I'll have to clean up your mess . . . but not before I punish you. Tick. Tock. You're about to run out the clock . . ."

The exit door is starting to give under my onslaught, the wood and hinges buckling with each powerful kick. Just a few more should do the trick. Behind me, the demon is making matchsticks out of the entire bathroom. Then I see Its dark, bulky shadow emerging from the wreckage, and I turn away before I can get a full look and really go insane.

I thrust my hand through one of the restroom door panels I've broken away, scrambling for the rusty master key I can glimpse jutting from the lock. I twist it, and in my panic, I almost dislodge it. But I'm rewarded with a welcome click this time. I give the door a final kick and propel myself through.

"Bring him to me now, or pay the price," the thing hisses behind me.

I sprint across the pathway back to the inn to find the others. They're gone. Shit! Where could they be?

"Ray! Isabella!" I call, without getting an answer.

I hear El Bacá smashing Its way out of the bathroom, scrambling toward me in pursuit. Then I'm running and ducking into the nearest shelter. The Carousel of Chaos.

Instead of the usual colorful horses of most carousels, this one features different variations of La Jupia, the spirit of the air's stallions, ready to unleash their devastating effects on humankind.

I hunker down next to one of these horses, getting my bearings while I wait for the demon to pass me by. Its rantings peter out as It moves away, until eventually, It's gone, and everything goes quiet again. That was a final warning. Either I sacrifice Ray or I'm next.

Chuckling behind me. I whirl. There's something moving on the carousel. More than one thing. At least half a dozen sets of glowing eyes are on me, attached to shadowy figures that I can't make out in the darkness.

"Who's there?" I ask reflexively. "Show yourself."

More laughter. Kids.

I remember this ride, Papi holding my hand as we rode the scary-looking steed together. He assured me it was all make-believe, that La Jupia was only a myth, that there was nothing to be afraid of, as Mami dutifully stood on the platform, taking pictures every time the carousel revolved and we were in her loving sight again.

The carousel music comes on at full blast. The ride begins to spin. Faster and faster. The carousel is filled with the chilling laughter of children, but it's going so fast, all I can see is the glow of their eyes. I back away, transfixed, despite the terror gnawing at me.

There's a loud crack in the air. I recognize that sound. It's a sound that's etched into my soul. One that I could never forget. It's the sound of gunshots. One after another.

With each shot, one pair of glowing eyes is snuffed out. It's as if the invisible shooter is using these ghostly children as target practice. Then the realization hits me. What I'm seeing isn't just some random supernatural phenomenon. I'm experiencing the psychic imprint of what actually happened here, when these very real children were murdered.

All the horses' eyes have gone dark. The carousel music warps to its end. The ride finally stops. But the laughter continues.

Give him what he wants, Joaquin, the chorus of dead children whispers all around me. *La Jupia is coming soon. It is coming soon. Then you can ride with us over and over and over again.* . . .

I shake my head in response, backing farther and farther away toward the exit. Tears stream down my cheeks. These poor lost souls, destined to relive the moment of their deaths over and over again. Adrenaline surges through me. I stagger out of the exit in search of Ray and Isabella without daring to look back.

ISABELLA

Ray should have been back by now. What was he thinking? Coño. Here we are doing the one thing you should never do in a horror movie: split up.

How many times had they all gotten together for a movie night and literally screamed at the characters for being so stupid and going their separate ways, and now here we are, our lives hanging in the balance, doing the same thing.

I'll never judge another horror movie character again. That is, if I survive this shit.

To calm my fears, I take out my camera, which at this point has become more of a security blanket. Coño. Battery's at only five percent.

The battery indicator starts to flash, so I shut the camera off, saving the last precious few minutes for something spectacular.

I stoop to look down into the hole again. "Raymundo! Give me a sign you can hear me."

"I'm still breathing, Izzy. Just give me a moment."

His voice sounds strange. Not sure what to make of it. Very emotional. Maybe he really is losing it, just like in that vision I had back at El Asilo.

I turn away, spotting a marquee on one of the shops off to my right.

HECTOR'S SPECTER DETECTORS.

I walk over, glancing through the darkened windows of the shop. According to the displays, they carry everything you need to capture evidence of spectral presences, from EMF detectors, to ectoplasmic sample containers, and special infrared camera systems. What if there's a spare battery in there? It's a long shot but worth investigating. And beats the hell out of staying out here in the open, waiting for Ray or Joaquin to get back.

I reach for the doorknob and barely touch it before the door creaks open, accompanied by the sound of a tinkly little bell. Don't go in, Isabella. If there's a chance I can extend my battery life and capture footage of live ghosts, how cool would that be? But that's not what I'm about now. Northwestern will just have to make due with non-exploitative Isabella. And if that's not good enough for them, there are other colleges to consider. But first I have to get out of this mess.

Ignoring my gut, I step inside. Using the flash from my dying camera, I sweep the area, checking out the aisles meant to store equipment. Most of these are empty, which would make sense, considering they could sell off most of this merch. But there are a few items left, and I grab one of the remaining ghost hunter backpacks and fill it with a couple of EMF detectors, bypassing the ectoplasmic sample containers.

There's a noise off to the right that startles me. Some kind of bumping sound that freezes the blood in my veins. Right next to the aisle labeled Infrared Cameras. What's causing that? I hesitate. I could find exactly what I need in there.

And something I completely don't need. Get out of here right now, Isabella. More bumping noises. It's only a rat. Or the result of the ongoing storm out there.

Just dart in, grab some batteries, and get out. Just a moment. Then you'll be out of the shop, where Ray and Joaquin are probably waiting for you already. The three of us will have a good laugh and get the hell out of this land and find a way off this island.

Taking a deep breath, I flash my light over the area in question. The light dies, leaving me in pitch blackness. I break out into a cold sweat. Fuck my life.

Inching my way into the aisle, I grope around for what I need, my fingers brushing against one empty cold steel shelf after another. I'm about to give up when I feel the familiar shape of camera batteries. I grab a few and shove them into my backpack.

A dim, reddish light zips through the room, like an insect. A firefly. A powerful camera flash comes on, blinding me.

"Are you gonna pay for that, mija?" the strange voice asks.

JOAQUIN

No sooner do I exit the carousel than I run into one of the last people I ever expected to see again: my dead father. My heart practically stops, but I'm too consumed by the sight before me to obsess about that.

He's standing about ten feet in front of me—no, hovering is more like it. The fact that he's standing at all is crazy enough, but his whole body has this kind of glow about it, as if he were a hologram. Aside from that, he looks . . . healthy. No gunshot wounds. No blood. Nothing. He's grinning at me with that infectious smile of his that I remember so well. A flood of emotions breaks through the dam of my fear, tears of joy, of sorrow, streaming down my face.

I know you're shocked to see me, Joaquincito. But you have nothing to be afraid of.

He doesn't speak the words. His lips aren't moving. It's like his voice is being projected into my mind.

"This can't be happening," I say, stupidly, because it is happening, and I'm experiencing every second of it. "You're dead, Pai. I saw you die."

In a manner of speaking, yes. I've . . . transitioned . . . you might say. But it's still me. That's what I've come to tell you, hijo.

His body shimmers, as if it's engulfed by static. Then he disappears and reappears a few feet away.

I know you have questions. I know you're afraid. But everything's fine. I feel better than I ever did when I was alive, at least by your interpretation of the term. I actually feel more alive now than ever. Healthier. More vibrant. De verdad.

His chuckle echoes all around me. He does that static flutter and reappearing thingy, materializing next to me.

You can leave this island and live a long and happy life. The life your mother and I would be proud of, never having to worry about a thing . . .

The sound of his words is like a balm to my brain, a drug, promising the peace I've been craving ever since I was a kid and this whole nightmare began. Imagine, no more obsessing about death. No more looking up symptoms, diagnosing myself with every illness in the book. No more popping pills just to get through the day. No more horrible dreams and waking up night after night shrieking, drenched in a cold sweat. Isn't that what I've always wanted? And here it is, staring me in the face.

I can't control myself. My body's shaking. Tears streaming down my cheeks. Pai's promising everything I ever dreamed of. It almost sounds too good to be true.

"What's the catch?" Because if it's one thing I've learned from being raised in my grandparents' coven, there's always a catch.

My father flutters again. He reappears in the exact same spot.

No catch, Joaquincito. All you have to do is let go of your fears, give in, perform that one simple little task.

"Simple little task? You mean sacrifice Ray? The murder I've been trained for?"

Don't think of it as murder, mijo. A bargain was made that has to be honored. Think of it as a chance to honor your family.

My hope turns to bitterness. "I know what I have to do, but it's so hard, Pai . . ."

Sí mijo. I understand. But It has such grand plans, Joaquin, such vision. And a very special destiny for your friend. Un honor. It's only a matter of time before It can reach out and embrace the whole world.

"You mean El Bacá?"

My father's fluttering more rapidly, disappearing and reappearing at random points around me. The air turns colder, and various crates and park paraphernalia shift and tumble.

It's angry. It knows It overplayed Its hand. And It's shown how desperate It is. With Carlos and Sofia gone, It has no other human minions It can possess to do Its bidding. It needs me now.

You ask way too many questions, Joaquincito. You haven't had a good swat with a chancla to keep you in line.

"You're not my father! You're El Bacá. You're never going to let me go, verdad? I wish it had been me, not Rudy, that died in the massacre. But that wasn't supposed to happen, was it?"

Pai's expression changes to one of sorrow.

Follow your instincts, Joaquincito. Find your strength. It's too . . . powerful. Not to be trusted . . . don't listen . . .

It's my real father now, come to the surface. I try and clasp his hands, but mine go right through. That static electricity between us is comforting. "I have no choice. If I don't do what It says, then I'll have to pay the price. Tell Mai that I love her."

His expression contorts into one of pain. Then he flutters again, and when he reappears, I know my father is gone. Forever this time.

The entity wearing his spirit grins, projecting a malevolence that makes me physically recoil. Then Pai's image transforms to the state he died in, pale, bloody. My legs buckle from the psychic onslaught, draining me. I drop to one knee, head bowed, terrified to look It in the eye.

Bring him to the mountaintop tonight, or your soul is mine.

The malevolent presence fades from my mind, and when I look up, there is nothing there.

ISABELLA

The unseen shopkeeper keeps the bright light pointed at me, blinding me. "We don't tolerate thieves at Malicia, no matter how pretty they are, mija."

I'm grateful I can't see the owner of that voice. It's gravelly, like something clawing its way out of the grave spitting out mounds of desecrated earth.

"I—I wasn't . . . stealing . . . we'll pay you back . . ." With each word, I blow puffs of frost into the suddenly ice-cold shop. I back away, slipping fresh batteries into my camera, holding it in front of me like a shield, shining my flash, despite my fear. Two can play this game.

The thing behind the counter chuckles. "Sí, vas a pagar. You will, really pay, oh, yes . . ."

I still can't make out its face. Just the sound of it shuffling from behind the counter, coming toward me, cutting me off from the exit. Think, Isabella. You're in a ghost hunter supply shop. What is it that they do on TV and in the movies? Salt. I back into the aisle, throwing things out of my way. There it is. Salt. One box left.

"You naughty carajita," the thing says. "Looks like I have a bone to pick *from* you . . ."

I grab the salt, pop the cap off, and sprinkle it in a circle around me, just as the icy fingers graze my back. There's a loud screech that shatters the shop's windows and threatens to burst my eardrums, despite having my palms pressed against my ears.

"Puta," the thing bellows. "No fair!"

All around me there's chaos, the shelves toppling, equipment flying all over the place, shattering against the floor and counter. But nothing touches me. It's as though I'm protected inside an invisible bubble. The realization fills me with confidence.

Bacá's bitch, or whatever it is, can't touch me.

Destruction rains down around me, horrifying and mesmerizing all at once. A splinter pierces my flesh. Everything stops. The bright light goes out. The items whizzing through the shop crash to the floor. All is still. Nothing but blackness all around me.

My confidence dissipates like puffs of frosty breath. Coño. What am I supposed to do now? If I break the circle and try to leave, that demon dickhead will have a clear shot at me. But I can't just sit and wait for Ray or Joaquin to rescue me. What can they do against a spirit that I can't? Besides, the odds are they're dead too.

My heart rate and breathing are in a race. The idea that I

could be the only one alive on this island is too much to process right now. It suddenly feels colder in here. As if I were hunched over a grate instead of the shop's wooden floorboards.

Floorboards.

Panicked, I stare at the tiny gaps between the wood. No. The salt should protect me. I maneuver myself on all fours, careful not to dislodge the barrier surrounding me, pressing my face against the wood, peering into the dark below.

Red eyes blink at me. I scream as the floor collapses beneath me. Next thing, I'm rolling, my body banging against what I assume is the basement stockroom. It tricked me, coming in from underneath. I guess it found a salt barrier loophole. There's something they never tell you about in the movies. There's no bright light aimed at me. Just a swirling outline of mist bubbling from the shadows.

"You thought you were going to get away from me, mija. But I've devoured craftier meals than you and will tear through plenty more once I've swallowed you . . ."

I frantically search my surroundings as the mist advances. Nothing but empty boxes, a couple of uniforms—Uniforms. That's it. It has to be.

I scramble to the uniforms, grabbing the pile, as a force throws me across the room. The pain makes me suck in my breath. Feels like I've cracked a rib or two. But I can't stop. My life depends on it. If this spirit was attached to the counter, it must have worked here once, still tethered to this plain by one of its possessions.

I whip out one of the camera batteries and grab a metal souvenir keychain, jamming it against the positive and negative terminals simultaneously, conducting the electricity until it bursts into flames. Ignoring my burning fingers, I toss it onto the pile of uniforms, praying that at least one of these belonged to my ungracious host. And if I succeed in destroying it, it'll send this thing back to hell.

A force lifts me into the air. I can feel pressure as if I'm being crushed by an invisible vise. Then I'm dropped to the ground. An inhuman howling fills the air.

"Cuero sucia!" the poltergeist screams the curse words at me. "We'll filet your flesh for this!"

The mist coalesces into a fireball, radiating pure hate. Then, just as quickly, it explodes, spattering me with slimy, ectoplasmic fluid before vanishing completely.

I collapse, laughing, crying, grateful to be alive. Until I hear footsteps up above, tromping through the shop. Then descending down the basement steps toward me.

"Isabella!"

I look up to see Joaquin offering me a hand to lift me to my feet. I throw my arms around him, despite the pain in my side.

"I was passing the shop and heard screaming," he says. "What happened here?"

I shake my head. "Never mind about me. We have to get to Raymundo. He might already be dead—"

Joaquin's eyes nearly bulge out of his skull. "Where is he? Tell me!"

I grab my pack and lead the way, hoping we're not too late.

RAYMUNDO

Damn it! Where the fuck are you Joaquin? If anything has happened to him it will all be my fault. More crashing. I stare in disbelief as park benches are flung through the air with such force, they smash through the sides of buildings. All around, pipes are bursting, cables lashing like whips, storefront windows cracking and smashing open, sending sharp, glass projectiles across the park. Edgar's already passed. This is something else completely.

Two figures stumble into view. Joaquin and Isabella, both shielding their eyes against the deadly onslaught. Our gazes connect, and I rush to meet them, the three of us doing our best to dodge the maelstrom of debris, its intensity increasing by the second.

"We have to get out of Paranormal Place ASAP," I say. "Our best bet is the mountaintop." I tackle both of them to the ground, just as one of the carousel horses whips through the air and smashes into the space we were occupying. "Looks like El Bacá's stepped up Its timetable."

I pull them both to their feet but can't bring myself to look Joaquin in the eyes. The three of us run as fast as we can across the path leading from Paranormal Place to the entrance of Angel Falls.

A shard of flying glass propelled by the psychic storm stabs me in the leg and I stumble.

"Help me get him up," Isabella shouts at Joaquin.

They haul me to my feet, half dragging me the rest of the way. I grit my teeth against the pain, trying to ignore the blood oozing from the wound.

Behind us, the paranormal activity is reaching a crescendo, screeching wind, swirling masses of poltergeists swarming through the rides and concession stands, uprooting everything in their path like psychic tornadoes, each swallowing the other, forming a gigantic cyclonic mass headed straight for us.

Joaquin points at the funnel cloud. "I think El Bacá has assumed the form of La Jupia, the spirit of the air. Some dead kids at the carousel warned me she was coming."

I know he's trying to be helpful, but the wound of Joaquin's betrayal is too fresh. He lied to me. But am I really any better?

Up ahead, the exit to Paranormal Place looms. We fight the strong winds, struggling to reach it before we're consumed by that wave of evil.

"We're almost there," I shout, my head reeling from the pain, the storm, the emotions, the blood loss.

LEAVING SO SOON? A voice echoes through the

loudspeakers, so loud that we spot a few of the speakers sparking and ripping free of their hiding places throughout the
park. *YOU CAN'T MISS THE GUEST OF HONOR AT THE
PARANORMAL PARADE. LA JUPIA IS ON THE WAY. AND
SHE'S IN A SACRIFICIAL MOOD!*

Behind us, the maelstrom is quickly approaching, ready to
engulf us. We've run out of time. The cyclonic mass of psychic
energy bears down on us. I can see swirling forms inside, flying
corpses, their jaws opening and closing as if they're chomping at
the bit, ravenous, ready to devour our souls. The hellish funnel's
blocking the exit. I turn to them, probably for the last time.

"Whatever happens to me, get to the mountaintop. That's
the best chance the chopper has of reaching us." I grab Joaquin's
hands. Our eyes lock. I can barely control the flood of tears
streaming down my face. "I believed in you, pana. Why?"

Before he can answer, I thrust my backpack into his hands.
Then I tear myself away and run in the opposite direction, trying to ignore the pain and blood rushing from the wound in
my leg, doing my best to lead La Jupia away from them and
follow me as I head away from the mountain base to clear the
path for Joaquin and Isabella to the rescue chopper.

The glowing funnel cloud's taking the bait, moving away
from the exit in pursuit. Isabella drags Joaquin toward the now-
clear exit as he fights to break free and come after me. But with
the cloud moving in between us, he's blocked.

I squeeze my eyes shut as I hear him call my name, over
and over, killing me again and again with each cry as I fight my
instinct to go to him. I can't. The moment I do, the cloud will
follow.

Something with glowing eyes is moving ahead of me. It's one of the horses from La Jupia's Carousel. Except this one is riderless.

As I approach, I recognize it as the steed Rudy and I would always ride together. There's no way this animatronic horse can be alive and moving on its own. But somehow, it blinks, eyes glowing blue, stopping in front of me, and I know Rudy sent it.

Without thinking, I grab ahold of its synthetic mane and hop on its back, galloping away, leading the deadly force of La Jupia's psychic cloud as far away from Joaquin and Isabella as possible, before turning to face it.

La Jupia herself emerges from the funnel, wind whipping across her dark, naked body, revealing a smooth stomach with no navel. It may be wearing the form of La Jupia, but I know that it's really El Bacá, and that the time has come for me to pay for my father's sins.

My horse rears up on its hind legs and neighs loudly as she approaches, the funnel behind her, waiting to devour everything in its path.

"For you, carajito," I whisper.

I turn back to the cloud. "I'm the one you want. My family built this place. I'm a Delvalle. La misma sangre de mi padre. Take my blood!"

Then I gallop off and the cloud moves in, bent on engulfing me.

JOAQUIN

With Isabella's help, we close the door of the elevator leading into the Angel Falls portion of the park, sealing us off from that deadly storm—and Ray.

Then we flop against the elevator's walls, drained. Even though the rest of my body is numb, my heart hurts at the memory of the way he looked at me before he was ripped away, the pain of betrayal etched in his face.

"He's not dead." My voice feels like it's coming from a million miles away.

Isabella turns to me. "What?"

"Ray's still alive. I can feel it. And he's heading up that mountain. That's where we need to be as well."

"He's dead. You saw him. La Jupia's tornado swallowed him whole . . ."

We both let loose silent tears, holding each other close for what seems like hours.

Isabella finally breaks the spell. She surveys the elevator then turns back to me. "I know we've lost our park guide now. But you've been here before. Where do we go from here?"

I stand, examining the walls, relieved to keep going. If I stop and dwell on Ray, I'll have a total meltdown. The sooner I get us through, the sooner I'll reach the top of that mountain and face my destiny. "This isn't really an elevator. It's designed to look like one. If we pry open the other side of this door, it should lead directly into Angel Falls, the final quadrant of the Malicia experience."

She smiles at me. "You're beginning to sound just like Ray."

"Maybe I'm channeling him." Under normal circumstances, that might be a joke. But we left normal in our rearview miles ago.

"I'm not as up on the lore of this place as you are," Isabella says. "Why would a horror theme park have an area called Angel Falls?"

"It's called Angel Falls as in Fallen Angels, demonios seeking to infect the human race with their progeny."

"Hold up. That sounds like the plot of—"

"*The Infant* movie franchise," I finish for her. "The story of genetically engineered demons that are placed in unsuspecting hosts by Fallen Angels through in vitro fertilization."

"I stopped watching after the fifth sequel."

"This whole Fallen Angel setup at Malicia is a prequel to the entire franchise."

"So, according to the movies, Fallen Angels mate with humans and spawn demons."

"You got it, Iz. Welcome to hell."

Using a tool from Ray's backpack, I jam it into the groove between the doors on the opposite side of where we came in. "Give me a hand with this."

We pry the doors apart, just wide enough to grab our gear and squeeze inside. It's some kind of cathedral, a very large one by the looks of it. Stained glass windows leer down at us from every side, depicting horrific images of a violent battle in heaven between angelic creatures and monstrous beasts. Hanging down from the ceiling above the altar is a massive cross, only it's inverted.

"Subtle," Isabella mutters.

"Not as subtle as those." I point to a row of computer banks resting on the altar.

Isabella nudges me. "What the hell are computers doing in a gothic cathedral?"

"This isn't just a church. It's an archaeological dig."

She follows my gaze down each of the four corridors branching out from our location: long and dark, their stone, gothic design interspersed with sleek computer monitors embedded in the walls. Rows of test tubes and beakers compete with votive candles and incense in an anachronistic mishmash of ancient religion and modern science. As we make our way down one of these passages, the flickering candles create a maze of distorted shadows, as if the place itself is alive. Every ten feet or so, the walls are broken up in intervals by thick metal supports, protruding like vertebrae on an emaciated spine. There are a lot of exposed wires coiled around old, crumbling statues. Only these aren't effigies of saints. They're sculptures of demonic creatures with wings, claws, hooves, massive coiled tails. Trudging through these unnerving corridors feels like slinking through the carcass of some behemoth, maneuvering through its guts. Our steps echo down the corridors, accompanied by the steady moan of the storm raging outside.

We make our way through the catacombs and into what appears to be some kind of monastic commissary, featuring half-eaten food and drink still on stone plates and in stone mugs. But here again, there are signs of the modern world. A tablet. Briefcase. File folders. I lift up the nearest folder and glance at the label.

Bacá Project

The circular, horned symbol is engraved on the folder, just like it was carved in those trees at Boneyard Bayou and on that chained box Ray's father buried underneath the park.

I leaf through the folder and scan drawings of El Bacá in different forms. In some, It's a dog with burning eyes made from hellfire. In others, It's a black cat, or a bull. These illustrations are interspersed with clinical jargon dealing with genetics. I set the folder down. I can't shake the feeling there's something I'm missing here.

I point to a serving of meatloaf and cornbread that's still steaming. "Looks like somebody didn't get a chance to finish their dinner."

Isabella picks up a steaming mug and sniffs.

"Lipton® tea." She looks up at me. "What's up with that? This park's been shut down for years."

"Maybe there are more crew members working this part of the park?"

"Posiblemente."

From there, we make our way to the monks' sleeping quarters, where we find bunks that look like they've just been slept in, the outlines of bodies pressed into the spartan mattresses.

A further search reveals a makeshift laboratory in one of the monk's cells, which looks like someone was in the middle of some sort of dissection, though the specimen appears mostly melted.

After a bout of silent exploration, we make our way back to the cathedral's altar and the blinking banks of computer monitors. Of course, there's no Wi-Fi connection.

"What do you think happened here?" Isabella asks, studying some readouts on the nearest monitor.

"I'm guessing in the original ride, there were Malicia cast members who assumed the role of the monks assigned here, but they're all long dead now."

"Here's something interesting." Isabella points to a flashing amber light, accompanied by text on a screen announcing *Bacá Project log, Outgoing Transmission.* "Looks like our missing monks sent one final message before they met their mysterious fate."

I press play.

ISABELLA

here's a burst of static on the computer console before the transmission plays.

Joaquin and I gasp as we recognize both figures on-screen: Sofia and Ray.

At least, they're pretty reasonable facsimiles of the real thing. It's as if the two have been completely body-scanned and converted into photo-realistic computer images, like they do in movies sometimes—to replace dead actors.

The figures are definitely in uncanny valley territory, appearing close to human, but not quite. The eyes are always the giveaway. There's something about them that's off. Soulless.

Instead of their normal clothes, they're dressed in religious robes, hoods around their heads, a circular horned symbol embroidered on their cloaks, accompanied by the text *Bacá Project*.

All of their robes are disheveled, even ripped, in some cases, their faces smudged and scratched, as if they've undergone some kind of crisis.

"Greetings," Uncanny Ray speaks. "This is Brother Delvalle, highest-ranking survivor of the Order of El Bacá."

His voice, while close, also sounds a little iffy, as if recordings of him saying certain words were spliced together into a patchwork of dialogue, resulting in an unnatural rhythm.

"After our order uncovered this ancient church buried in the Arctic ice, we've been able to ascertain that it is indeed built on the location where the angel Bacá was cast out of heaven," Uncanny Ray says. "But after recovering Its body from Its icy tomb and awakening It, we were unable to contain Its evil, and one by one It has possessed our brethren, an evil parasite intent on inflicting pain and suffering on all humanity."

The Sofia clone says, "It's imperative that El Bacá doesn't escape from the isolation of the Arctic and find Its way to civilization."

The Ray doppelganger moves in closer to the camera. "Should El Bacá reach any populated area, It'll immediately enact Its diabolical plan to infect humanity with his progeny, creating an army of demons that will wreak havoc over the earth and enslave every man, woman, and child in a cloak of darkness and despair for all eternity."

Sofia cuts in again. "We have no choice but to initiate the self-destruct sequence and destroy this entire unholy cathedral, or risk outsiders finding this site and becoming possessed pawns for El Bacá's will. The explosive device contains holy—"

The two uncanny brethren whirl as loud banging on the massive arched wooden doors behind them erupts. The camera moves erratically, highlighting the splintering of the doors. Something's determined to break through.

Each of them inputs a code sequence into the console. Flashing amber emergency lights spin and strobe as alarms blare throughout the ancient church.

Emergency destruction sequence has been initiated, a robotic voice says.

Uncanny Ray faces the camera once more. "We pray that our sacrifice will save the lives of countless others. If El Bacá should ever make it back to highly populated cities, It will extinguish the light forever."

Joaquin and I exchange looks.

"Can this get any more cliché?" I ask.

The door behind the uncanny duo bursts open. Then all hell breaks loose.

Screams fill the altar speakers. It's as if something is tossing the camera around. Snippets of running. Close-ups of frightened eyes, splashes of blood as something enters. Is It attacking them? Eating them? Everything's a blur of motion, hard to make out. At one point, something large and dark moves into camera range for a moment and then disappears. Joaquin and I glance at each other.

I force myself to look back at the screen. The pleas of the uncanny duo are growing fainter as they're overpowered by the dark, shadowy figure slinking through the cathedral. There's one final gurgle from one of the victims—I can't be sure who it is—then the image flickers and cuts off for a minute.

When it reappears, the uncanny duo is grinning, horrible, monstrous leers, drool and bile leaking from their mouths, eyes yellow slits, almost reptilian, skin cracked and a sickening gray-green.

Brother Delvalle floats. "You've already lost," he says, his voice deep and gravelly. "We'll eat your souls."

The Sofia-thing cackles like an old crone. "El Bacá is the one true god."

Her fingers dig into her face and she tears away at the skin, layer after layer, laughing and spitting out blood, which drips down the screen in clumps.

"Wherever you go," the Ray-thing says, "we can see you. . . ."

He reaches toward his eyes and digs them out of their sockets, even as he hisses in glee.

Part of me wants to throw up. The other part can't take my eyes off the dark figure barely glimpsed behind the possessed duo. The image erupts into a chaotic montage, an orgy of cannibalism, maniacal laughter, then finally flicks off for good.

"El Bacá did this. It's trying to mind fuck us." Joaquin's as pale as snow.

"What was the point of showing us that at all, Joaquin? And how did El Bacá create those images of Sofia and Ray? Use their voices?"

Joaquin slowly shakes his head, opens his mouth to speak but doesn't say anything.

I try and take a deep breath but notice that's become a little difficult. I'm just about to say something to Joaquin about it when I notice he's studying the readouts near the console intently.

"That wasn't just a pre-show video. The temperature's dropping all through this church," he says through puffs of frosty breath.

"What are you going on about?" I join him at the monitor and stare at the scrolling data. "You mean to say part of the Malicia experience is to actually have visitors freeze to death in arctic temperatures in the spirit of realism?"

"It looks like it is now."

"That's messed up."

The candlelight grows dimmer on cue, and the emergency self-destruct alarms begin to blare, like they did in the video we just saw. Startled, we turn to study the sanctuary door, at least the remnants of it. Whatever crashed through it must have possessed impossible strength, enough to shred thick wood like cardboard.

"This doesn't make any sense. What's to stop us from high-tailing it out of here and going outside, getting fresh air. It's not like we're actually trapped in Antarctica."

"Aren't we?"

"This shit's crazy."

"Let's go." Joaquin pulls me by the arm. "According to the data, there should be one snowcat left outside the church. We need to be on it before this whole place blows."

JOAQUIN

The intense cold's making it very hard to breathe. It's kind of ironic that for the first time I can remember, the symptoms I'm experiencing—shortness of breath, shivering, drowsiness—actually have a physical cause, just as I've begun to get a grip on the manifestations of my anxiety.

Don't think about any of that. Think about getting to that mountain peak. Your life depends on proving your worth.

My knees buckle, and I use an arm to brace myself against an ancient pillar. I point toward a bank of lockers nearby. "The winter gear should be . . . right in there . . . according to the schematics. . . ."

Isabella isn't faring any better than me—maybe even worse. Her skin has a blue tinge, eyes bloodshot.

"I just . . . need a sec . . . to get my . . . bearings," she mumbles.

Problem is, we don't have a sec to spare.

Mustering the last of my energy, I stumble to the lockers. It takes me a couple of tries to get them open. Hand-eye coordination isn't what it used to be when I could actually breathe. I pull out articles at random—thermal underwear, waterproof pants, jackets, boots, hooded parkas—tossing some her way.

We help each other slip into the bulky winter gear, saving the thick, protective goggles for last. The effort is so much that I almost pass out. I can't imagine how cold it must be outside. And then it hits me how crazy this all is. We're off the coast of the Dominican Republic, for god's sake. How can we be experiencing the effects of sub-zero temperatures?

Isabella's teeth are chattering. "Did I mention . . . this is my least favorite ride . . . in the . . . entire park?"

I examine the temperature sensor around my gloved wrist. Almost ten below.

"It'll be warm inside the snowcat's cab."

She pulls the hood of her parka completely over her head. "What if that snow-thingy isn't working? What if it doesn't have enough fuel? What will happen to us then?"

I grip her by the arm. "Can't think about that now. What-iffing is for quitters. We need to get a move on." My voice sounds muffled through the heavy scarf bundled around my neck and head.

I lead the way down through the catacombs. If that schematic I saw on the computer was correct, there's only one more passageway to get through before we reach the doorway leading to the snowcat.

"Wait up!" Isabella grabs me before I can take another step, holding me back.

Something rips through the corridor from floor to ceiling. Something big.

We peer down the edge of the torn floor, revealing several levels of smoking, sparking destruction. Above us, things aren't looking any better.

"We have to find another way to the snowcat."

I shake my head. "We don't have enough time."

"We can't just stand here and—"

"That could work." I point toward a grated opening in the stone wall beside us, hunching down to get a better look. "We might be able to use it to get through to the other side."

I'm already working on pulling the rusty grate open, and with Isabella's help, it finally rips free.

She peers into the dark opening. "I'm not sold on this, but I guess there's no time to debate it."

We whirl at the sound of something approaching us. All I can make out in the darkness, on the far side of the catacombs, are flashes of teeth, claws, and writhing tentacles.

"El Bacá," I whisper.

"Not exactly a rosy-cheeked cherub by all appearances."

Isabella scrambles inside the aqueduct, and I'm right behind her. Because of our bulky gear, it's slow going. Despite the primordial fear and fight-or-flight instinct kicking in, I pause to block the opening with a nearby boulder.

"What are you doing? Let's go!" Isabella shouts.

"As soon as I seal this, I'll be right behind you. Ándale!"

I don't have to tell her twice. She's crawling, disappearing around a corner.

The slimy mass of teeth and flailing limbs is getting closer to the vent. El Bacá has assumed the form of the park mascot, Master Crawly, to terrify me like he did when I was a child. I can catch glimpses of that evil grin, growing wider and wider as It gets closer. At this rate, It'll be large enough to devour me in one gulp as soon as It reaches me.

Just as I succeed in rolling the boulder against the vent's opening, something large plows into it, caving in the opening, practically pinning me against the tunnel. But I squeeze my way out. I crawl as fast as I can, hoping I can make it to the snowcat before I feel those fangs and talons ripping into my body.

Behind me, the vent implodes with a loud crash and rumble of stone. It's inside. And It's after me just like before. But I'm not a kid anymore. And I will prove to It just how worthy I am.

Behind me, the Fallen Angel's thrashing, making horrible screeching noises. But in between, I swear I can hear something else. A voice. Calling out to me. Taunting me. Don't let It in your head. Just reach that mountain. Show It what you're really made of.

There's a light up ahead and something waving. Someone. Isabella.

"Hurry!" she screams, eyes wide in terror, focused on something behind me.

The adrenaline kicks in, and I pick up the pace, slipping through the grate. Something reaches for my leg. Isabella pulls me out just as Crawly, El Bacá or whatever Its real name is rips into my pant leg. Luckily, I'm so heavily layered it barely grazes my skin. The two of us are in the blinding snow, grabbing on to each other for support as we stumble into the cab of the nearby snowcat. Something clutches my leg firmly this time.

There's a deafening slam. I turn around in time to see Isabella securing the door lock. She saved me from El Bacá's grasp.

I yank my booted foot free from the severed tentacle wrapped around it, still jutting from under the cab door. Then I squeeze myself into the driver's seat and start the vehicle. It takes a couple of agonizing tries before the engine finally turns over and roars to life.

"Punch it!" Isabella shouts.

I floor the gas pedal, steering us away from that unholy cathedral. There's a blinding flash and it erupts in a ball of hellish flame.

ISABELLA

We're going to die in this snowcat.

The turbulent aftershocks spin us out of control, buffeting us to and fro. The next few seconds are tense. I'm not sure this vehicle's going to hold together. For a heart-stopping moment, it looks like we're going to roll right off a steep embankment and careen down a mountain. I stifle a scream.

At the last minute, we crash into a small building—a Malicia souvenir shop called Prized Possessions—which jolts us to a stop and prevents us from tumbling over the edge.

A thought hits me. "This is only a ride, right?" I ask Joaquin. "We aren't really on unholy ground in Antarctica."

He shakes his head. "I'm sure that was true when this ride was originally in operation, but so much has happened, who knows?"

When the snowcat's rocking finally settles down, I unbuckle my straps and take out my camera to shoot footage outside the windows, displaying the burning church and the vast, empty loneliness of the frozen tundra.

"Where to now?" I put down the camera.

He's bent over, studying the console display. "I'm not sure where to go next. We have to find a way off this ride and back into the rest of the park."

"Why would we want to do that?"

He turns the key and there's only a click. "That little tumble we just took fried the engine. We're not going anywhere. And after that fire burns out, it'll be forty below around here. No way we can survive that."

"Glad I didn't opt for the annual pass."

Joaquin ignores my sarcasm and heads to the back of the cab, rummaging for supplies. He pulls away a tattered tarp, uncovering a coffin-like glass tube.

"Interesante . . ." he mutters.

I have my camera out in a flash. "What's so interesting?"

"Some sort of stasis tube. This must have been where they kept El Bacá's specimen after they dug it up. Kind of like a hyper sleep thing."

The two of us slump to the floor, exhausted. Silently staring out the windows at the wintry night sky, alive with billions of stars.

I finally break the ice, so to speak. "If the park really does have an agenda, why do you think it took us way out into an arctic wasteland, if that's in fact where we really are?"

Joaquin considers this. "It wants to keep me from getting to Ray."

"How do you know that?"

He stares out the window again. "I think El Bacá wants the park to reopen."

But I'm not listening. I'm staring at the door of the cab.

"We've got other things to worry about right now," I say.

"What do you mean?"

"That tentacle that had you by the ankle and got severed when I slammed the cab door shut."

"What about it?"

"It's gone."

We both stare at the empty space under the cab door and the gelatinous smear disappearing into the shadows.

JOAQUIN

I peer into the dark corners of the cab. So many cracks and crevices the tentacle could have slithered into, hiding, waiting for the right moment to spring and catch us by surprise.

"We have to find It before It finds us," I whisper, more to myself than to Isabella.

"Let's say we do. And then what? El Bacá is demonic. Who knows what It could have morphed into?" she whispers back.

She has a point. Finding it is only half the battle. I mull our options. "It must still be inside the cab here with us."

"You don't know that. Maybe It found a way out and is lurking just outside, waiting to ambush us."

I shake my head. "I'd rather take my chances outside than in such close quarters. I say we crawl out the other door and into the gift shop. Then we mess with the gear shift, tie a weight to the gas pedal—I don't know—something . . . and send this snowcat over the edge and into the canyon, along with our little fallen angel tentacle. Follow me."

I crawl slowly over the passenger seat and try to push the door open. I have to shove it hard before it finally gives.

The two of us stare at each other, the only sounds our heavy breathing and the moaning wind. I muster my nerve and slither out the door, crawling with Isabella at my heels, and make my way into the remnants of Prized Possessions. As soon as we're both clear, I slam the cab door shut, hopefully trapping that tentacle inside.

Besides the chunks of crumbling wall where we crashed through, the shop's floor is littered with the remains of souvenir items. Isabella extends her arm and helps me to my feet.

It's freezing here, too. The temperature must have dropped another ten degrees. We adjust the hoods of our parkas, as well as our goggles, basically covering our entire bodies. If anyone saw us right now, they'd never be able to tell us apart.

When we're done, Isabella hunches over the snowcat's hood and presses both hands against it. "Let's rig something to push the gas pedal, send this thing over the edge and get it over—"

Something slithers through the floor of the shop, sending a display of hooded black robes crashing to the ground. We stumble into each other, cling to each other in fear.

The tentacle is in the shop with us.

"How are we going to flush It out and get It back into the cab?" Isabella whispers.

I point toward the wall in the opposite corner of the shop. "We could use that."

313

I carefully step through the debris and pluck a fire extinguisher from its perch. I give the lever a slight pull, releasing a burst of foamy powder and compressed nitrogen through the hose.

"This should do the trick," I say, not entirely convinced.

Isabella's eyes bug. "Coño. I forgot my camera in the cab."

"Forget it. Remember what happens to people who wander off—"

"El Bacá's thingy is out here, not in the snowcat, remember?"

Before I can stop her, she heads off toward the back of the cab.

It's taking every ounce of self-control to think about the ritual on the mountain peak and keeping the what-if thoughts at bay. I brandish the fire extinguisher like a weapon and make my way into the dark recesses of Prized Possessions, with nothing but the flickering light of the fire raging nearby to guide me.

I get a deep urge to scratch a sudden itch on my forehead and have to fight it because of the thick goggles protecting my face. What if the temperature drops so low the air freezes in your lungs and your heart stops, Joaquin? What if you suffocate, alone in the dark? Get a grip. Don't have time for this shit anymore.

Something long and tubular drops down from the ceiling on top of me, and I nearly have a heart attack. Just some sort of extension cable. I toss it away and plunge deeper into the darkness, my heart doing a drum solo in my chest and ears.

Something makes a squishing sound. I whirl. Was it on the floor? The walls? There it is again.

"Isabella?" I call.

No answer. She probably can't hear me because of the

wailing wind. Up ahead are the remnants of a first-aid kit, strewn across the floor. Someone must have been trying to render aid here when the massacre occurred. I continue my sweep, heading back in the direction of the snowcat. A dark shadow engulfs me, and I whirl. I almost trigger the fire extinguisher before I recognize the shape. Izzy. Arms crossed against her chest. I guess I can't blame her for being moody.

"Carajo. You scared the crap out of me, Izzy. Just stay behind me and keep up."

"Whatever you say."

Something's moving behind a display of Angel Falls T-shirts stashed in the corner. I can't quite make out what it is, but it has to be our little severed friend waiting to ambush me.

Lifting the fire extinguisher and positioning it like a rifle, I slowly make my way toward the display, dreading every step, every breath, as I creep closer.

Who knows what the severed horror that's been stalking us looks like now?

Before I can lose my nerve, I take a deep breath and push away the display rack, barely able to stop myself from letting loose with the extinguisher.

"There's nothing hiding back there, Joaquincito. It was right in front of you the whole time."

I spin and Isabella is grinning, drool dripping from her lips, a big parasite crawling in and out of her mouth, another one around her neck.

"I was wondering how long it was going to take for you to figure things out," she continues in a raspy voice that is so unlike her, at least the non-possessed her.

I swallow hard.

Dark wings sprout from her back, tearing through her suit. She rips off her goggles, revealing glowing, red, reptilian eyes.

"A little splinter pierces the skin, a parasite enters her blood . . . and now your part in this little drama is over, except for the soul I'm going to relish." She licks her lips, her tongue now long and snakelike.

Its face is morphing. Are those Raymundo's eyes? Sofia's nose? Carlos's shape?

"We don't need to wear masks anymore, do we, Joaquincito?" possessed Isabella croaks.

Then she's tearing at her face with sharp claws, tossing chunks of flesh and blood everywhere, revealing a familiar face. Master Crawly. El Bacá.

The child me, the one who's been buried under layers of fear, guilt, and insecurities can hear the blasts of gunshots ringing in my ears, hurting, echoing, smell the stink of spent cartridges and fresh blood, the stench of vomit from panicked victims, their screams searing into my soul. My hands are hot with a gooey mix of blood and brain matter as I clutch at my dying mother, staring down at me with half her remaining face, the other a smoking, unrecognizable crater.

As many times as I've woken up to these images, drenched in the cold sweat of night terrors, there's something different this time, as if the scenes have zoomed out, revealing another perspective I've been unable to face even after all these years. One that I still can't. Not yet.

"I'm not afraid of you anymore." I force myself to hold Crawly's wicked gaze.

Its grin grows impossibly wider and Its cackles raise every hair on my body. "Yes, you are afraid." The face contorts into a snarl. "And now you're going to pay for not delivering on your end of the bargain."

A dark, slimy tentacle shoots out of Its mouth, and I barely have time to dive to the floor, out of Its way.

The thing opens Its mouth and begins to chant in some kind of ancient language. It's deep and guttural, filling the air and rising above the wind. Growing louder. I shudder at the thought of what this ritual represents.

The chanting grows even louder, almost as if it's taunting me, egging me on. Though most of it is unintelligible, one word stands out.

Bacá. Bacá. Bacá.

I dart from my hiding place, rushing toward the snowcat, but something grabs my ankle and yanks me away, slamming me on my back.

Despite the pain, I look up to see the writhing creature that was once Isabella towering above me, slime drooling from Its myriad orifices, tentacles flailing, wings flapping, smaller parasites chittering and suckling against It.

I struggle to get away, but it's like my foot's being held in an iron manacle.

Isabella's abdomen pulls apart, dripping slimy tendrils all around me. I can only watch in horror as something emerges from Its gut, a long, ribbed tube with a razor-sharp point. There's nothing I can do. I'm trapped against the floor, desperately trying to squirm free of Its grasp.

That sharp point. It's going to dig itself inside me, like a needle.

The chanting reaches its apex.

Bacá! Bacá! Bacá!

The sky beyond the snowcat shimmers and glows. I can see the mountain just beyond it. Then it's closing in, a circular patch of horizon that grows smaller and smaller. Crawly's ritual is shutting some sort of dimensional gate. If I don't make it through before it closes, I'll be trapped here and cut off from the mountain, and Ray.

Everything vibrates around me. Items from Prized Possessions rise into the air before being sucked into the quickly dissipating vacuum between worlds. The snowcat's also vibrating. Inching closer toward the gate.

I should be terrified, should be unable to breathe, my heart finally giving out in a very real heart attack. But I'm not. In fact, as I turn away, all I can think about is how I hope it's over quickly, that the moment the slimy hook pierces my flesh, it'll strike some vital organ and it'll be over.

Who am I kidding? That's not how Bacá operates. Nothing's ever quick and easy. If It wanted me dead, I'd be dead already. This is punishment for my failure to deliver Ray to the sacrificial altar. My body might be destroyed, but my soul will burn in torment forever.

The tube descends, the sharp blade swiping at the air with a sickeningly sharp *swoosh*. I'm about to shut my eyes when I spot it in the corner. The nozzle of the fire extinguisher, only a foot or two away. I reach out my arm, stretching it as far as I can, my fingers grazing against the nozzle, trying to get a grip, pulling it closer, unable to get a firm grasp on it.

Above me, the tip of the demon's razor talon rips through

my layers of clothing and pricks my abdomen, pulsing as It gets the first taste of my blood. I can feel myself weakening. It's too late. The extinguisher, so frustratingly close, is beyond my reach.

This time, I'll finally die.

ISABELLA

Everything feels hazy, like I could pass out at any second. So hard to breathe. But I can't give up now. I've been fighting this thing possessing me. With every ounce of willpower and strength I have left, I whip the tentacle away from Joaquin.

I thrust the tentacle deep into my own body instead, reeling from the agonizing pain. But I can feel my body's other inhabitant stumbling and then screaming, a sound filled with fear and rage that echoes all around me.

Joaquin, now free from El Bacá's grasp, struggles to his feet, staring at me, confused.

"Isabella!" he shouts. "Fight It. We need to get back inside the snowcat and let it pull us through before the gate closes!"

Gate? I'm not sure what he's going on about, but it doesn't matter. He's going to be fine. That's all that really matters.

Nothing can compare to having a friend. I can only muster enough energy to hug him once through his tattered winter clothes. "Get the hell out of here!"

More pain explodes in my side. This time, El Bacá is using my own body against me. Joaquin and I share a look of horror. When I glance down, his clothes are coated with something dark and red. My blood. Along with some of my internal organs.

Before I'm pulled away by the tentacle that's impaled me, I thrust my camera in his hands. He shrieks, reaching for me.

I shake my head. "Get inside the snowcat. Strap yourself in," I call to him.

The wind's really fierce now. Everything not nailed down's being dragged into the void. My eyes dart to Joaquin. He barely manages to crawl into the snowcat. He presses his face against the windshield, tears streaming down his face as he slumps back into his seat and fastens the safety belt.

El Bacá raises Its hand, my hand, which looks more like a talon, to smash the glass. I manage to take control of my other hand just long enough to reach into my pocket, grab the blessed wooden cross, and stab It, over and over again into my own heart. In that moment of distraction, the snowcat's sucked into the void, carrying Joaquin away with it and through the gate.

A rush of fiery air engulfs us as the gate is sealed. I smile, tears rolling down my cheeks. One last thought goes through my mind before everything goes dark.

I'm so glad I wasn't live streaming this shit for once—

JOAQUIN

"Isabella!" I cry out.

But it's too late. She's trapped in that hell dimension. And with her, that thing, that Fallen Angel, part of El Bacá.

All I can hope for is that she'll bleed out quickly. Sofia. And now Izzy. With Ray's fate unknown. I have no more tears left. I could be the last of the Quisqueya Club. And if that's the case, and Ray is already gone, then I'll be joining El Bacá in hell.

I shake my head. No. Ray. Isn't. Dead. And if I get to that mountain, I may be able to escape El Bacá's punishment after all.

My seatbelt feels like it's about to snap, and when this thing crashes, I might end up joining Isabella in the endless dark. I strap her waterproof camera as securely as I can to my body. The seatbelt gives and I'm hanging on by the straps for dear life. The vacuum of hell dimensions beckons, trying its best to draw me in through the opened rear door of the cab. My arm feels like it's about to be ripped free from its socket.

With a cry, I try and grip the steering wheel, willing myself to hold on. Everything I've been through, both before and now, has been for nothing—I lose my grip. My body plunges toward the open rear door, just in time to smack into it and grasp the handle, using my legs to push my body back inside the cab, before shutting it.

I can only lie there, spent, muscles aching, relief and sorrow washing over me in waves. It's not over yet. As soon as I get my bearings, I'm crawling back up to the driver's seat, even though it's pointless. The snowcat's not on solid ground anymore. There's nothing I can do to steer it, control its speed.

Something looms through the windshield. I'd recognize that unholy silhouette anywhere. It's haunted me almost my entire life, a great burden, at times impossible to bear. Malicia.

While the mountain's shape is the same, there's something about it that's different, as if I'm staring at it when it was first formed, still smoldering and pulsating with volcanic activity, the sky around it dark and red, filled with billowing clouds of fiery ash.

Is it a prehistoric vision from my hell or another? It's hard to say. But one thing's certain, the mountain's radiating power. I can feel something dark and malignant emanating in waves, filling me with nausea and revulsion while simultaneously drawing me in, drowning my thoughts.

The snowcat rocks violently through the dark clouds. I strap myself into the passenger's seat, as if that's really going to help, as the mountain looms ever closer.

Water below. The moat Ray had talked about so gleefully when we first arrived here and explained the history of the castle. The memory causes a deep pang in my heart.

Crashing into water is probably a slim chance for survival but better than none. I'll have to swim out of there if I'm going to have any chance at all. Which means I'll have to shuck the winter gear.

I shed the layers of clothing until I'm down to my long johns. I can only hope I'll be able to hold my breath as long as it takes to make it to the surface once I hit—assuming I survive the crash, that is.

The snowcat goes into a nosedive, and I brace myself for impact. After everything that's happened, I can't wimp out now. I can do this. I strap the pack on and pop open one of the doors. I will do this.

The water rushes up to the windshield. And then it feels like something's slammed into the vehicle. The dashboard bursts into sparks. The sound of grinding metal fills my ears, followed by shattering glass. Everything flickers and goes dark.

There's a rush of ice-cold water filling the cab. But I'm ready for it, pushing open the door and plunging into the moat. I fight the current trying to drag me deeper and break free. Which way is up? I can't tell. Panic sets in, my old friend, but I shrug it off as best I can, kicking out with my feet, swimming toward the dim light of that red sky, upward, despite the aching of my starving lungs.

I burst free at last, spitting out water, clawing my way out of the embankment. I spot another snowcat, completely intact off to my left. Then a second. And a third. There's a whole line of them resting on tracks that loop into the sky and through an ancient gothic cathedral, flanked by snow-covered mountains. A rollercoaster.

A sign warns, You Are Now Leaving El Bacá's Lair. Make Sure You Have All of Your "Possessions."

I almost lose my balance and slip back into the moat a few times from the weight of the backpack, before collapsing on solid ground—

My eyes spring open. Did I fall asleep? How long was I out for?

I'm still too weak to move. But I can listen. At first, the sounds I hear make no sense at all. Everything's too muffled. Then, little by little, each sound becomes distinct. Voices. Is that . . . music? Laughter. And screams. And those smells. Roasting peanuts. Cotton candy? The sizzle of hot dogs and burgers . . . Fireworks.

Taking a deep breath, I raise myself to a sitting position and look around me. No. This can't be happening. This can't be real. But of course, it's real.

Malicia is alive and open for business.

The entire park is bustling with activity. Couples laughing and prodding each other to face the next terrifying ride. Others enjoying hot snacks while scouring the park map, deciding which haunt to visit. Still others make their way through the souvenir shops, draped in Malicia caps and T-shirts, small children tugging at their arms, pulling them toward the tot-friendly attractions. Everything looks like it must have that fateful last day when the park was open—except all these people are already dead.

They're all in varying stages of decomposition, some barely

more than skeletons, while others are puffed out with rotting flesh. Many are missing limbs or have great holes in their chests and heads. One woman, giggling to her male companion, is basically a neck and half a jaw, the rest torn away and dangling over her shoulder, dripping blood and brain matter as she meanders across one of the plazas, stopping to pose with a corpse that's burned beyond recognition for a selfie.

The act reminds me of Isabella. How I wish she were here right now and that I had her strength. Despite our differences, I'd do anything to take one last selfie with her, with all my friends. I see them in the distance. Just a glimpse really.

Sofia, holding the hand of a little boy. I recognize him from the news photos and the séance. Ray's brother, Rudy. Then they're gone, swallowed by the undead crowds.

Everything goes quiet. Activity stops. There's a huge drum roll from the loudspeakers, and an all too familiar voice booms.

Welcome, one and all, Master Crawly shouts. *Tonight's Midnight Mayhem Parade is going to be extra thrilling. We have a very special guest among us, this evening. A naughty little boy that thought he had escaped his Malicia family but tonight will discover we'll forgive him, if only he'll own up to his transgressions and finally fulfill his duty! Let's give it up for Joaquin Talavera!*

I'm ducking into the shadows, past these perversions of humanity, desperately trying to avoid detection, not sure where I'm going, just knowing I have to get as far away from here as possible, before—before I remember.

Spotlights pan all around me.

There he isssss! Crawly squeals. *Snatch him up! Don't let him get away!*

One by one, the dead, who up until now had paid me no mind, focus on me, reaching out rotting limbs, some even aiming cell phones with cracked or smashed screens toward me.

Come! Let's take a sssssssssssssssssselfieeeeeeeeeeeeeeee. . . .

I'm running as fast as I can with nowhere to go.

You're not getting away this time, Joaquincito! Crawly croaks.

Bullets whiz all around me, some striking the already dead crowd, whose corpses collapse from the blasts, while their deceased comrades look on. They're taking pictures of the carnage as if it was a concert or a sporting event.

You belong to me, and you're going to do your duty!

Up ahead, the parade is blocking my pathway, as Crawly steadily gains behind me. More gunshots, barely missing me, one even nicks my ear. I leap onto the nearest float as the crowd roars, pointing and taking more pictures, the multiple flashes creating a strobe effect that disorients me. I leap from float to float, Crawly's bullets dogging my every step.

Why the hurry? His voice echoes like a god. *It's time you faced the truth! What are you so afraid of, hmmmmm?* He breaks out in a long, hair-raising cackle.

It's the one that's in a hurry. If I don't sacrifice Ray, It has just as much to lose as I do.

The horde of undead visitors follows me, a massive throng in relentless pursuit, cutting off each of my pathways, except for the one leading to the very center of the park and—

Malicia's mountain itself.

That's where I need to go. That's where Ray is. I'm convinced he's still alive or El Bacá would have no further interest in me. There still might be time to perform the sacrifice and redeem myself to escape the demon's punishment.

With nowhere left to go, I run toward the mountain, skirting its perimeter until I spot the pathway carved into its side, leading up and up. My lungs feel like they're going to burst from the exertion, my muscles on the verge of collapse. But still I press on, not just to escape Crawly and that horrific mob of corpses, but to flee from the most terrifying thing of all, the thing that makes all these serial killers, creatures, ghosts, and aliens pale in comparison, the one thing I've never been able to face even in my deepest, darkest nightmares.

The truth.

There's a part of my brain that's always known there was more to what happened here than I consciously remembered. Despite the brainwashing from my abuelos and the rest of the coven, it's always been there, deep down inside like a seed waiting to bloom.

I make my way higher up the mountain, skirting a precarious ledge. I have to face the truth at last

Below me, the parade's degenerated into utter chaos. Screams. The sound of bullets. Explosions. Now that's more like it. That's what I remember. Tears are streaming down my face as I finally reach the mountain's peak, staggering onto the precipice, collapsing to my knees from pure exhaustion and sorrow.

I bury my face in my hands. It's all coming back to me. First the events as I remember them, all the people running, the screaming, the gun shots, Crawly chasing me, hunting me down to finish me off—but It didn't kill me then, when It had the perfect opportunity. Why? That's the unspoken question that's haunted me, the one not even the reporters or the conspiracy theorists ever seemed to ask out loud. Why was I alone spared?

Those memories fracture, like a double-exposed negative, my memories overlapping with a hidden layer just below the surface, my mind now peeling away the top coat of paint, the lies fed to me by my abuelos and their coven, to cover the raw truth lying just beneath.

Crawly isn't pointing any guns or hacking away at the park visitors that day, nor is there a mysterious team of assailants stalking their victims, taking them out in rapid succession. They're doing it to themselves. Couples turning on each other. A man drowning his wife in Lugaro Lago, the ride operator on It's a Small Underworld bludgeoning a patron with his own cane, fathers pushing their children off rollercoasters, a server at one of the eateries stabbing a guest through the eyeball with a fork. All over Malicia, the guests are murdering each other. Crawly may have provided the caches of weapons and explosives, but the park visitors are doing all the work themselves. They butcher each other in a primal frenzy that leaves the pathways and rides, as well as the rivers and lakes of Malicia, awash in crimson. It's as if someone took a bucket of red paint and splashed it on a canvas with reckless abandon. And with Crawly's supernatural hijinks at play, no forensic team will ever be able to figure out what really happened.

I can see Crawly's face, Its distorted grin, El Bacá's grin. "You all wanted thrills, the chance to live out your horrific fantasy, to be scared and scare others, and I've granted your wishes. But there's always a price when you make a bargain with me."

It's the very last memory that breaks through the dam in my mind that's the hardest one to relive. Mami aiming the semi-automatic at Papi and blowing his head off, his brain matter splattered across that lovely yellow sun dress she's wearing. Then she turns the gun on me with shaking hands, her face twisting in anguish, body trembling, as she fights Crawly's malevolent influence.

Always remember I love you, Joaquincito, she says through her tears.

At the last second, she turns the gun on herself instead, and fires.

Then Mami is no more, just a pile of smoldering meat, brain and bone matter, staining that lovely yellow dress, leaving me as the sole survivor of the Malicia Massacre. She sacrificed herself in order to save me from Crawly. And a part of me deep down inside has known I was the reason for her death all along.

Someone approaches and I look up. The statues from El Salon de Leyendas. All those infamous horror icons have shed their pedestals and made their way up the mountain, staring at me silently, forming a ring around me, boxing me in. La Jupia. El Ratoncito Perez. Las Ciguapas. Los Biembiens. Los Duendes. El Galipote. Los Chupacabras.

And then they all merge into one towering figure. Master Crawly. El Bacá.

It's not grinning, only staring at me. It transforms into a million shapes before settling into that of a hideous bull-like creature that walks upright on its hind legs, with twisted, pointy horns jutting from its skull and paws that end in razor-sharp claws. I can feel something crackling in the air like static electricity, along with a rising heat.

Kill him and join with me.

The thought slams into my head with the power of a sledge-hammer, knocking me to the ground. I pick myself up, blood oozing from my nostrils from the psychic assault.

"Why are you doing this?" I ask.

Long, cold fingers touch my face.

I know there's no point in trying to renegotiate my family's bargain with the demon. I spent my life in my abuelos' coven being groomed for this moment, so that El Bacá could take possession of Ray's body and enter the mortal world to enslave humanity. That's why I was spared. I had to be the one to bring Ray back to fulfill his destiny.

Ray emerges from the shrubs, bruised and cut, but very much alive. I drop the backpack with Isabella's waterproof camera and run into his arms. Despite everything, he hugs me back tightly, pulling back and looking into my eyes. "I'm sorry I pushed you away, pana. What's going on here is so much bigger than both of us. We can still make it out of this. Just wait it out with me. The rescue chopper should be here soon."

As if on cue, the sound of a distant helicopter approaches. Several of them. Along with a ship. Coast Guard by the looks of it. And when I stare down the mountain, I can see why. The fire that Izzy set in Serial Springs is now blazing like a wildfire. Half the park is in flames, sending up the biggest signal flare we could come up with. They'll be here in a matter of minutes.

I whisper in his ear. "Please forgive me, tiguere."

Then I plunge the hypodermic that Sofia had originally planned to use into his neck.

He collapses to the ground, his eyes opened wide, in shock

and hurt. "Why . . .?" is all he can muster before the paralytic effects of the herbs kick in.

Now he won't be able to stop me from doing what I need to do.

As the helicopters soar closer, I notice one of the logos belongs to a popular television news station. There'll be reporters aboard, along with cameras, ready to interview the lone survivor of this latest Malicia tragedy. Imagine what a story that'll make. The footage will go viral, broadcast all over the world, millions of social media clicks, posts, comments. The new Izzy would have hated every last bit of it.

Soon Malicia will become a household name again, and the entire world will get the opportunity to experience the most frighteningly fun family adventure for themselves, in ways they could never ever imagine.

The helicopters circle above, and I can already see the cameras, hungry for the first live footage, which is probably streaming on news stations everywhere already.

They're all speaking to the island, the conversation growing and growing. And the island's answering them. Louder than it ever has before. The park is awakening again, the music, the laughter. The screams. Growing stronger and stronger. Strong enough for every single television, cell phone, computer device to hear.

El Bacá is grinning, already tasting Its victory, relishing the fact it will be him leaving the island in Ray's body, leaving this cursed island to eventually enslave all of humankind.

Ray's eyes flutter open and he tries to reach out for me. "Joaquin . . . why can't I move, pana?"

"Everything will be okay, tiguere. I promise."

I stare deep into his eyes. "I need you to understand that everything that happened here, none of it was your fault. Your father made a deal with El Bacá for fame and fortune, but he couldn't pay the price." I lean in closer. "You were that price, Ray."

Ray's eyes search mine. "He lost everything for betraying his covenant with El Bacá to protect *me*?"

I nod and squeeze his hand. "Yes. He thought he could outplay a demon. He was wrong."

"And his decision doomed so many more."

I sigh and lift the end of my shirt, exposing the scar on my hip, now pulsing with a symbol instead of a bullet scar. The mark of El Bacá. "I'm a loose end, tiguere. My grandparents were Brujas. Raised me in a coven after my parents were killed. I was also supposed to die in the massacre, along with everyone else. But my mother's love saved me, creating a loophole that El Bacá needs to close. It can't let love win. But It can corrupt that love if I sacrifice you myself of my own free will."

"What happens if you choose not to?"

I smile. "Then I lose my own soul."

"And that's why you did this. It had nothing to do with me."

I brush his lips with my finger. "None of that matters anymore. I needed you to know . . . before I do what I must. I love you, Ray. I wish I would have told you sooner. But better late than never, right?"

My tears drip onto his cheeks, and his lips. He tries to lift his head, and when he can't, I lower mine to meet his, pressing my lips to his in our first, and last kiss, savoring it, etching it into my memory.

He stares deep into my eyes. "Whatever happens, there's something I want you to know, too. Te amo, pana. I love you with every fiber of my soul. I always have, since the first awkward moment we met. You're a wonderful person. Smart, sweet, funny. And strong. Don't ever let anyone tell you otherwise. Now do what you have to do. I'm ready."

The time to pay your price has come, El Bacá croaks.

I carry Ray's body onto the stone altar, positioning him as comfortably as I can. Then I reach underneath and remove the sacred dagger that's been waiting for this very purpose.

El Bacá is practically drooling when I position the dagger over Ray's heart and raise it high . . .

Before plunging it deep into my own.

The demon lets out a roar and pounces. But I'm ready for It. With my last bit of strength, I barrel into It, grabbing hold, driving the dagger deeper into my body as we tumble off the mountain, our bodies intertwined in our death throes.

El Bacá's animal cry is drowned out by Ray's long, agonized wail.

As we fall, I picture Ray's beautiful smiling face, before all the darkness, before the tears. For one glorious moment I'm soaring through the air and into the sunrise, like a bird, not a care in the world. Free at last.

RAYMUNDO

I can't bring myself to set foot on the island ever again. All I can do is watch it from the boat, storm clouds on one side, clear skies on the other, keeping the darkness at bay. All throughout the flight from Los Angeles to Miami, and then to Cibao International airport, I thought of nothing but this moment. Once I landed, I made my way to the dock and chartered this boat so I could arrive just as the sun was rising over the horizon.

After what happened last year, Malicia was totally leveled. Whatever plans were underway to rebuild were totally scrapped, with no plans to ever touch it again. Good riddance.

And now I'm back here.

This is something I have to do alone.

Tears well as I stare at the blooming colors of sunrise on the crystal Caribbean Sea and breathe in the crisp, salty air.

Tranquilo y tropical.

Peaceful and tropical, the Quisqueya Club's motto. I shed tears for Sofia and Isabella.

He's all I ever think about, no matter how busy I get with school, no matter how many new people I meet. None of them will ever be him.

People tell me I'll heal, just like I did with my father. The two of us talk now, even laugh on occasion. They say healing takes time and I'm willing to give it a shot.

I hear a sigh in the air, and when I look up, I see his silhouette on the island, all alone, staring across the sea at me. Some people might say it was just the shadow of a tree fluttering in the wind, or the angle of the sun, but I know better. I squeeze my eyes shut, feeling the warmth of his fingers on my face, and touch my own cheeks to feel closer to him.

I bask in the warm feeling for a while, before pulling out my notebook and flipping to the next empty page.

"What story are we going to write today?"

I listen carefully to the wind, and jot down the title *La Leyenda del Tiguere y su Pana*. I continue to listen, filling each page with love and hope.

He once told me if he could rewrite the legend of El Tumbador y La Bruja, he would make it so that they'd be reunited a year later, finding their love again, creating an ever-lasting legend. I believe that what you speak into the universe is a much more powerful spell than El Bacá could ever cast.

I whisper his name. The fireflies begin to appear. Las Nimitas. First dozens, then hundreds, reflecting off the water around my boat like brilliant stars. That's when I reach into my pocket and pull it out, the tiny charm in the shape of an arrow, the one that used to be part of a couple.

I close my eyes and concentrate, picturing his face. Hearing the lovely sound of his voice in my head, reaching a tentative hand out. Soon, the boat rocks gently with a sudden added weight. I smile and open my eyes.

ACKNOWLEDGMENTS

While we writers spend a great deal of time alone in our caves, crafting our tales of unspeakable horrors, romance, adventure, and the like, publishing a book is a much more collaborative process. You wouldn't be reading any of this now if it wasn't for all of the encouragement and support of these wonderful individuals who I have been so fortunate to have in my life and be a part of the process.

First off, my eternal gratitude to the faculty and mentors at the Naslund-Mann Graduate School of Writing at Spalding University, where I received my MFA, including Kathleen Driskell, Sena Jeter Naslund, Karen Mann, Katy Yocom, Lesléea Newman, Susan Campbell Bartoletti, Edie Hemingway, Lamar Giles, and Beth Bauman. You were all there when *Malicia* (then known as *Malice Mountain*) was in its infancy, and gave me the inspiration to forge ahead on this long journey toward publication.

Next, I want to give a huge shout out to my fabulous agents, Lynnette Novak, Nicole Resciniti, and the entire crew of the Seymour Agency, who have guided me every step of the way, providing words of solace and wisdom during every challenging junction of this publishing adventure. Thank you all for your patience and belief in me, even when my gas tank was running on empty!

I can't even begin to express how lucky I feel to have the awesome team at Page Street in my corner! I want to give a special thanks to my incomparable editor, Tamara Grasty, whose insights and attention to detail have really elevated this manuscript and realized its full potential, despite my frustrated grumblings along the way. I see what you were saying now, Tamara, and you were so right! I'd also like to express my gratitude to Page Street's design team, including Laura Benton, Rosie Stewart, and Meg Baskis for taking my words and wrapping them in such an enticing package! To my copy editor, Susan Lovett, thank you for asking all the right questions in order to make sense out of the nonsensical. And Aleksey Pollack, your cover illustration really brought my vision of Malicia to life and conveyed all of the dreadful atmosphere from the deepest corners of my imagination into a thing of dark beauty!

Finally, to my beta readers and dear friends, Stacie Ramey, Joyce Sweeney, and Marjetta Geerling, what can I say but muchas gracias for all of the time spent reading the early drafts of *Malicia* and recognizing its potential, even when I did not! And to Claudia Love Mair, who helped keep me motivated through our check-ins when I was trying to finish the very first draft of *Malicia*, you will always be my (WoD) Write or Die!

ABOUT THE AUTHOR

Dominican/Portuguese-American author Steven dos Santos is the author of The Torch Keeper series and *Dagger: The D.U.S.T. Ops*. His first novel, *The Culling*, was a top ten selection of the American Library Association's Rainbow List. Steven is an English professor and a passionate advocate of LGBTQ+ rights. He currently resides in Miami, with his beloved Great Dane mix, Dagger, his constant companion and loyal friend. When he's not writing, you can probably find Steven at the movies or playing board games.